FLY AWAY *Home*

JUDE WILLHOFF

Mary,

Happy Reading!

Jude Willhoff

Fly Away Home ~ Sweet Home Colorado ~ Book Two
A Contemporary Romance

ISBN-978-0-9896380-3-6

Cover and Book Design by
THE KILLION GROUP
www.thekilliongroupinc.com

This book is a work of fiction. Names, characters, places and incidents are either products of the author's imagination or used fictitiously. Any resemblance to actual events, locales, or persons, living or dead, is entirely coincidental.

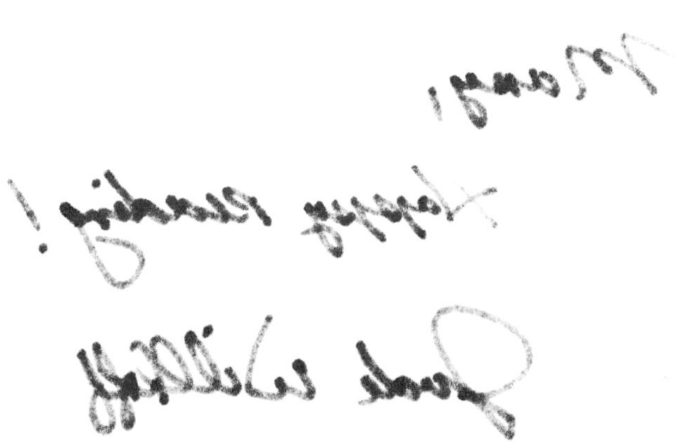

About The Book ~ Sweet Home Colorado ~ Book Two

FLY AWAY HOME

SHE'S NOTHING HE EXPECTED…

After being betrayed by her cheating ex-husband, Cindy Dawson makes a major decision to go after what she wants—a family of her own. Being the last single woman in her group of friends in Cedar Falls, Colorado, Cindy decides she needs to leave town—their happiness is killing her. She takes a job in Denver and joins a singles group to find her soul mate. For love and to realize her dream she'll take the chance of rejection. She learns she has to date a lot of frogs to get to the prince.

BUT EVERYTHING HE NEEDS…

Officer Jack Riley wants nothing more than to be left alone. He works the night shift and does free lance writing. When he goes undercover to get the story about dating in the singles scene he hates the whole idea. He's anything but a swinging single and he'll never be ready for the dating scene again. When he meets Cindy, he begins to realize there is more to life than grieving the loss of loved ones and fighting his own demons. He realizes he isn't really living, if he's not out there experiencing life in all its messiness—the good, the bad and the love.

Cindy Dawson and Jack Riley must learn to forgive the past in order to embrace the bright future that beckons them.

DEDICATION

To the people, the sights and sounds of downtown Denver on the Sixteenth Street Mall. This place is what inspired me to write *Fly Away Home* so I dedicate this book to them. The mile high city never sleeps. There's always something fun to do, shopping, museums, bookstores, parks, theater, and sporting events, with entertainment options for everyone.

TO MY HUSBAND

Robert J. Willhoff Jr.
My hero, the love of my life who stands beside me through my trials and tribulations.

AND TO THE REST OF MY WONDERFUL FAMILY

Robert and Elizabeth Willhoff III,
John, Aimee, Lydia and Hannah King,
Kevin, Jessica and Natalie Willhoff,
Robert, Jennifer, Makaela and Jayda Powilleit.

Thanks for the way you've all shown your love and support with my writing.

AND TO

Rosecolored Ink, my critique group, my writing sisters who keep me on track when I go off the rails. Thanks, ladies. You rock. Always!

TABLE OF CONTENTS

CHAPTER ONE

"Great buns. Muscular thighs...mmm Baby, come to Mama."

The dusky light of evening played along the Denver skyline, but Cindy Dawson could see enough of the nearly naked jogger to cause heart palpitations. The tight, skimpy shorts covering his backside brought a whistle to her lips. For a split second, her eyes wandered from the road as she reached for her cell phone, then glanced back to see the flash of red tail lights. "Oh, God."

She swerved and stomped the brakes to the floor.

The sound of crunching metal and breaking glass drowned out her scream as the air bag exploded. Slamming into something solid, everything came to a halt. The noise of the accident reverberated into a million tiny white shooting stars pulsating in her head. A shiver of panic forced her brain to function. Over the deflating air bag the front of her red Jeep Cherokee curled around the back of a police cruiser. The clanking of the engine stopped as a last shuddering breath of white smoke puffed from the motor spraying water everywhere. "I'm so sorry, Matilda," she murmured and patted her dashboard with an unsteady hand.

The sound of a siren pierced the false calm. Her face tingled from the impact, but nothing seemed to be broken. In the glow of the early evening streetlight, her head tipped toward the jogger racing up to the car. Looking old and tired, he didn't seem to be as cute close up and personal. And to think she had whistled at *this* guy. Clearing vision brought a disturbing thought to the surface. *Leopard print Speedos on a pot belly old bald man—didn't do a thing for her.*

Someone called from the driver's side of her car. "Hey, are you all right?"

More shaken than she cared to admit she glanced toward the voice. "Yes, I'm okay." A wave of apprehension swept away the brief calm as she wished to be anywhere else. A tall man stood outside the broken window. The sleeves of his shirt were tight against his swelling biceps. A thick shock of dark, wavy hair fell in careless disarray over his forehead. Blazing from a handsome face were his eyes—dark brown like melted chocolate. Their glint mirrored the shiny badge on his chest. He looked pissed. *Great...just great.*

"Are you hurt?" he asked and quirked a brow.

She blinked and met his eyes without flinching. "No, I...I think I'm okay." Guilt nearly caused the words to lodge in her throat. The smarting on her face from where she'd been smacked by the airbag was minor compared to what this man could do.

She managed a tremulous smile and tried to size up the situation. The man's brooding good looks made her stomach quiver but she hesitated at the spark of anger in his eyes. *I'm in so much trouble.*

She brushed a long strand of dark hair behind an ear and focused on him. Noting the name on his badge, J. Riley, she said, "I'm so sorry Officer Riley. I only glanced away for a second and when I looked up there you were." She cringed at the strained expression on his face. "I tried to stop."

"I'm sure you did." He lifted the radio unit from his shoulder and growled into it, then turned back. "I'm Officer Jack Riley. I'll get you out." He worked on the jammed car door. "The paramedics will be here in a few minutes." Reaching through the window he pressed a handkerchief to a small scratch on her brow. "Keep pressure on it."

She hadn't been aware she was bleeding. "Thanks, but I don't need them." He pushed the deflated air bag back and tugged the door open. She rubbed her face, stepped out of the wrecked auto and stood on jelly legs surveying the damage. Broken glass and pieces of twisted metal littered the roadway.

The front of Matilda hugged the patrol car. "I...I have insurance."

"Well, ma'am, that's a good thing. Now, please go sit on that park bench." He pointed to a spot near the street. "I have to direct traffic around the accident."

"Okay."

A slight grin crossed his face as he looked at his car and shook his head. Another police car pulled up with its lights flashing. Jack spoke to the policeman and came to stand by her. Just then an ambulance drove up with a tow truck close behind.

"I don't need an ambulance." She tried to object.

"Just a precaution, they'll check you out."

Jack took in the mangled front-end of the jeep and his car. "Looks like neither of us is going to drive too far tonight." The other officer glared at her. "Lady, you about ran over him at a red stoplight. What were you thinking? Tell me what happened."

"I...I guess, I wasn't thinking. I was just reaching across the seat for my cell phone." *The police officer was right, she had been a fool.* Unshed tears burned the back of her gritty eyelids at the thought. "I'm sorry."

The policeman nodded and penciled something on a notepad. "I need your license, registration and insurance information."

Cindy crossed to the Jeep and reached in to grab papers from the side pocket on the door and handed them to him as Jack stood silently by.

He returned the car registration and continued to write. "Ms. Dawson, do I detect the presence of alcohol. Have you had anything to drink this evening?"

Her heart tumbled in overtime when she glanced at Jack. As if to smell her breath, he moved closer to her side. His jaw clenched and his eyes narrowed while his friend continued the questioning.

Heat rose to her cheeks as she stood between the two policemen and glanced from one to the other. "Just a couple of drinks with my friends, but I'm not intoxicated." Folding arms across her chest, the rapid rhythm of her heartbeat matched the nervous ache swirling in her tummy. "It's my birthday," she muttered under her breath.

If looks could kill, she'd be on the ground twitching. Jack hesitated for a second. "Ma'am, there are two kinds of drunks...those who are sorry and those who soon will be."

She cringed at his scathing words, but just then the yellow lights of the tow truck flashed down the street, hauling the damaged jeep off to the impound lot. She sighed deeply. How could I have been so careless? She tossed a long braid over her shoulder in a gesture of defiance to keep from crying and waited for their next move.

Four long hours later, she arrived by taxi at her downtown condo. All she wanted to do was take a shower, crawl into her pajamas, settle in with a hot cup of herbal tea to watch the latest episode of *Grey's Anatomy* she'd recorded a few nights back and put this behind her.

She'd never been arrested for anything in her life—until now. She always believed she could turn adversity into opportunity, but this time... Her car was trashed and she had a ticket for careless and reckless driving. She stared at the front of the towering downtown high rise and pulled out her security card. With the card clutched in her hand, she realized what a horrendous mistake she had made. She could have hurt someone. She shuddered at the thought.

The elevator door opened on the thirtieth floor. Several people stood around the hallway holding drink cups and talking. Loud music poured out of her condo. *What now?* Puzzled, she stepped through the open doorway.

Samantha, Cindy's co-worker and new friend from down the block rushed toward her and shouted, "Surprise! Happy Birthday."

This explained why Sam had taken the day off, supposedly sick. "You didn't have to." Cindy groaned, not in the mood for a party. A few hours ago with the two policemen at precisely nine-thirty-eight p.m., she had turned thirty. She sighed. Tonight she wanted to put herself on hold and forget birthdays...especially this one.

"Yes, I did. I read the Tarot cards and they said you would meet your soul mate today."

"My soul mate?" Cindy snorted. Normally fascinated by Sam's belief in the cards, crystals and strange exotic things, she wondered grumpily why Sam hadn't foreseen the accident and warned her. "Sorry. It didn't happen." She'd only met the surly police officers. They certainly didn't count.

"That's why I threw this party," Sam explained. "Look at the single men I found for you." Sam's long blond hair bounced on her shoulders as she waved her hand around the room.

"I don't know what to say." The number of men and women crammed into her condo astounded her. People sat on her overstuffed floral sofa and loveseat. Some stood around the fireplace, deep in conversation, others in her open kitchen mixing drinks. Music blared from her stereo. One couple danced on her balcony. Cindy glanced around her home and wished they'd all disappear. *This is the last time I ever give anyone an extra key to my place.* "Where did these people come from?" She didn't know any of them, but it looked like everyone was having a great time—at her expense. Her home was a party zone.

Sam pulled her farther into the room. "Where have you been? It's gotten so late. We expected you hours ago."

"It's a long story." She craved peace and quiet. How could she get everyone to go home, without offending them? She wanted to be alone with her misery.

Sam frowned and handed her a glass of champagne. "Sure, tell me later. Here's to the birthday girl." She toasted Cindy and sipped from her glass while scanning the room.

"Thanks." Cindy grimaced. After the accident, the last thing on earth she wanted was a drink. She cringed at the memory of being tested to see if she was over the drinking limit. She held the obnoxious glass at arm's length and watched Sam checking out the guys. Sam became a real trip when she went on the prowl for a new man. A sweetheart of a friend, but she would go after anything with tight pants and a big wallet. Cindy watched her drift from one guy to another to end up on the open balcony with an older man.

The chance to slip into her bedroom had arrived. Sam had meant well, but the last few hours had taken their toll. Cindy worked her way around the room as her head pounded. The ticket stuffed in the bottom of her purse dominated her mind, absorbed her focus. The thought of what could have happened if someone had been sitting in the backseat of that car became unbearable. She could've killed someone. She shivered and set the untouched drink on the bookcase next to her bedroom door. Of course, her insurance would go up. And there went the new clothes she had been saving for. *Damn.* She shouldn't have reached for her cell phone.

"Oh, no you don't." Returning from the balcony, Sam caught Cindy's arm before she could make a clean get away. Her friend grinned with a mischievous twinkle in her eyes. "I thought you were going to miss your own party."

"This is nice, Sam, but it's been a long day."

"Don't be a spoiled sport. I have a surprise for you." Sam laughed. "And you know every woman should have one, especially on her birthday." She led Cindy into the kitchen.

There on the white porcelain tile floor lay a puppy with a huge red ribbon tied around his neck. Part tan Shar-pei and part traveling salesman he was wrinkled like a raisin that had been left in the sun too long. "I present your very own Prince."

Cindy laughed and released some of the pent-up frustration from the past few hours. It was love at first sight. "Oh, you did it. You found my soul mate." She scooped him up and scratched behind his ears. "Hello little guy, how are you?" The puppy licked her face with approval in his dark brown eyes. She hugged him to her chest. "Where did you get him?"

"Animal Rescue. His owners were transferred overseas and they couldn't take him with them."

At last something good had come out of this day. "Thank you. I've always wanted a dog."

"If, for any reason, you change your mind, the agency will take him back. And I checked with the management office. They don't have a problem with you having a pet."

Cindy rubbed his soft, furry head against her cheek, drawing some much needed comfort from the puppy. Her heart hammered with happiness for the unconditional love the sweet animal offered as he sniffed her fingers. "Oh, I adore him. How did you arrange all this without me knowing?" She swallowed hard and appreciated the warm friendship Sam had shown.

Sam laughed. "I know how to be sneaky. Now, go mingle with these men. I had the girls bring a throw-away date."

"Huh? A throw-away date, what's that?"

"You know. A good guy you don't want for yourself." She sighed. "We meet mostly women so this is a way we help each other out." Sam grinned. "I thought about a theme party—come as your favorite condiment—but decided the throw-away party would be better for your birthday." She winked at Cindy and wriggled her way back to the older man across the room.

Now Cindy had heard everything. A condiment party, things were sure different in the city. She sighed. She held the puppy and walked out onto the empty balcony to avoid the party crowd and stared across the way at the tall skyscrapers lit up like shiny jewels against the jet black sky.

She sighed and thought about home. If she were in Cedar Falls, she probably would've gone to a quiet dinner with her best friends, Grace and Jenna. Grace had married Seth, loving his little girl Jamie, adopted Joey, had twins and had her hands full with four children. Jenna was happily engaged. Cindy was happy for them, but that was part of the reason why she had moved to Denver. Tired of being the only single one in the group, she had needed a change—their happiness was killing her. She'd come to the city to find a man, someone who was father material. She craved a family of her own.

When she'd been offered an opportunity to teach Cosmetology at the Vocational Community College in Denver, the position had been too tempting to pass up. After she accepted the job, she sold her salon in Cedar Falls and bought her condo and joined a singles group to start her new life. Maybe, just maybe, if she were lucky, she'd meet someone interesting. But, who was she kidding? There was nothing easy about dating. So far the prince had been hiding...the only men she'd met were frogs.

Yes, she was single and ready to mingle, but tonight she didn't have the energy. The truth hurt. With a deep breath, she moved back into the living room and settled down in her favorite overstuffed chair with the puppy on her lap. She removed the red ribbon from his neck and kissed him on top of his head. He shivered and snuggled close. "Don't be scared, little guy. I'll kick them out soon as I can." All of a sudden her landline rang. "Now, what?" she muttered to the puppy and moved to picked up the receiver. "Hello."

"Ms. Dawson, This is Dean at the front desk. We've received a noise complaint from your neighbor."

"Oh, I'm sorry I'll turn the music down."

"Thank you, have a good night."

Someone must've moved into the vacant apartment next door while she was at work. This wasn't the best way to meet the new neighbor.

CHAPTER TWO

Jack rubbed the palm of his hand against his temple. "For Pete's sake, hold it down." He stared at the blank beige wall. He'd closed on the condo and moved in a couple of days before, and never suspected he would be living next door to party central.

It had been a bitch of a night. First, he'd had to deal with the careless driver ruining his patrol car. Even though he was pissed at her he had to admit she was a babe. She came in a small package with the right curves in the right places. The woman had beautiful dark hair, skin like refined silk and green cat eyes a man could get lost in—too bad, she was a flake.

And then, if that hadn't been enough. When he'd arrived home a message from his editor on his answering machine had asked, 'Where is this month's magazine article?' He had miscalculated, thinking it was due next week.

He'd worked on the police force for several years, but the extra money from his freelance writing had helped him buy his new place. His goal was to pay off the condo in five years. But now he needed quiet. "Turn it down," he mumbled to himself. The front desk should have talked to them by now.

Someone adjusted the music to a dull roar. "Better," he grumbled. He could go next door and flash his badge, but in his first few days here, he didn't want to make enemies. Besides, someone in the hall had said it was a birthday party. At least these folks were doing their drinking at home.

Getting his frustration under control, he glanced at the colorful fish as they swam in their salt-water aquarium. The graceful way they glided in and around the lighthouse never failed to soothe him. It wasn't entirely his neighbor's fault. This article taunted him. With the nosie next door he couldn't concentrate.

Jack rechecked his notes, looked for a new angle and pushed away from his computer, annoyed as he listened to the party going on next door. Life hadn't always been this way. A few years ago, he'd been happily married and easygoing until he'd accidentally shot a kid on the job. When the kid died, he had sunk to the bottom of a bottle. And then his family was gone, too.

He sighed. With Briggs' help and the department's support, he'd conquered rehab and crawled up from the seventh level of hell. To this day, he carried an underlying fear that if he ever took another drink, he'd never be able to stop. Since he'd dried out, he cared little about socializing with anyone—especially a bunch of rowdy people.

Today, he was sober, a loner and he liked it that way. Rubbing his eyes to erase the pain, he realized he needed to finish the article and get some rest. He wanted to be fresh for the meeting with his editor, Briggs, in the morning.

The music became louder. *Damn it.* He glanced at the offending wall.

Cindy covered her mouth and yawned. "It's getting late and I have to work tomorrow."

"Now don't be like that. It's not that late." Out of breath from dancing, Sam leaned against the side of Cindy's chair. "I met your new neighbor yesterday when I was sneaking stuff in for your party. He's cute, but not very friendly. He should come over and join the party instead of calling the front desk and complaining."

"No, he's right. It's time to get these people out of here."

"Are you sure? The party is just getting started."

Far as Cindy was concerned, it had ended before she walked through the door. She glanced around the room at the overflowing ashtrays and drink cups sitting on her fireplace mantle and coffee table. Some couples gyrated against each other, lost in the moment. Having these strange people around made her feel more lonely than when she was by herself.

She looked at Sam. "I'm sure. I appreciate the party, but it's time to call it a night. I need to go to bed." Not used to partying to the wee hours of the morning, she mumbled under her breath. "How do these people do it?" *Oh, Lord, it's happened. I'm old.*

"Okay." Sam flipped off the stereo, "Time to close up shop. The birthday girl has had enough fun for tonight." She turned and gave Cindy a hug. "Everyone can come over to my place. I'm at the Barkley, just a few blocks down the street," she shouted to the others. She grabbed a bottle of Merlot off the table and headed out the door. "Follow me." Sam danced through the entrance way with a twinkle in her pretty blue eyes and the older man on her arm.

Cindy watched the last of the stragglers follow Sam out and closed the door and locked it behind them. Silence, glorious silence, finally, she was alone. With a heavy sigh, she wandered around the room with a trash bag. "Great way to spend my birthday," she muttered as she tossed in another cup.

And so much for meeting Prince Charming, would she always have to be content with toads? Of course, the kind of prince she wanted would be different from Prince Charming in the fairy tale. She didn't need somebody to rescue her, but someone to lean on occasionally wouldn't be bad.

What did it matter if she was a lonely divorcee, sneaking up on the down side of thirty? She could handle it. Sure, she wanted someone to love, but she refused to be some man's doormat. Been there, done that, and had no desire to repeat. However, with the men she had met in the singles' group so far, there were no princes. For now she was content with the puppy, but someday she wanted a child of her own.

As if on cue, a low whimper came from under the table. "Oh, Prince, come here, you poor baby. I bet you need to go out. Come on. Let's take a walk." Being the considerate gift-giver, Sam had left a collar and a leash along with several bags of *Puppy Chow.*

Grabbing her coat and keys, Cindy locked the door behind her. At least after taking Prince out, she'd be able to catch a few winks of sleep before she had to turn around and go back to work. She glanced toward Prince in time to see him lift his leg over the next door neighbor's newspaper. Oh, wow, we're really earning brownie points with the new neighbor.

Morning came way too early. Jack sipped his strong black coffee and realized how much he would enjoy living in the condo. No more mowing the lawn or shoveling snow. Selling the house in the suburbs had been the right thing to do, too many memories and regrets lived there. And with less household to manage, he'd have more time for writing.

His neighbors were noisy, but they were probably young and just having fun. If it got to be too much of a problem, he'd go over and quiet them down. At least they turned the music off after he called the front desk.

He fed his fish and headed for the door to retrieve his paper—his only pure joy in the morning. He hated mornings. That's why he preferred to work the night shift at the station. With the move, he was totally out of sync.

He picked up the paper. It was damp. Holding it out, the smell of urine stung his nostrils. "Damn... Somebody has a dog." Squinting toward the party animal's condo, a suspicion formed in his mind. He'd bet a dollar to a donut the culprit lived there. Was this retaliation for last night? "I'll get you...and your little dog, too." He must be losing it. He shook his head. *That's what happens Jack, old boy, when you don't get enough sleep.*

He tossed the ruined paper in the trash and went into the bathroom, no time to read it anyway. Briggs expected him with the article and he still needed to shower and shave. After today, he would be glad to get back on schedule at the department and back on track with his writing. Work nights, sleep and write days, avoid the daylight crowd—that's the way he liked it.

A rumble of water sounded in the pipes from the next door bathroom. Back to back bathrooms, huh? Oh, yeah, the Realtor had warned him everything in the building had been upgraded, but the new plumbing was still being installed on this floor. It didn't matter.

He listened to the low hum of a woman's voice singing in the shower. Oh, well. If she couldn't have any consideration for him and his newspaper, then she deserved whatever she got. Besides, he didn't have a choice. He needed to run. He reached down and turned on the water. Jack stepped into the shower and grimaced when a muffled shriek sounded from next door. Maybe he had been too harsh, should've waited till her water stopped. Then he thought of his soiled newspaper. Nah....

Cindy squealed as her soapy fingers slipped around the cold water handle. When she finally got it turned off, she heard the neighbor's water running. She wiped her face as shampoo dripped in her eyes. "Couldn't he tell I was in the shower?" she mumbled, more upset by the minute.

Wrapping a towel around her hair, she squinted when a glob of soap worked its way into the corner of her eye causing it to sting. Wiping it away, she yelled at the white tiled wall and hoped he could hear her. She dried off and pulled on her robe. Leaning over the sink, she proceeded to rinse the remaining shampoo from her hair.

Bothered about the way Prince ruined the paper, she had planned on going over to apologize, especially for the noise last night. Ha! Forget it! This was war. Throwing on her clothes, she blew her hair dry and flew out the door to face her obnoxious neighbor.

Cindy took a deep breath and rang the doorbell, waiting for the confrontation. Ridiculous, they were neighbors and two grown adults surely they could work out a system. Angry, she pounded on the door and repeatedly rang the door bell. "Are you in there?" No answer. She fumed. She couldn't stand around here all day. She had to get to work. "Jerk," she whispered to herself and caught the elevator.

"You want me to do what?" A few blocks away at the Adam's Mark coffee shop, Jack's mouth fell open and he stared at his editor, Jim Briggs, as if he'd grown horns.

"You did so well on the last article about dating from the personal ads that I want you to be our sixty-minute man," he answered. "Go undercover and write an expose about singles dating in the new millennium."

"Why me?" Jack asked with a critical squint. "Sounds like this would be better as a fluff piece, maybe from a woman's point of view."

"That's just it. I want a single man's angle. From some information I've come across, it seems the dating tide is changing and soon there will be more single men than women. And with this high-tech generation, there isn't time for the old-fashioned way of dating." He leaned back and steepled his fingers. "The professionals have given up on the tried and true, the bar scene, meeting someone at church or through family and friends. With the hours they put in at their jobs, the bottom line is they don't have the time." His mercurial black eyes sharpened as he said the words with the certainty of a man who was accustomed to getting his way.

"Okay, I'll bite. If they don't go out and meet people the usual way, what do they do?"

Briggs threw back his head and let out a great peal of laughter. "I guess we're both out of the loop these days and I do mean literally. It seems there's a new singles group for professionals in town. They have their own website with singles boards and meet several times a week in person for an hour."

A secretive smile softened Briggs' lips. "During this hour, six men and six women show up for cocktails. They are preselected by a computer—having similar interests and all. Technically, it should be a pretty well-rounded group." He moved closer to the table.

Jack's full attention had centered on Briggs. This was so not what he wanted to write about.

"A good time is had by everyone," Briggs added persuasively. "Anyway, the women sit at separate tables and there's a coordinator who sends the men to the tables and they switch partners every ten minutes." It was obvious he wanted Jack to see the opportunity with this assignment.

"You see, at the end of the hour they've met six people instead of your normal one or two over the weekend. They exchange business cards and information about themselves and e-mail addresses. Then, if something clicks, they contact the person for a date."

"If you were into that sort of thing I guess I can see where it would save time," Jack said grudgingly. "Meeting six at a whack would cut the odds down on finding Mr. or Ms. Right." He let out a long sigh. "Why me? I still think this is a woman's article."

"I figured you would, but statistics show there are as many lonely men out there as women." His features became more animated, his mood buoyant as he plunged on in his efforts to persuade Jack. "Besides, other than me, you're the only single reporter I have."

Jack's defenses began to crumble. "Now, we get to the truth." He eyed Briggs with his cop instincts and knew something else was going on in the man's editorial mind.

"I want you to date a few of these women, make friends with the men and get both angles on what's happening in the professional dating climate today." Briggs cleared his throat. "I realize you haven't dated much since Janet's passing, but it's been five years," Briggs' eyes widened in false innocence. "It'll be good for you. Of course, your membership fees and expenses will be covered by the magazine."

If the words had been spoken by anyone else, Jack would have decked the man, but Briggs had taught him the secrets to freelance writing. He had always reminded Jack of a big teddy bear, soft on the outside, but with a heart of steel when it came to business. Jack ran his finger around the rim of his coffee cup and thought about the type of article he could write.

He didn't want to date anyone, but the subject intrigued him. And the kicker—the money was good, too good to pass up. He shot Briggs a twisted smile. "Okay. I'll do it, but on my terms. No interference from you or anyone associated with the magazine." He ran a hand through his hair. "When do you want me to start?"

"Immediately. And as you said on your own terms." His face split into a grin. "We've already signed you up."

"Signed me up, pretty sure of yourself, weren't you?" Jack frowned into his coffee cup.

"I know how bad you want to get your condo paid off. I took a chance. Here's the information." He handed Jack a packet. "You start today." An expression of satisfaction warmed his eyes. "I'd like you to do the dating game for a few months and I'll run the article in a later edition." He picked up the check. "I hate to run, but you know how my schedule gets crazy."

"No problem." Jack sipped his coffee and watched Briggs shuffle his six-foot frame out of the room as if he owned the place. If a person didn't know the man, he could be intimidating as hell. Being his late wife's cousin, Briggs had been his good friend for a long time.

Jack sighed. What could he possibly find in common with these desperate people on their quest for love? The job would be a piece of cake...except the part about dating. What kind of women joined clubs to meet men? And what kind of man signed up for this sort of thing? Jack had to chuckle. As of five minutes ago, *he* was that kind of man. "Crap."

CHAPTER THREE

A few days later, Cindy awoke with a start. Sitting up, she brushed sleep from her eyes. The dream had returned—her mom telling her to go to the car. It had been ages since she'd dreamt it. Being at the police station must have triggered something. Before she could ponder further, Prince jumped on the bed. "Good morning, fella. It's Saturday and we have the whole day off." She cradled him in her arms and patted his soft furry head before she put him on the floor. After pushing the warm covers back, she climbed out of bed and went into the bathroom. Not hearing anything from next door, she figured it should be safe to shower.

It seemed the man was never home, and she still hadn't met him—probably for the best. Prince yelped. "I'll be quick and take you out in a minute, little guy."

After she threw on jeans and a sweater, she stepped out onto the open balcony. Not a cloud in the sky. The warm sun beat down on her wrought iron patio furniture. The smell of spring was in the air. The clock tower located in the middle of the Sixteenth Street Mall struck nine times. She looked down from her thirty story balcony to see bits of green grass growing along the edges of the sidewalks. Small buds had appeared on the tree tops and the sound of birds chirping lifted Cindy's spirits.

Springtime in Colorado was great. One day she could have

snow and the next it would be in the seventies. Today was one of those days that made her feel good to be alive.

She grabbed her cordless phone and punched in Sam's number.

"Hello." A sleep-filled voice answered.

"Hey, want to meet me on the Mall at Starbucks for coffee? Go out on your balcony and look at all the people. It's a beautiful day."

"Huh...what time is it?"

"It's a little after nine, wake up sleepyhead." Then it dawned on her. Sam might have company. A casual one-night stand meant nothing to her. "Oh, I'm sorry. Are you with someone?"

A ripple of laughter flowed over the line. "No, it's just me. Guess I slept too hard." Cindy heard her yawn. "Yeah, give me a half hour and I'll meet you."

"Great. I'll take Prince for a walk. See you at Starbucks."

She clicked off the phone and went to find Prince. "Here, Prince. Come on boy." He ran from the open kitchen with his tail wagging and his toenails tapping against the hardwood floor with the resemblance of a smile on his wrinkled tan face. Could dogs smile? It looked like a smile. "Let's go, boy."

Opening the door into the hallway, she saw the backside of her new neighbor. Dressed in a towel twisted with a loose knot at his waist, he bent over to retrieve his morning paper. Before she could stop him, Prince ran toward the dangling towel. The dog grabbed the edge between his teeth and yanked. The towel fell to the floor.

Hello, Mr. Lover.

The man jumped back and tried to cover himself with the newspaper while he reached for his towel with the other. As if in slow motion, his door shut behind him. Cindy stood transfixed, with her mouth hanging open, staring at all his naked glory. Her libido hit overload. She hadn't been intimate with anyone for over a year and the last time wasn't that great. *Wow.*

"Hey, come here," he growled at Prince. The pup ran down the hall with the towel flapping from the corner of his mouth.

Cindy found her tongue. "I'm sorry, he usually..." She'd barely uttered the words when the man glanced in her direction. She stopped—horrified. Officer Jack Riley stood there with a frown on his face and only the sports' page to cover himself. Unable to speak, she tried to deny the pulsing knot that had formed in her stomach.

"I'm sure you've seen one before." Sarcasm dripped from his lips.

Life isn't fair. That glorious body belonged to the policeman...her pain-in-the-ass neighbor? And—*oh my God*, he was naked. "You. What are *you* doing here?"

"I live here. Lady, you need to do something about that damn dog. He's a menace. I should have the pound come and pick him up. They'll keep him—where he belongs."

"That will be the day." The mention of someone taking Prince pulled her out of her stupor. "He's an innocent puppy. You come near him and I'll have *you* arrested." Then it dawned on her to whom she was speaking—a policeman. Her face flushed with heat while he glared at her. "I'll send up someone to help you." She turned on her heel and ran after Prince, leaving Jack standing naked in the hall. Still angry, she hurried around the corner to find Prince.

Cindy caught up with the pup at the other side of the building near the elevator. Her heart thumped in overtime against her ribcage. He sat there innocently chewing on the towel. "Bad boy. Bad boy. No. No. No." She hooked him to the leash and pulled him in the elevator, taking the incriminating evidence from him. It was warm in here. The image of Jack Riley's muscular chest filled with soft dark curly hair trailing down to a well-endowed happy land would be forever imprinted on her brain.

Exiting on the first floor, Cindy saw Dean—the usual security person—working the front desk. A good thing. "Dean, could you go up and help my new neighbor. He's locked himself out of his condo and he's...naked."

"What?" Dean glanced at her and frowned.

"Prince stole his towel. I'm sure he'll explain it to you. Oh and here." She handed the towel over to him. "Give this to him with my apologies."

"Okay. I'll check it out. You have a nice day, Ms. Dawson." He chuckled and moved from behind the desk to the elevator.

She cringed. Her work was done. She and Prince needed to hightail it out of there. She didn't want to be anywhere near when Jack found his clothes.

Jack had stood there and watched her run away. Of all the neighbors to have...his just happened to be the luscious babe and her hell hound. "Some days it doesn't pay to get out of bed." He groaned, hoping no one else would see him.

"Looks like you have a problem," a small voice echoed from down the hall.

Jack turned to see a little old gray-haired lady two doors down peeking out of her chain-locked entryway. "You might say that, ma'am." He continued to hold the paper in front of himself and realized she'd already caught a good look at his backside.

"Did you get locked out?" she asked.

Dumb question lady. "Yes, ma'am, I did. Would you have something I can cover myself with until security gets up here to let me in?"

She closed the door and locked it behind her.

His hopes plummeted as goose bumps dotted his exposed flesh.

The woman's door cracked open a notch. "Here, young man. You can use this." She threw out a pink fluffy robe that had seen better days.

"Thanks, ma'am..." She shut the door before he had a chance to finish. He put on the threadbare robe and tied it around his waist. The sleeves were too tight and came to mid-elbow, but it covered him to the top of his thighs. *Better than nothing.* He could feel her watching him through the peep-hole. He smiled at the closed door and pulled the robe tighter. There would never be a dull moment—living next door to the raven haired vixen and her hellhound.

A short time later, Jack tugged the belt on the pink robe and gave the smiling security guy a look that could freeze water. "Don't say a word. Just let me into my condo."

"Sure Mr. Riley. I think this is yours." He handed Jack his towel and placed the master key in the lock. The door clicked open. "There you go."

"That woman is a pain in the ass," he mumbled.

"Sir, she did send me up to help you and she said she was sorry for her dog's actions. I don't think she meant any harm."

"My neighbor is a disaster waiting to happen. Believe me I intend to stay clear of her and the mutt."

"That might be a good idea, sir. Well, I have to get back to the lobby. If there's anything else I can help you with, let me know."

"Uh...Dean thanks for getting up here so quickly."

"Anytime, sir, it's my job."

Jack knew the man had to be snickering under his breath as he strolled down the hall. He entered his condo in a foul mood. "Damn woman." Why did *she* have to be his neighbor—his neighbor?

The next evening, Jack Riley sat in the back of the stretch limo with his date—willing the night to be over. The woman clung to him like a cheap suit on a hot summer's day. He had thought he'd be safe with an older woman. Wouldn't have to talk much, wouldn't have to worry about sex. Damn, the woman's hands had been working overtime, constantly stroking and groping.

"Do you like my hair?" Rhonda leered at him and placed her well manicured fingers against the side of her head.

Miss Blond Beehive 1965. He didn't want to be rude or hurt her feelings, so he did the only thing he could think of—he lied. "It's very becoming," he said behind a smile as fake as her three inch nails.

She slid close to his side, leaned her head against his shoulder and pushed the ratted, sprayed mess in his face. "Why don't you touch it?" she asked playfully as she gazed into his eyes and batted her lashes. Caught off guard, he felt her red lacquered tentacles slither up his leg.

Why had he agreed to go to dinner and the opera with this woman? Oh, the magazine article, his freelance editor...the money. Aspiring author or not, when Jack got his hands on his editor, Briggs was going to rue the day he fixed Jack up with the human octopus. Briggs called this research. Jack had handled drunks in the tank who were more manageable.

"I have a feeling you kind of like me," she whispered.

Why me? He'd been in uncomfortable positions before, but this was nuts. Feeling drugged from her heavy perfume, he tried to ease away. "Of course I like you, but I have a busy day tomorrow and I need to make it an early night."

"That doesn't matter. We can have our fun right here on the way to your place." Her husky voice grated on his nerves as she pressed the button to close the privacy divider. Digging into her suitcase-size purse she pulled out an envelope and handed it to him. "Maybe this will change your mind."

"What's this?" Opening it a shudder of revulsion shot through him. The envelope contained five one hundred dollar bills peeking back at him. The cloying woman thought he was a gigolo. This had gone far enough. An officer for the Denver Police Department, Jack could arrest her for solicitation, but he'd never hear the end of it from the guys down at the station. "There's been a misunderstanding. I'm not for sale."

Her long fingers kneaded his thigh through his trousers. "Honey, everybody has their price. What's yours?" She grabbed his family jewels and caressed him as if he were her latest prized possession. "Come on. Rhonda won't hurt you. Let's have some fun."

Feeling dirty and angry, he grasped her wrist and pushed her hand away from his body."Look lady," he growled, "I'm not interested." *I couldn't get it up right now if you were a pair of sexy twins in a vat of Mazola oil.*

"You're hurting me." Her eyes glittered in the dim light of the limo. She reached for him with her other hand. "So...you like it rough."

"Stop it. This isn't going to happen." He released her and slid away with his back against the side of the car.

She glared daggers at him with her hard cold eyes. "Fine. It's your loss," she shouted, then pressed the button for the chauffeur. "Charles, stop the car. Mr. Riley wants to get out."The limo slowed to a crawl along the deserted street and pulled to a smooth stop. Jack didn't care that he was several blocks from his place or it had started to snow in downtown Denver. His top priority—escape.

He stepped out into the cold evening under the overcast sky and slammed the car door. The red tail lights of the sleek auto disappeared around the corner. Savoring his freedom, he took a deep breath of fresh air. It was okay. He needed time to clear his head. He hoped all his so-called dates for this article didn't turn out like this one.

At this rate, his search for information would probably lead to dating dope addicts, lesbians, and women who kept dead cats in their freezer. Some people might not think there was anything wrong with that but it sure as hell wasn't his idea of a good time.

Moving along the sidewalk, he got over being disgusted. Instead, he tried to think about why she'd done what she did. Tons of money and no love. He shoved his chilled fingers in his pockets and felt some pity for the older woman. But still....

He should have listened to his gut. It never steered him wrong. When she had insisted they leave the opera early in her private seduction wagon, he knew she was up to something. And—that something was getting lucky with him.

Did he look like a gigolo? He glanced at his reflection in the shop windows on the Sixteenth Street Mall. A tall muscular man in his mid-thirties stared back at him. He hesitated and pushed his dark wavy hair to one side of his forehead. The tux was rented and he looked...

He laughed. Maybe he did look the part but he had been a perfect gentleman during the evening listening to her prattle on about her deceased husband and the millions she had inherited. So sad. And in some way he had to admit, deep down, he was sorry for the lonely woman. Maybe she thought her only chance at happiness would be to buy her way into a relationship.

How could a person let themselves become so needy? The woman had lots going for herself. Fairly good looks for her age—if she'd change her hideous hairdo—good health and money to burn. He grimaced. Everybody has something broken. The less broken have to take care of the more broken.

He'd learned that early on, but he'd be damned if he'd take care of *this* one.

However, she made an interesting character for his article. He sighed and let go of his hostility. Welcome to the Lonely Hearts Club...people who were desperate and would do anything to get what they wanted. The snow came down harder. He didn't have an overcoat. The Mall trolley had shut down for the night. He shivered as goose bumps rose on his arms. Steam hissed from the grates in the center of the street. He continued down the empty sidewalk, alone with his thoughts. At times he liked to stroll the quiet avenues late at night, with only the skyscrapers to keep him company, glad he didn't need or depend on anyone to make himself happy.

Sure, when his family was alive things were different. Missing them still hurt, Jack swallowed the lump in his throat and carried his guilt tucked deep in his soul. On that fateful morning, he'd been passed out in the back area of the family SUV. The place where he'd decided to sleep it off, instead of going into the house to face his wife and child...once again, drunk on his ass. He was dead to the world while inside the house on a Saturday morning his son watched cartoons and his wife made pancakes. This was their way of coping with his problem. Janet cut her finger slicing fruit for the pancakes and put their son in the SUV with her to head to the emergency room.

A drunk driver ran a red light and hit them head on. The steering wheel pinned her in the car. He slept as his young son died on impact and the jaws of life pried her from the car. She breathed her last breath. He awoke in the aftermath. Alone in the hospital room, he cried. His family was gone. If only he had gone into the house to be with his wife and son...if only.

After the accident, there had been times he'd been close to kicking the radio into the bathtub. He'd been lost—working through his pain with alcohol until his friend, Jim Briggs, fished him out of the bottom of a bottle and showed him how to pour his sorrow out on paper. What counted in his life today was who showed up to live it...the hopeless drunk or the sober cop who did freelance writing. For the past four years, the sober cop had won.

CHAPTER FOUR

Cindy was happy to see Sam already sitting outside at the downtown Starbucks enjoying the day when she arrived.

“Hey, it’s about time you got here,” Sam said.

"Yes, I got caught up with something. I'll grab a coffee and be right back." Prince plopped down on the sidewalk next to Sam where Cindy tied him to the black wrought iron railing.

"Cool. I'll be here enjoying the people watching."

A few minutes later, Sam sipped her latte while Cindy gave Prince a cup of water. "Okay, now tell me what’s up? You look all flustered."

"It’s such a nice day I just wanted to get outside.” She frowned. “Okay, I’ll come clean. You'd never believe who I ran into this morning."

"Who?" Sam arched her eyebrow, waiting for an answer.

"Of all people, it was Jack Riley, the policeman who I hit with my car." She grinned at the recent memory of him standing naked in her hallway and laughed.

"Oh, my God, you’ve got to be kidding. Where?" Sam waited patiently for the rest of the story.

Cindy hesitated. "You’re not going to believe it but he's my new neighbor. When I opened the door this morning, there he was, getting his newspaper, wearing only a towel. Prince grabbed the towel and took off with it. I saw *everything*."

"Wow, you got beefcake for breakfast? Lucky woman." Sam laughed.

"I left the man there in the hallway...naked."

"That's funny." Sam's uncontrollable laughter flowed around them. Erasing the smile from her face, she said, "Wish I'd been there."

Cindy couldn't help but giggle, too. It was humorous. "I...I guess I should've let him into my place, but my first thought was to get Prince out of there. Do you think he can have my dog taken away because of what happened?" Cindy glanced down at Prince and watched him snore his way through the conversation.

"No. He's a playful puppy and he's had his shots. The fact he didn't bite anyone should help." Sam chuckled. "I don't think Mr. Cop will do anything. The man's pride was bruised. He reacted to the moment. After he calms down, he'll get over it."

"I hope you're right. He was really upset."

"I'm sure he was, but think about it. This is something he wouldn't want to get around the police station. The realization a small dog could outdo him will be his best kept secret."

"Maybe, but I'm going to keep a sharp eye on Prince. He goes nowhere without his leash."

"Tell me...without his clothes, would Officer Friendly be worth the aggravation?"

"Sam, you're incorrigible." Cindy sipped her drink. "I hate to admit it, but he's really cute...until he opens his mouth." The imprinted image of a naked Jack was still fresh in Cindy's mind. "What about you and the guy you left my birthday party with? How'd that go?"

Sam laughed. "It went fine. I like older men. You know it's not until they're past fifty before you can have an intelligent conversation with them."

Cindy was surprised. "He isn't *that* old, is he?"

"It doesn't matter. He's done the great foraging through the years and can give me the answers." A dreamy look came over her face. "I'm going over to his place this evening." She wriggled her eyebrows. "Let me tell you, Larry is a keeper. We've gone out on a few dates and I'm having a ball."

"Oh, yeah? And what did you do?"

Sam hesitated. "Last night we had a lovely dinner at the Broker and went back to his place." A cloud settled over her features as she leaned toward Cindy. "To look at the man, he's a walking, talking sex machine. But when I got him alone, up close and personal, there was no life on Pluto."

Cindy burst out laughing. "That's a good one. You know, I envy you being such a free spirit."

"Honey, there's nothing free about me. The man is loaded." She grinned. "Trust me...give me time and the phoenix shall rise again."

"You're too funny." Cindy sipped her coffee as thoughts of Jack Riley intruded once again. *If I was more of a free thinker, like Sam, I'd have the guts to do something about Jack—even if he is a policeman.*

Later that evening, Cindy sat at her laptop and checked Mark Smith's bio one last time. After meeting at one of the single's dinners they had agreed to go on a date. In about ten minutes, she would see this latest man at the Rock Bottom Brewery. The stats were good—an executive at Qwest with an interest in sports, nature walks, rock climbing and having a good time. Plus, he was easy on the eyes. The rising executive had short brown hair and sparkling blue eyes with a Michael Douglas dimple on his chin. Yes, she could stand to gaze at him over dinner.

Satisfied, she shut down her computer and looked through the peephole into the hallway. With no sign of Jack, she quickly rushed out the door and caught the elevator. Being late was one of her pet peeves. It drove her nuts when people weren't on time. Fortunately, the Rock Bottom was on the Sixteenth Street Mall and she lived only a block away.

The open air street mall stretched through the heart of downtown Denver for over a mile. Filled with elegant dining establishments and wonderful shops, it was always an adventure. Traffic was restricted, except for the free shuttle buses that ran up and down the Mall, lucky for her, since her car would be in the shop for a long time. She shook her head at her stupidity and sighed. In the meantime, she could get to work and make the best of it with the city transit system.

Regardless, she preferred to meet her dates on location. That way, if things didn't work out, she could leave on her own power. She shivered in her light coat and hurried along the busy sidewalk. The temperature had dropped like a stone when the sun went down.

When she stepped through the wide double doors of the Rock Bottom Brewery, warm air caressed her skin. The minute she came inside from the cold blustery evening, Mark walked toward her. "Good evening, Mark."

"Hello there." His gaze moved slowly up her body and finally reached her face. The way the man looked her over made her uncomfortable. Glancing around, she noted the upscale brewery and sports bar was filled to the rafters. When they moved further into the entranceway, the buzz of the restaurant surrounded them, which made conversation nearly impossible. Warm and welcoming, the atmosphere made it appear like a big happy family reunion.

Huge silver brewery vats were placed in the center of the restaurant behind glass partitions. Customers could see the ale being made. Large TVs were suspended from the ceiling with different sporting events being broadcast for the pleasure of the crowd. Early evening diners sat in comfortable padded booths enjoying their meals.

"I'm glad you could make it." Mark pulled her to his side, making her tense with anxiety.

She wasn't used to her personal space being invaded this quickly by a total stranger. *For heaven's sake, it's only a hug. Get a grip.*

"I hope the restaurant is okay with you," he said.

She moved away from him, regained her space, smiled and tried to disguise her annoyance. "It's fine. Looks like a fun place." A small voice echoed what she had said. *Fun place. Fun place.* She shook her head, thinking she must be imagining things. Cindy glanced around the restaurant liking what she saw.

"They have great food." A distinct hardening appeared in his eyes as if he could read her mind. "The buffalo fajitas are fabulous," he said.

Cindy glanced at the nearest monitor for a second, hoping to catch the score of the hockey game.

"Do you like hockey?" Mark snuggled closer to her.

"Yes, I go to as many games as I can." She moved slightly away from him, hoping he'd take the hint. Listening to Mark, it dawned on her as to what he had said—something about eating buffalo.

"You eat buffalo?" Her nose crinkled before she thought to control it. She realized buffalo were no longer endangered, but she still didn't want to eat one.

"Yeah, they raise them on farms, you know. Just for eating. Less fat, they say. Anyway, you have to try it."

"I think I'll pass," she murmured, an image of the proud majestic beast of the old west forefront in her mind. She glanced at Mark. She hadn't anticipated his interest in nature ran to eating it. *Strike One.*

"Your table is ready," the hostess said. Cindy and Mark followed her into another room where the noise from the sports bar became muffled. They were seated and the waiter brought menus, tall glasses of ice water with lemon and took their orders.

After ordering their meal, Mark rested his chin on his hand and studied her. His gaze roved over her body, giving her the creeps when he spoke. Why hadn't she noticed at the singles' dinner he wasn't the shy type, but instead a man with a huge ego...on the make.

"Do you live near here?" he asked.

"Yes, at Brooks Tower, a few blocks away." She clamped her mouth shut and wanted to cut out her tongue. Why had she told him where she lived?

He acknowledged the waiter as their meal and drinks were set in front of them. "I've heard of the building. Quite nice." His gaze lowered to her modest cleavage. She squirmed, wishing she'd worn a turtleneck. "It's located near the center of the Mall, over a block, isn't it?"

Mentally, she kicked herself for telling this creep her address. Thank goodness the building had twenty-four hour security and a doorman. "Yes, it's an older building."

"How's the view from the top?"

"I'm sure it's awesome, but I don't live in the penthouse. I'm on a lower floor but it has a great view of the city and the mountains." She placed the white linen napkin on her lap and focused on getting through the dinner.

"Maybe you can show me your view sometime?" He raised his eyebrows in anticipation. "I like to be up high, away from the average peon on the street."

Jerk. During the course of the conversation, she realized he wasn't what she had expected, not what she had hoped. She sipped her hot tea and only half-listened to the man ramble on about his possessions, his fabulous job, and his new BMW. It would be a long night and a cold day in hell before he saw her view. She had lost her edge. Usually she could spot this type a mile away. *What a pompous ass. Strike Two.*

"Rock Bottom has marvelous food," he continued to stuff the buffalo fajitas into his mouth, finally shutting up for a minute.

She forced herself to be polite and at least finish the meal. She attempted a smile. "Yes, the Brown Ale Chicken is delicious." Cindy had enjoyed the meal, the service and the atmosphere, but couldn't say much for the company. She tried to think of a graceful way to leave when she heard something from under the table.

She peeked under the table and saw nothing. Glancing around, no one spoke to her. A strange voice called out, "*Oh, Mark, you're so handsome.*" To her surprise, he showed no reaction. She glanced at the table and wondered who was playing games. The voice sounded again, much louder this time. "*You're too sexy for yourself.*"

Cindy felt a red flush crawling up her neck and face as she glanced at the other diners who had started to stare at them. The voice spoke up once more. "*Cindy, this is your lucky night,*" the voice said. Her embarrassment turned to annoyance.

"These are for you." Mark pulled a bouquet of silk flowers out of his sleeve and handed them to her. He spoke loud enough for the whole room to hear, but gazed only at her. Apparently, the man was a ventriloquist. He had been throwing his voice, entertaining the crowd at her expense.

She hated being the brunt of his joke. Mark sat across from her looking pleased, as if she were going to announce that he was the man of her dreams. She reached into her purse and laid a twenty by her plate, along with the napkin. "That should cover my meal." Standing, she graciously took the flowers and plunked them in her water glass. "They look a little wilted." *Strike Three.* She walked away, putting distance between the arrogant man and the still staring crowd.

Another frog...this one with warts.

Jack pushed send and let the e-mail to "Snow White" fly into cyberspace. After finding her on his singles board, he had left it to the fates. *A funny thing about fate—you never know where it might lead you.*

It took guts to put your heart out there, not that he intended to do any such thing. But, it was apparent from a name like Snow White she was looking for Prince Charming. He would play along...sorta. He'd be her e-mail buddy, gather information from her about her dating experiences. He did admire the woman for having the courage to put herself on the market so blatantly. And after all, he'd already been out with Cruella Deville. Why not Snow White?

"Jack, you're a genius," he told himself. Since they belonged to the same group they could discuss their dates without naming names. He could keep this one on his monitor screen if he chose, and never have to meet her in person. Yeah. He hoped she would answer. If nothing else, he could use some good insight from the woman's angle.

It probably wouldn't be wise to tell his dates he planned to take them out strictly for research. He laughed. No, that would go over like a dead fly in the punch bowl.

Stretching his arms out in front of the computer, he caught the time on the screen. He needed to get to the station. Johnson's wife had gone into labor and they were short-handed so he'd volunteered to work a double-shift. Besides, he wasn't quite ready to go out on another date. The memory of the last one left a bad taste in his mouth. Thinking of the red polished talons, he cringed.

Back at her condo, Cindy decided the evening had exhausted her. With many more dates like this one, she'd just hunker down with a bucket of fudge and call it quits.

Prince snuggled against her side and fell asleep while she sat on the bed with her laptop and looked out at the city. Lights winked from the skyscrapers across the way, shining like expensive jewels against inky black velvet. She'd never grow tired of the view. Still early for a Saturday night, every now and then, she heard voices float up from people having fun on the Sixteenth Street Mall. With several colleges nearby, students partied until the bars and restaurants closed in the wee hours of the morning.

Denver was alive. Back home in Cedar Falls, they rolled up the sidewalks at six o'clock. If you were up for it, something was always happening in this town. Sports, opera, theater, movies—the choices were endless. The city had a pulse of its own. The heartbeat soothed her as she gazed at the Qwest building across the way. Moving here was the best decision she'd ever made.

The sign high atop the Quest building's fifty-two story headquarters spelled the company's name with an eighteen-foot high "Q" followed by four ten-foot high letters in sky-blue neon. It had become a favorite landmark of the city. She watched it slowly disappear among the falling snowflakes. Sitting atop her own little world, secluded in clouds of snow, she contemplated her horrific date.

With a sigh, she returned to her laptop and checked her e-mail. When she thought about the voice she'd heard from under the table, she had to smile. It was comical. Back in her condo, away from Mark and the staring crowd, she could laugh at the whole thing. The man was stuck on himself. She checked the screen. Cool, she had an e-mail from Grace, one of her friends from Cedar Falls.

From:GraceTaylor
To:Snowhite

Hi Cindy,

How's it going? Did you have a good time on your date? Tell me about it. Cedar Falls isn't the same without you. The twins are starting to crawl and get into everything.Jenna said to say hi. We all miss you.
Love You Like A Sis ~ Grace

Prince woke up and rubbed his nose against her arm. She reached over and tucked him close to her side. Cindy missed Grace, too, but she wasn't ready to pack it in and go running home. If she'd learned anything since moving to Denver, it was she'd fallen in love with the city. Leaning back, she sipped her favorite Celestial Seasonings Cinnamon Apple Spice tea. *Ummm...she could get into tea.*

How should she answer Grace? Her date had been a disaster from beginning to end. Sure, she knew going in there would be false starts in the dating game, but this guy couldn't get off the line. At least she had a good support system with Grace, Jenna and Sam. She could tell them her secrets. Laughing or crying, they were there for each other.

She'd known it wouldn't be easy to step out of her comfort zone. Going after what she wanted was the hard part. Pushing her hair behind her ears, she typed the e-mail. Dating was tough for her, but from what she'd heard while talking to the other girls in the singles' group, it was difficult for them, too. She liked her independence and could live without a man if things turned out that way. Companionship would be nice, but she had achieved her own brand of happiness. She had a fun job, great friends—a good life and if she never met a prince, she could still adopt a child of her own. The thought warmed her heart.

The girls told her the key to playing the dating game was not to be serious about every date. Like in sales, where you went through so many no answers to get to a yes, in dating you had to kiss a lot of frogs to find a prince. Could this be worth it? Maybe...maybe not—time would tell. She stroked Prince's back. He whimpered in his sleep and snuggled close to her side. Turning back to the monitor, she noticed she had an e-mail from someone in the singles group.

From:JPrince
To:Snowhite

Hello,
I picked your address from the singles group list. I thought we might have something in common. You know, like Prince Charming and Snow White. Great minds think alike. How is the singles group working for you? I just joined. What do you want in a relationship?
JPrince

Finally a charming prince had come to call...or at least he lived out there in cyber space. She laughed. Here she had been searching everywhere for him and he was on her singles' board all the time. What did she have to lose? The only thing she knew for certain was no matter what happened, it was going to be a year she'd remember for the rest of her life.

CHAPTER FIVE

Before she spoke, Cindy gave Sam the once over the next evening at work at the Vocational Beauty School. She leaned against the counter and watched Sam. "You had something done. You've been sucked and tucked...or something."

"I have not...I'm in lust." She grinned.

Cindy glanced at her friend. "Are you sure?"

Sam laughed. "Yes, I swear. I haven't done anything. It's the afterglow of having the best sex imaginable, even after the condom broke." She sighed. "The Phoenix has risen and Larry knows his way around my body. The best lover I've ever had. I could easily fall for this guy."

"Be careful. You haven't known him long."

"Yeah, that's why I'm holding back."

"Holding back." Cindy laughed, ribbing her friend. "Since when?"

"Not with my body, with my emotions. I'm going to give this relationship some time before I let myself fall totally off the ledge."

"Smart. But how do you control your emotions? I'm always too sensitive about those things."

"It comes with practice. You'll figure it out." She gave Cindy her usual wink. "I'm teaching the freshmen haircutting for the next couple hours. I'll see you after class."

"Okay, see you then." Cindy hoped she didn't have to go through as many men as Sam had, to get to her soul mate. She was cut from a different cloth, but she wanted to have a night of incredible sex, too. It had been a long time for her and the recurring vision of a naked Jack had given her too many wild dreams. So she was horny—she was entitled. What was she going to do about it?

"Ms. Cindy, Ms. Cindy. Come quick. Brenda needs your help." A young cosmetology student with spiked burgundy hair caught Cindy as she came out of the classroom.

"What's wrong?" The girl looked stricken. "You look as if someone died."

"Oh, worse than that, ma'am. Brenda gave Mrs. Smith a perm and her hair is falling out."

Cindy hurried to the scene of the crime. Her jaw dropped when she peered into the shampoo bowl where Mrs. Smith lay back waiting for her perm to process. There in the bottom of the sink were two perm rods still wrapped with hair. They resembled two perfect, fat little Jimmy Dean sausages.

"Aahh...good evening, Mrs. Smith." Cindy faked a smile. "I need to check your perm." She glanced at Brenda and warned her with her gaze not to alert the customer to what had happened. "Brenda, who gave you the perm solution and how long has it been on her hair?"

"Miss Dotty. Fifteen minutes," Brenda croaked.

Cindy unwrapped one curl on top of the woman's head to see the usual 's' shape pattern which indicated the perm had processed. "She's ready. Let's rinse out the solution and start the neutralizer."

She grabbed a dry towel from the shelf and handed it to the customer. "Here, Mrs. Smith, we don't want to get any water on your face." The customer covered her eyes with it, unaware of the situation.

Another perm rod plopped into the shampoo bowl—hair and all. Cindy swallowed a gasp and went to work. The woman's hair was breaking off at the scalp.

After a thorough rinse, she grabbed a bottle of neutralizer and applied it to every rod left on the woman's head. This would stop the breakage before any more damage could be done. But there was no getting around it—the customer would have a few bald spots. Picking up the three rods—complete with hair—from the bottom of the bowl, she shoved them into her smock pocket.

The two students looked over her shoulder in fear. She'd explain to them later what caused the damage. Right now she had to deal with the customer. Once the woman knew her hair was falling out, she'd have a hissy fit. And who could blame her? Right now Cindy had to protect her students—and the school.

Placing a folded towel under Mrs. Smith's neck, she smiled at the customer. "We have to leave the neutralizer on for another five minutes. Are you comfortable?"

"Yes, I'm fine." The customer lay back on the lip of the shampoo bowl and closed her eyes.

The dinging of the timer matched Cindy's heartbeat as she gently removed the perm rods and feared more hair would fall off in her hand. She worked the neutralizer through the ends of the hair. Things could've been much worse. The woman wouldn't be totally bald.

Cindy let out a sigh of relief when she saw the perm liability card had been signed and was on the counter. She knew what had happened, had seen it many times throughout her years as a cosmetologist and instructor. The customer failed to mention she had done some other chemical treatment to her hair, such as a color and Dotty had given the student the wrong perm solution.

Changing the towel around Mrs. Smith's neck, Cindy covered her hair with another. "Come on. Let's finish at Brenda's station." The sound of blow dryers, snatches of conversations, and the chemical smells of the beauty school surrounded them as they went back to Brenda's work area.

After Mrs. Smith was comfortably seated, Cindy unwrapped the towel around her head, blotted out the excess moisture in the hair, and clamped the towel around her neck. "Have you frosted your hair or put color on it recently?" Running her fingers through the damaged, curly hair, she met Mrs. Smith's gaze in the mirror.

"Why...ah, yes, but that was several months ago. I frosted it at home and didn't like it so I colored it back to my natural color." The woman broke eye contact and glanced away.

"I see. Well, because of those two chemical treatments and now your perm, I'm afraid you have some breakage." She hesitated for a second. "I recommend you recondition your hair with a good moisturizer and protein mixture. I'll send you home with a couple of samples. But don't do anything to it for the next forty-eight hours. Just wet it down and let it dry. It takes that long for the perm to settle into its new shape. The breakage will have to grow out."

"It's okay. This looks wonderful." Mrs. Smith squeezed the bottom of her curly hair and glanced at Brenda. "I knew that other beauty school was worked up about nothing. They refused to do it, so I came to you. Besides," she smiled. "I knew I'd have some breakage. I've done this before."

Cindy did a double-take. *The other school refused to do her hair. She knew she'd have some breakage. This customer is a **real** gem.* She sighed, making a mental note to add Mrs. Smith to the list of clients to watch closely when they came in for services. There were always those customers who weren't honest about what they put on their hair and wanted problems so they could sue the school or get free services. She'd never understand it. Why would someone ruin their looks for a few measly dollars? It was something the schools always had to be on the watch for—whether it made sense or not.

"Thanks for doing my hair." Mrs. Smith looked in the mirror at her curly do.

Sheesh, the woman didn't have a clue. Fortunately, most of the breakage had been in the back and underneath.

Cindy and the girls finished up with Mrs. Smith and chalked it up to another day in the life of working in a beauty college. The students had to learn the customers didn't always reveal the truth—either by choice or sheer forgetfulness.

Thinking of those hair-wrapped rods now resting in her pocket, Cindy shivered. Things could've been much worse. She'd use them for a class demonstration on what not to do.

Sam came over to Cindy. "Look what I found in the break room." She held up a can of beer. "Everyone knows alcohol isn't allowed in the school. Someone is trying to get us in trouble."

"Do you have any idea of who would do that?" Cindy lifted

the clean perm rods from the shampoo bowl and spread them out on a towel on the counter and glanced back at Sam.

Sam scooted in next to her, holding the beer can over the shampoo bowl. "I can't say for sure, but it's probably Miss Dolly. I know she wants to get me fired." She sighed. "I'll pour it down the drain and none will be the wiser." She pulled the tab back and smelly beer spewed out, splashing both of them. "Oh, crap." She giggled.

Cindy tried to wipe the warm spray from her clothes with a towel. "We stink." She laughed. "It's a good thing we've already closed the doors to any more customers for the evening."

"I'm sorry. What can I do?" Sam looked upset.

"Don't worry about it. I'm going straight home after we lock up." Cindy blew her bangs out of her eyes. "What a day."

"Yeah. By the way, you handled that bad perm situation beautifully. When I saw those hairy rods in the sink, I about died." Sam emptied the remains of the beer can and threw it in the trash.

"Thanks. Brenda used the wrong solution. If anymore of Mrs. Smith's hair had broken off, you could bet there would've been a lawsuit, and you and I would have been named as instructors on duty." She sighed. "Some days you eat the bear and some days the bear eats you. Today, we ate the bear."

Sam's gentle laughter rippled through the air. "Cool. Hey, how did your date go the other night?"

Cindy laughed. "You won't believe this one. It was a mess." She glanced at Sam. "The guy was cute, but totally stuck on himself. He was some kind of ventriloquist who talked to me from under the table."

"Talked to you from under the table? You're joking."

"No. I kid you not. It about embarrassed me to death. Everyone in the restaurant stared at us."

"What a schmuck." Sam shook her head.

She winked and went off to help another student check a haircut.

Sam came back to stand by Cindy at the reception desk while the students cleaned up for the night. "Now, that things have slowed down, I can finish telling you about Larry. I experienced romance in a bottle."

"What do you mean?"

"Remember, I told you, when I wore my magic bra and panties, Larry still couldn't get it up. Well, this new Niagra drink is the cure. It's the woman's answer to Viagra and it comes in a pretty blue bottle, kind of like wine coolers."

"But that's for women. I don't get it." She grinned. "Does it work?"

"Yeah, not that I needed it. I've never had a problem in that area." She giggled. "But I think it was mostly the fact that I drank it for him. That's what got Larry so turned-on. All we had were a couple of bottles of Niagra and he took some Viagra. It was great."

Cindy could hear the purr of satisfaction in Sam's voice. "Good for you. Have another bottle for me."

"Oh, honey, I sure intend to. Larry is fridge worthy and I'm going to stock up."

Cindy laughed. "Fridge worthy? Too funny."

"You know how small my fridge is well it's not just any guy who gets his own space."

"Oh yeah, I forgot."

Before Sam locked the doors to the school for the night, Cindy grabbed a mannequin head. She needed to brush up on making finger waves before she taught a class on it the next day.

She and Sam went their separate ways as she stepped out of the building and was greeted by a blast of street noise. Near the intersection, a car had stalled, blocking the tram. The police were directing traffic around it. She moved with the crowd, when lo and behold, who did she see, Officer Jack Riley. She cringed. Her heart beat faster at the sight of him. Horns honked and people in a hurry drowned out the thudding of her heart.

"Murph, move those people back so we can get the tow truck in here." Over the sounds of the city, she heard Jack, loud and clear as he spoke into his radio unit with cool authority. Juggling her books and the mannequin head, she tried to blend in with the group of students crossing the busy street, hoping he wouldn't notice her.

But she had to walk right by him, under the bright street

lights, to get to the other side. Her luck didn't hold. He saw her and recognition dawned in his eyes. She stopped, frozen, like a bug under a fly swatter. Someone bumped into her and ran on by. Her stuff tumbled to the ground.

"Murph, cover for me." Jack rushed after her mannequin head as it rolled down the street. He grabbed it by the long hair and turned back to face her. He gave her a black look and bent down to pick up the rest of her scattered books.

The man had left his post to come to her aid, but he sure didn't like it. He handed her the head. When his fingers touched hers, she had the wildest urge to jump back. The touch had triggered a spasmodic trembling that tried to surface. She fought it back.

"Lady, I'm surprised you don't have the mutt with you." He frowned and seemed to sniff the air. "Have you been drinking...again?" Placing a gentle hand on her arm, he guided her to the sidewalk.

Her stomach lurched as she realized he had caught the smell of beer on her clothes. She glared daggers at him and ignored the remark about Prince. "Not that it's any of your business, but no, I haven't been drinking."

"Maybe it is...maybe it isn't." He glared right back at her as she stepped onto the street corner, gripping her mannequin head like a lifeline.

"Look, it was spilled on me." *The man had a lot of nerve.* "Anyway, I'm not driving. Remember, I don't have my car...it's in the shop. I'm going to catch the tram." *Control my temper, take a deep breath.* She didn't need another ticket and didn't want him messing with Prince. "Did you know I could hear you speaking into your radio all the way across the street?" *What a dumb ass thing to say.*

She tried to change the conversation and sounded like a blathering idiot. Now, he would think she was drunk for sure. But the man flustered her brain with his very presence. His natural animal magnetism caused her heart to pound erratically. He made her feel things she resisted with all her might. A primitive warning sounded in her brain. The last thing she needed was an attraction to a moody cop.

"The idea is to keep the volume turned high so the people

will stay out of our way." He cleared his throat and frowned. "Are you interested in the police force?"

His response held a note of impatience while she stiffened under his withering glare. The image of him, naked in her hallway flashed through her mind. To her annoyance, she felt herself start to blush. "Me...uh...no, I don't think so." *If he only knew.* Police work would be the last thing in the world she would be interested in.

"That's what I thought." A sparkle in his eyes caused her heart to hammer foolishly. She didn't need this. One minute he gave her dirty looks and the next he flirted. Standing there on the street talking with him made her lose track of time. Against her will, she felt an immediate and total attraction to the man. A brief shiver rippled through her. No way would she get involved with a cop.

"Are you cold? Why don't you step inside the student center where it's warmer? We'll have to get that car moved before you can catch the tram."

She followed alongside him in a sort of daze. What was wrong with her? For heaven's sake, he was only a good-looking man and she'd seen cute guys before, lots of them. Maybe not naked, but... *Shake it off, nitwit.*

"Thanks for your help." Her mouth was dry and dusty like old paper. She took the rest of the books he handed to her. He grinned, and the reasons why she shouldn't let herself like a policeman went right out the window.

"Have a good evening, Ms. Dawson. Go home and sleep it off." She was acutely aware of his broad shoulders when he smiled, turned and walked back out into the night. Then common sense slammed into her.

Sleep it off? How dare he assume she had been drinking. *Damn him.* With mixed emotions she stood there with students wandering around her in the entryway. Her stomach churned with anxiety and excitement at what had happened.

Memories flashed through her mind. *A young girl sits in a crowded police station sipping a soda while the business of busting criminals goes on around her. A dim memory of her mother coming to tell her she'll only be a few more minutes and they can go home...*

Shaking her head to bring herself back to the moment, she left the student center and attempted to push the thoughts of Jack out of her mind. She'd learned to live for today because life went so quickly.

Not wanting to run into him again, she decided to walk downtown. It wasn't far to her place. Again, a vivid image of her mother surfaced. This time her mom lay bleeding on the floor with no one to help her. Cindy's heart had healed, but sometimes excruciating pain crawled to the surface. She could never date a cop...cops died.

CHAPTER SIX

Cindy stuck her head out and glanced up and down the hall before she stepped off the elevator. It'd been quite some time since Prince had stolen Jack's towel and she'd seen him on the street. However, she remembered his reaction and grimaced. So far her luck had held. She and Prince had successfully avoided Jack. She hadn't heard anything from Animal Control and Prince was safe, tucked away in her condo.

Just as she reached her unit, his door opened and luck beat a nasty retreat. Jack stood there in his uniform, looking strong, sexy, and capable of dealing with any situation. He held his black Oakley sunglasses in one hand, keys in the other. His cool stare washed over her, leaving her with a slight case of frostbite.

"Hello," she said and smiled. She would step up and be friendly—for Prince's sake. Never mind the man looked like the tempting icing on a three layer chocolate cake. And besides, there was the old saying about keeping your friends close and your enemies closer?

"Hello, Ms. Dawson. Is it safe to come out or is your mutt lurking around the corner?"

Cindy's temper climbed a notch. After all, she was the one extending the olive branch. Picturing Prince playing with his chew toy, she let the insult slide off her like raindrops off a duck's back. "He's in the condo." She placed her key in the lock and glanced back at him. "Please, call me Cindy."

"Okay, Cindy, call me Jack." He held out his hand.

She shook his hand and pulled back as an intense warmth passed between them. It happened again. Why did she get this feeling every time he touched her?

He watched her. "Today, it sounded like he was having a great time over there. I heard a couple of crashes." Jack smiled.

There was something lazily seductive in his look. "You must've been mistaken. He's the perfect pet." Cindy swallowed the white lie. That is if she didn't count the shoes he'd chewed beyond repair, or the bathroom door he'd scratched when he accidentally closed it on himself.

She hesitated, dreading what she might find on the other side of the door. She realized arguing with the man was only going to get her and Prince in more hot water. "I should have said something earlier, but I'm sorry about him taking your towel. It won't happen again."

Jack cleared his throat. "It's forgotten."

"He's a sweet puppy if you'd give him half a chance."

He snorted. "Yeah, sure, just keep him away from my newspaper." Jack slipped on his shades and nodded toward her. "Good day, Cindy."

"Whatever." She watched him walk down the hall to the elevator. As Sam would say, he looked as good going as he did coming. Jack turned and grinned when he stepped into the elevator. With a flush on her cheeks from being caught appreciating his backside, she slipped into her condo.

Jack had been right. Prince had thrown a party while she'd been at work. A small round table had been overturned and a cushion had been ripped apart and half of it hung from the edge of a glass and wrought iron coffee table. A trail of foam stuffing led across the living room floor and into the bedroom. Cindy held her breath and wondered what he had done to the bedroom. Peeking through the door, she found him fast asleep in a corner with the remains of the pillow under his head. The chew toy she'd given him this morning lay across the room untouched. The scamp looked peaceful in the remnants of condo demolition.

After she cleaned up the mess, she grabbed the phonebook and settled into her favorite overstuffed chair. Prince needed to go to obedience school. She rubbed his head as he snuggled next to her, peacefully unaware of what she had in mind.

An image of Prince stealing Jack's towel flashed before her. Damn, she just couldn't get the naked vision of her surly neighbor out of her head.

Jack sat at the station in front of a computer. Johnson's new baby had a high fever and had been rushed to the hospital. He had volunteered to work desk duty with ulterior motives. He was hoping for an easy night so he could work on his article.

Unwarranted thoughts of Cindy raced through his mind. Reluctantly, he had to admit she was a babe. Cute, in an old fashioned sort of way, with dark raven hair and a sprinkle of freckles scattered across the bridge of her nose. And those green eyes could cut glass when she was riled. Such an easy target, he did enjoy teasing her about the pup.

But damn, when he had seen her on the street, she had just gotten off work and smelled to high heaven of alcohol. He couldn't stand the thought of hooking up with someone who probably had a drinking problem—it would be a betrayal to his wife, his child...himself. He'd never let that happen. Today, the only things he had left were the memories. Added to his disappointment was a feeling of unending guilt. *I'll never put myself through that pain again—ever.*

Shrugging off the thought, he logged onto the computer. While things were slow he could get away with doing some personal work. He'd check his e-mail first. There was a message from Snow White. It had been several days and he'd thought she wasn't going to respond.

From: Snowhite

To: JPrince

Hi, the dating game has been pretty much a disaster for me. How about you? You asked what I was looking for in a relationship? Well, here it is. He has to be someone who's not afraid to commit and show his feelings. And he has to like children, animals, classic movies, sports and hiking in the mountains. Must have a sense of humor and be able to make me laugh. And he should be able to show a girl a good time without being possessive. Later ~Snow White

Well, I'll be dammed. It isn't just me. This woman wasn't having the time of her life in the dating game, either. He hated going on these phony dates. But for the article's sake it had to be authentic. He'd added her e-mail address to his instant messaging and sure enough she was on line.

JPrince: *Hi, Snow White. You seemed a little shy the other night in the chat room. Chat rooms are overrated. Hope you don't mind that I added your address to my instant messaging.*

Jack blinked at the blue box on his screen. Would she answer? It would be more interesting to pry information out of her in a personal e-mail than in a chat room.

Snowhite: *Hello, Prince, surprised to hear from you. I don't mind if you e-mail me. What are you doing tonight?*

JPrince: *Messing around on the computer. How about you? It's a warm night for May. With the snow last weekend and now this beautiful weather I have a bad case of Spring Fever.*

Snowhite: *Same here. I always like to go to the mountains this time of year and hike the trails. Do you hike?*

JPrince: *I haven't done much of that lately. Used too.*

Snowhite: *Why not?*

JPrince: *Long story.*

Snowhite: *I have all night.*

Jack tensed as he sat at the computer. Should he tell this complete stranger how he and his wife used to spend almost every free moment hiking, snowboarding or white-water rafting? Well, why not? He had no intention of ever meeting her. If he opened up to her, then she would do the same for him. He bit his lip. The Internet sure did free up the inhibitions.

JPrince: *I lost my wife and son in a car accident five years ago. I haven't been to the mountains since. Too many memories.*

Snowhite: *My heart goes out to you. That had to be tough. Tell me more about you. Who you are, where you live? What you do?*

Damn. What should he tell her? He couldn't tell her the truth. *Make up something.* She'd never know. *Think.* Then ask her those personal questions for the article.

Jack glanced up at Murph who stood over his shoulder reading the screen.

JPrince: *Got to go. Talk to you later.*

"What are you doing?" The older officer asked with a twinkle in his pale blue eyes.

"Surfing the net. What's up with you?"

"Not much. Heard you were going undercover in a singles' group. Is it true?" A grin split his face while Jack cringed.

Jack had known if Murph found out about this freelance assignment he would tease him unmercifully. And now someone had snitched to the old coot. *Damn.* "I'm working on an article. What's it to you?"

"You're my partner. You should tell me these things instead of letting me find out through the grapevine." Murph looked slighted. "I'm curious. Are you meeting any babes?"

Jack pushed away from the desk. "It's a dirty job, but somebody has to do it." If he told Murph how distasteful he found it, then he'd never hear the end of it. Maybe he should set Murph up with the human octopus? Now that would be fun. He grinned. "Actually, I met a lady you might want to get to know.""Oh yeah? What's she like?" His eyes lit up with excitement.

"About your age, blond, rich, and lonely." Jack didn't mention how needy the woman could be.

"Sounds like my type." He sighed. "Especially, the part about being lonely." He laughed. "Can you get a picture for me?"

"Sure, why not? There's only one thing. You'll have to meet her on your own. We didn't leave each other as the best of friends."

"What did you do? You horny old dog."

"Let's say we didn't have the same idea of a good time and leave it at that."

"Sure, get me the picture. I can arrange to meet her on my own. Funny, how she might have a tail light burned out and I might have to let her know. You know how it works."

Jack laughed. "Okay, I'll get it for you. Have a good one, Murph. You be careful out there." Normally, Jack would be out there, too, but tonight he was stuck behind the desk.

Glancing at the computer, Jack wondered if Snow White was still on-line. He checked. Nope, apparently she had better things to do. Couldn't blame her. He looked up at the big black clock above the booking area. It was coming up on midnight. He yawned and went over to pour a cup of coffee.

Sipping the strong brew, he rehashed his on-line conversation with Snow White. She liked to go to the mountains and classic movies. They had a few things in common.

Sitting back at the desk he decided to send her an e-mail answering her last questions...sorta.

From: JPrince
To: Snowhite

Hi, Snow White,

Sorry. I had to leave. I live in Denver and work for the city. Let me see, I'm older, five foot eleven and weigh a hundred-eighty-five pounds, with brown hair and brown eyes. At least that's what it says on my driver's license.

I grew up in the San Luis Valley, but I've lived in Denver for the past fifteen years. I like sports, especially football. Let's see, I hate broccoli, love chocolate donuts and brownies. My idea of a good time is going to the mountains, listening to classical music or reading a good crime novel. I'm pretty much a loner and like it that way. I'm not ready for a relationship right now, although I am looking for an e-mail friend. Are you interested? Your turn. JPrince

He sat back and reread the message and pushed send. He didn't actually lie to her...just bent the truth. He did work for the city and everything else was true.

A strange sensation settled in his chest. For reasons beyond his understanding, he hoped Snow White would answer.

Cindy rubbed Prince's ears and settled back against the sofa cushion, wondering why Sam had called her to come over to her house this late on a Sunday evening. Traces of unshed tears shimmered in her friend's red puffy eyes, but she would let Sam get to what she wanted to talk about in her own good time. Something important was on her mind.

"So, what's new with you? Have you met any new men?" Sam asked, looking like she was trying to keep from crying.

"No, the only person I've seen lately is my obnoxious neighbor on his way to work." She hesitated, torn by conflicting emotions. She was unwilling to give in to the attraction she felt for Jack.

"You saw Jack? He does look sexy in his uniform. What did he have to say?"

"Not much. He was cordial." Cindy smiled. "He caught me staring at his butt. My reaction seemed to amuse him."

"What? I love it. Tell me more." Her soft voice urged Cindy on as a flash of humor crossed her face.

"There's not much to tell. He was going out when I unlocked my door. I happened to glance at him when he was getting on the elevator and he turned and caught me." She sighed. "He gave me this wicked grin that seemed to be some sort of invitation, maybe a passionate challenge, hard to resist. And maybe I imagined the whole thing."

"Nonsense, you didn't imagine it. You have to go for it." She winked at Cindy and kept on talking. "This is too cool. He does have a cute tush."

Cindy sighed weary of the argument. "Yeah, but I'm not interested." He was nice to look at. Mentally, she caressed his attributes.

"For Heaven's sake why not?" Sam stammered in bewilderment.

Cindy's throat went dry. With a pang, she realized she hadn't told Sam about her mom, maybe now was the time. "I don't want to get involved with a cop...cops get killed." A flash of wild grief ripped through her. "I never told you, but my mom was a cop." She ached with an inner pain. "When I was eight years old, she died buying me a candy bar on her way home from work." She pushed a strand of hair behind her ear. Her sense of loss was beyond tears. "I was with her." The misery of that night still haunted her. "If she wouldn't have been wearing that damn uniform, I think the guy would've let her go." She settled back on the sofa. It was like dealing with an old wound that ached on a rainy day.

"Oh, honey, I'm so sorry." There was a slight tremor in her voice. "It must have been horrible for you. No wonder, you feel the way you do about policemen." She shook her head. "But this is different. Jack can take care of himself."

"Yeah...maybe." She became increasingly uneasy under Sam's scrutiny. "I wouldn't want to risk getting involved with him." Awkwardly she cleared her throat. "Anyway, I hate guns and he doesn't know I'm alive." Somehow, she had to steer this conversation back to what was bothering Sam.

"Well, I hate guns, too, but he'd be a fool not to want you." Sam spoke as if she believed what she said. "Besides, I love men in uniform. They are so masculine and heroic." She hesitated for a heartbeat. "You and Jack would look good together."

Cindy laughed. "Sam, you'd say that about me and Frankenstein."

"Not true." A momentary look of discomfort crossed her face. "You and Jack would make a cute couple. He has that nice wavy hair and those chocolate puppy dog eyes and you with your dark hair and green eyes. And he's matched to the right height with you, too."

"What do you mean matched by height?"

"You know when you're in bed it really doesn't matter, but you want to look good walking down the street, too, not like a Mutt and Jeff cartoon."

There was a pensive shimmer in the shadow of her eyes. This had gone on long enough. "Sam, you're trying too hard to be funny. Tell me. Why have you been crying? I'm your friend. I want to help."

"I'm that obvious." Unspoken pain was alive and glowing in her eyes. She took a deep breath. "Today, I went over to surprise Larry and found him in bed with two women." She sniffed. "I'm open-minded, but that was a bit over the top." Tears of frustration streamed down her face. "Especially, since I was going to tell him, I'm pregnant."

Cindy hugged her and let her cry on her shoulder. "Oh, honey, it'll be okay. You know, I'll be here for you every step of the way." She continued to comfort Sam.

"Yeah." Brushing away tears to see, she sniffled. "Oh, God. What am I going to do?"

Cindy handed her a Kleenex. "I don't know, but I'm sure you'll work it out."

Sam dabbed at her eyes and lowered her lashes quickly to hide the hurt. "The worst part is I knew all along he wasn't the one." She took deep breaths until she was strong enough to raise her gaze. "Sure, he was fun, but he's not Mr. Right."

"Then, it's for the best. You don't want to tie yourself to someone that you know isn't right for you." She said the words tentatively, hoping they would help Sam feel better.

"I know. I'm not crying about Larry. It's the baby." She blew her nose. "I've had all day to think about it and I don't know what I want to do. One minute I want to keep it and the next I want to get rid of it." Tears glistened on her heart shaped face as she swallowed hard. "I know I have choices, but this decision is going to affect me for the rest of my life." Raw hurt glittered in her big blue eyes.

"That's true. But you don't have to make this decision today. You need to get some rest. You're all worn out and you can't think straight when you're overtired."

"Maybe, you're right. This blubbering isn't any good for me or the baby." She blew her nose and dabbed tears from her face.

"Yes, you'll see things differently in the morning. It's amazing what a good night's sleep will do."

"There's something I have to do first. I have to cleanse my home of Larry. Help me remove all signs of Larry from my life."

"Okay. What do you want me to do?"

"Go to the fridge and get all the Niagra and put it in the box next to the stove. I'll be right back." She ran into the bedroom.

Cindy boxed up the Niagra and carried it into the living room and set it on the coffee table. She'd do anything to help Sam get through this.

"Here's Larry's picture, movies, flowers, everything he's given me." She threw the things into the box, ran into the kitchen and brought out a hammer. She held the picture over the box and smashed it. "Be gone from my heart and home."

Seeing the amusement in Sam's eyes, Cindy laughed. "Now, do you feel better?"

"Yes, and I'll feel even better once I've dumped this stuff down the trash chute." She grabbed the box and headed out into the hallway with the remnants of Larry.

Cindy held the door as she watched Sam stride down the hall with a purpose. The sound of falling bottles let her know the job had been accomplished. "Good for you."

"Yes." A glint of humor had returned to her eyes as she trudged back into the condo. "Like you said, tomorrow is another day. I am tired. I'll deal with the rest of it later." Her features became more animated. "When do you work tomorrow? And please don't tell anyone about this."

"Don't worry. It's our secret. Bonnie put me on the evening shift with her. I don't mind doing it from time to time."

"Yeah, I know what you mean. I plan to take the day off so I'll be on tomorrow night, too." "Listen, Sam, you really do need to get some rest and I need to go so I can take Prince for his walk."

"Sure, go ahead. I'm okay, now." She hugged Cindy.

"Thanks for being here for me. Since we talked, I do feel better. Go on, take Prince for his walk." She patted the pup on his head. "I'll see you at work."

"Prince, Prince, come here boy. Time for your walk."

The puppy slid across the hardwood floor with a silly grin on his wrinkled face. "You're such a good boy." Cindy rubbed his belly and hooked the leash to his collar.

Walking down the hallway, Cindy wondered what Sam's final decision would be. If she ever got in that situation, she'd keep the baby. Then JPrince overtook her thoughts. It must have been a terrible time when he lost his wife and son. She could relate to his pain. Losing her mother was the worst thing she'd ever experienced. He must have really loved his wife not to be ready to date after five years. Having a love like his, seemed hard for her to imagine. Deep down in her heart, it slowly dawned on her that was exactly what she craved. Was it a lost cause?

Later the next night, after work, when Cindy returned with Prince from his walk, she glanced at her computer screen. JPrince was on-line. Should she send him an instant message? Why not? She needed a man's opinion.

Snowhite: *Hello Prince, I'm curious. Can you tell me...what is love to a man? Does it really exist or is it a figment of my imagination?*

JPrince: *Hey, Snow White. It's late. I didn't think I'd hear from you tonight. I'd be happy to answer your questions. Of course, it's only from my experience. Yes, love exists. It's passion, lust, secret smiles, shared looks, the excitement of being together...this is falling in love. Real love is the left-overs, after the passion has cooled and the excitement has wavered. It's when the roots of each other are so intertwined with memories and times shared that you can't imagine ever being with anyone else...this is love.*

Snowhite: *I can't imagine having such deep feelings. Your*

love was like that?

JPrince: *Yes. I was a very lucky man. I had it with my family.*

Snowhite: *I envy you. At least you've experienced it.*

JPrince: *You'll find it. Be patient. Good things come to those who persevere.*

Snowhite: *Patient. Oh, my God...it's happened. I've turned into Snow White...waiting for my Prince to come. Heaven help me.*

When the hell had that happened? Cindy sighed as she waited for his answer.

JPrince: *LOL. That's not necessarily true. You're not sitting in the forest with seven dwarfs. You're out there experiencing life. You know...your Prince might be right down the street.*

Snowhite: *LOL. Sure, thanks for the thought. I'm really not as desperate as I sound. I would like a husband and children, but basically, I'm a happy person, just get lonely sometimes. Thanks for your sage advice. It's put some things into perspective for me.*

JPrince: *You're welcome. I'm here for you, anytime. Have a good night. JPrince*

Love is when the roots of each other are so intertwined with memories and times shared you can't imagine ever being with anyone else. A warmth spread across her chest as she rethought JPrince's words. Would she find a love like that? JPrince had experienced the love of a lifetime and all she had found in her search were shallow losers. Why couldn't she meet someone like him?

Remembering he said he wasn't looking for a relationship, she sighed. Now she knew why. When you'd experienced the love of a lifetime you could never replace it. What a great guy. Why couldn't she meet someone like that...even JPrince? No, it wouldn't work. He wasn't ready.

Were there any good men left? She sure as hell hadn't met any lately. And the ones she'd met weren't right for her. Usually they were obnoxious or too nice. Was there something wrong with her? Where is my Prince? Does he exist? Is he searching for me?

Too many questions and not enough answers. But as they say, life is what happens when you're busy making other plans so it's time to get on with it.

"I have to shake off this lousy mood." Looking on the bright side, she had lots to be grateful for. She had a good life, kind friends and a great job. Big deal, if she didn't have a special man. She'd get by. She clicked on the e-mail from Grace.

From: GraceTaylor
To: Snowhite

Hi Cindy,

Everyone at the ranch and the beauty salon in town misses you. Also, there's one lonely cowpoke, Travis said to say, hi. He sends his love and said for you to come back and see us sometime. He's finally getting over you. I heard rumors that he's dating the Widow Jones. How do you feel about that?

How is the dating game going? Your last date sounded like a hoot. What's happening with your neighbor? Hesounds cute. And how is your puppy? Rub his ears for me.

Seth and the kids are doing fine. The twins are growing like weeds. Nana is volunteering at the hospital gift shop. I think Sheriff Davis is sweet on her.

I hate to be the bearer of bad news but Jenna and Charlie are going through a rough patch. I'm sure she'll be telling you all about it. Everyone sends their love. Wish you could come for a visit. Talk to you later ~ Grace

She would answer Grace's e-mail tomorrow. She yawned. Shutting down the computer, she pushed away from the desk and headed for the fridge. "Chocolate, I need chocolate." Not quite time to hunker down with a bucket of fudge, but close. She and Prince would walk an extra mile tomorrow. It would be worth it tonight. Chocolate ice-cream and the classic movie, *Sleepless in Seattle,* just what she needed to take her mind off her sorrow. Tomorrow was another day.

Late, the next morning, when she and Prince returned from his morning walk, they ventured to the storage area in the parking garage. With the day off, she planned to unpack some more of her things. When she pulled down another box, Prince ran between them and tried to get her to play tag with him. Then, he ran around the corner and out of sight. With her fast on his heels, he darted farther into the parking garage, in and around the cars.

"Prince, come here boy, you know better." She chased him through the garage when all of a sudden a red sixty-six Mustang roared around the corner and slammed into him. "Oh, my God, you've killed my dog!" she screamed. Tears sprang to her eyes.

CHAPTER SEVEN

The minute he heard the yelp and felt the thump, Jack knew he had hit the tan blur that ran in front of his car. *Damn.* Cindy stood in the parking garage with one hand over her mouth, turning pale and about ready to toss her cookies. Jack jumped out of the car and rushed to the pup.

She stumbled over to where Prince lay. "We were in the storage area and he ran out here," she mumbled. She looked down at her pet. Then it dawned on her who had been driving the car. "You...you did this on purpose." Her eyes glazed over in pain and anger.

"That's ridiculous. I didn't see him in time to stop." Jack shook his head and touched the dog's neck for a pulse. It was faint, but there. "Come on, we have to get him to the animal hospital. There's one not far from here."

In a daze, Cindy watched Jack gently wrap Prince in his jacket.

"Get in." He pushed her toward his car. "You can hold him." Jack sped out of the parking garage. She sat in the bucket seat of the Mustang and held Prince on her lap. A small trickle of blood pulsed down his leg. The puppy started to shake. "Oh, thank God, he's alive."

"Yeah, but he's in shock. The shaking is delayed reaction."

Jack screeched into the parking lot of the Cherry Creek Small Animal Hospital and rushed around to the side of the car and pulled her door open. "Here, let me have him."

She snuggled Prince tight against her chest and pushed her way out of the car. "I think you've done enough." Her eyes filled with anguish as she spit the words out.

"Fine. Let's get him inside." He hurried in front of her, holding the door open. A woman behind the desk glanced toward them.

"My dog's been hit by a car." She swallowed a sob. "Please help him." She stood at the desk clutching Prince in her arms. She was as white as the receptionist's smock.

"Bring him in here and I'll get the doctor to take a look at him."

Jack followed behind her. She laid Prince on the long stainless steel table and stood back, handing him his jacket. The doctor came in and looked into Prince's eyes and at his gums. When he tried to lift Prince's back leg, the pup let out a blood curdling yelp.

"His back leg is definitely broken." He continued the exam. "I don't think he has any internal injuries, but I'll have to take some more tests to make sure." He pushed his wire-rim glasses up on his nose. "You can wait in the reception area. I'll come and get you when I'm done."

"Thank you, doctor. I'll be here," she said.

Jack tried to hold her hand, but she jerked away from him. It had been an accident and he wished she would let him comfort her.

They sat in the reception area not speaking, surrounded by animals that came and went with their owners. She wouldn't give him the time of day. Feeling low as dirt, Jack watched the interaction between the people and their pets.

Dr. Gerrard finally reappeared and guided them into his office, motioning for them to sit down. He glanced at the paperwork she had filled out. "Ms. Dawson, Prince Charming is going to be fine. However, he'll need surgery to stabilize the left ulnar fracture. I'll have to put in a titanium rod to hold the fracture in place until it heals correctly."

"Is there anything else wrong?" she asked.

"Nothing. Everything seems to be in good working order. With a simple procedure, the prognosis for a complete recovery is good...providing strict confinement is followed."

Relief shone on her face as she bit her lip deep in thought. "Will he have to stay in the hospital?"

"Yes, but only for a day or so. Then you'll be able to take him home. But when he goes home, he must be confined to a crate for a week or until advanced healing is evident. Short leash walks are okay to do his business."

"You mean he has to stay in a box?" Her face paled as Jack sat by her side.

"Actually, it's like a baby's playpen. It's for his own good, otherwise he could reinjure himself. You see, with this type of surgery, his leg won't be in a cast. You have to keep in mind any excessive licking will disrupt the wound. An Elizabethan collar will be needed when the pet is unsupervised."

He took off his glasses and tucked them in his pocket. "And you have to beware of excessive swelling, redness, or discharge around the surgical area. If any of these symptoms appear, you are to call us immediately and bring him back." He hesitated. "There is another matter we need to discuss." He cleared his throat. "The cost of the plate fixation is twelve-hundred dollars. Take a few minutes to think about it. Keep in mind Prince's leg will never be the same without this surgery."

"Twelve hundred dollars? That's a lot of money." She gave Jack a dirty look. "Go ahead with the operation. I want his leg fixed."

"Fine. I'll set it up for soon as possible. You can wait here or go home and we'll call you."

"I'll wait." Standing, she straightened her shoulders and glanced at Jack.

"I'll come out and see you soon as it's over," the veterinarian said.

"Thank you." She swallowed hard. The doctor escorted them back to the waiting room.

Jack wondered why it cost so much to fix a dog's leg. Couldn't they tape it or put it in a splint. Why did an animal need a titanium rod? Couldn't they use aluminum? He sighed, knowing it didn't matter. Even though the dog had darted out in front of him, the bottom line was he felt responsible. "Look, I'm sorry this happened. I'll pay for his medical expenses." His voice was quiet when he turned to face her. "It's the least I can do."

She glanced at him, wiping a tear from her cheek. "You hate him. Why would you offer to pay his bill?"

"I don't hate him..." Frustrated, Jack ran a hand through his dark wavy hair. He didn't hate animals. This one had just managed to crawl under his skin. "Look. I want to help." He swallowed a lump in his throat the size of a goose egg. "It's my fault. Let me pay for it."

Her shoulders slumped a little. "Okay...I...I guess." She sniffed. "I want him well."

"Glad that's settled." He held her hands and gently squeezed her fingers. "We have the best care for him. He's going to be fine." He was used to comforting people on the job, but holding her hand was different. From her touch, a soothing warmth spread up his arms and into his heart. He thought he could actually feel ice cracking.

She hesitated. "I don't know what I'm going to do with him while I'm at work. He's going to need around the clock care for awhile."

"I can help out." He'd say anything in order to keep holding her hands. He wanted to make things up to her and show her he wasn't a bad guy.

"Why would you do that?" A gleam of suspicion appeared in her eyes.

"Like I said, I want to help. Regardless of what you might think, I didn't mean to hit him." It hurt Jack to know he'd caused her so much pain.

"Oh, I know." She pulled her hands free. "I shouldn't have said those terrible things to you." Her features softened. "I was just worried about Prince."

He was at a loss when she took her hands away, but she continued to sit close to him. "Look, let me help you with his recovery." The subtle scent of her perfume tickled his nose. "I'm home during the day and can take care of him while you're at work."

"You'd do that for me?" Her eyes sparkled with the sheen of moisture from her recent tears.

"Sure, how much trouble can he be?" At this moment, he'd agree to anything she asked, just to take away the hurt look on her face.

She frowned. "You don't know Prince like I know Prince."

"True, but I'm sure we can work it out. What do you think?"

"I...I don't have much of a choice. Are you sure you want to do this?"

"I'm sure or I wouldn't have offered." He wasn't sure about anything. *I must be losing my mind, taking the obnoxious dog into my home...but what else can I do?*

"Okay, it's a deal." They sat there in companionable silence and waited for the doctor to return.

After what seemed to be an eternity, the vet came out. "The procedure went well. Prince is doing fine. He'll sleep through the night."

"Will he be back to normal after his leg heals?" Cindy asked with a tremor in her voice.

"Certainly. I don't foresee any problems."

"Thank you, doctor." Jack shook the man's hand. "When will we be able to take him home?"

"I want to keep him here for a few days to make sure there's no infection and he doesn't have a reaction to the medication. I'd say he'll be ready to go home by Friday afternoon."

"Great, we'll pick him up then." Jack grinned at her.

She glanced at Jack and then back at the doctor. "Can I see him before we leave?"

"Of course, right this way." The doctor led them into another room full of animals, to where Prince lay sleeping.

She leaned down into the cage and kissed him on the top of his head. "I'm here, fella, everything is going to be okay."

Jack reached out and rubbed Prince's ears. "He's innocent when he's sleeping." *A person would never guess he's a towel thief.* He smiled at the puppy.

She frowned at Jack. "He's a good dog."

"Hey, I'm not trying to start anything. You have to remember, he's the one who seems to have a problem with me."

"You're the one who wanted him taken away." Her mouth spread into a thin lip smile, her expression sharp and accusing.

"I was mad at him at the time, but that was then, this is now." Jack reached for her hand. "Soon as he's well enough, we'll take him to Washington Park. I hear the dogs love it there."

"Okay, I'll have to take your word for it." She let him hold her hand.

Jack watched indecision wash across her face. He knew he was going to have to do some quick shuffling to get on her good side. He wasn't sure what he could do, but he knew he had to do something. Then a shocking revelation came over him. Why did he want to get on her good side, anyway? God...where did these feelings come from?

At work the next day, Cindy ran a comb through a customer's hair checking the haircut and nodded her approval to the student. "You did a wonderful job. It's a great cut."

"Thanks, Miss Cindy."

She glanced up to see Sam cruise across the room toward her.

"Now that we have a few minutes, I need to talk to you." A frown appeared on her worried face.

They walked over to the front reception desk. Cindy put her elbows on the desk and read the appointment book. "Looks like we have some down time." Sam had decided to keep the baby. Had she changed her mind? "Is it the baby? Are you feeling okay?"

"We're fine." She grinned and touched her stomach. "But I have to ask you to do a favor for me."

"Sure, what is it?"

"Can you cover the afternoon perm class for me? I made a doctor's appointment and that's the only time he can get me in."

"That'll be okay. Teaching perms is one of my most favorite things. Yeah, I can do it."

"Great. I'll be back, soon as I can. Just keep an eye on Miss Dotty and make sure she gets her class through the afternoon testing."

"Oh, okay." Cindy glanced around and spotted the older instructor teaching a manicure class at the back of the school. As always, Miss Dotty sat on her big fat butt. The silver haired woman with the huge black framed glasses never pulled her share of the weight. She always managed to shove her work off on the new students or another instructor. Through the years, she had figured the angles of getting out of work and was always a thorn in someone's side. She resisted any change that came their way, unless it was her own idea.

"Don't worry about it, but I didn't get a chance to tell you what happened."

"What?" Sam leaned against the reception desk.

"Prince was hurt. Jack accidentally hit him with his car."

"Oh, no. I'm sorry. Is he going to be okay?"

"Yes, but he has a broken leg. They did the surgery yesterday." She bit her lip. "Jack is taking me to pick him up tomorrow."

"That little scamp." She winked. "He figured out a way to get you and Jack together. Animals always know who's a good person."

"Don't be silly, but you know, when I thought I was going to lose him, it about killed me. I didn't realize how much I love that dog." She grinned. "You know, he really is my soul mate."

"Yeah, sure. What about the real Prince...what about Jack?"

"Oh, he's not my Prince, but he was sweet about the whole thing. He agreed to pay for the vet bills, but now I've thought about it, I'm going to pay half." She sighed. "He did offer to watch Prince during the day when I'm at work."

"Are you going to let him?"

"Yeah. I don't have much choice. He needs to be cared for around the clock. I'm grateful for the help."

"Cool, now you can get up close and personal. You lucky woman."

"I don't think so. He's not my type...remember he's a cop."

"Yeah, I know. The heroic type. And you'll be seeing him every day." She winked at Cindy. "Wake up and smell the perm solution, he's perfect for you. The man is awesome."

"Whatever you say." She had to get Sam off the subject. Her emotions about Jack Riley were still too raw to discuss with anyone. She sighed and looked away.

"Anyway, I have to go check Sandy's perm. I'll catch up with you at the break."

"Sure, see you later." Could Sam be right? What would it be like to have Jack as her boyfriend? Her heart did a tap dance. *Don't go there.*

The next day, Jack pulled the dog bed on wheels into his apartment. *What was I thinking when I volunteered to watch Cindy's dog? The mutt ran in front of my car.* A splinter snagged itself into the palm of his hand when he pulled the wooden crate into position. *Damn. I should've sprung for the hard plastic one.*

He set the wooden box in the corner of his living room near his desk, and threw some old blankets in the bottom of it. Now, the bed was ready for when they brought the pup home from the vet. He glanced at his watch. Where was Cindy? It was almost time to go pick him up.

From what the doc said, he would be sleeping most of the time. His only job would be to give him his medicine and make sure the pup didn't hurt himself.

The doorbell rang. When Jack opened the door, Cindy stood there in a canary yellow sundress looking like a bright ray of sunshine. Her natural radiance nearly took his breath away. "Are you ready to go get Prince?" she asked.

"Yeah." He swallowed and lifted his chin and boldly met her gaze. "I have the bed set up. Give me a minute to find my keys." He motioned her into the room. "Come in."

"Oh, he'll be near your desk. I hope he doesn't cause you problems." For an instant her glance around the room sharpened as if she doubted his sincerity.

He scooped his keys off the table, trying to not let her know how she affected him. "Yeah, they delivered it this morning. He's not going anywhere in that thing. He'll be fine."

She boldly met his eyes. "It's nice of you to help me out this way."

"No big deal. Let's go." Jack shrugged. "I'm home during the day. It works out." He cast an approving glance at her tanned legs as they left the condo.

Jack turned the key in the ignition and the engine of his Mustang roared to life. "It won't be long now and you'll have your pup home."

For a moment she studied him intently. "Yeah, I can hardly

wait." A soft gasp escaped her. "I wish I didn't have to go back to work today." Her voice, soft and sensual, sent a ripple of awareness through him.

"How did you come up with his name?" Jack wondered if she was looking for her Mr. Right, like everyone on his singles loop.

"Oh, it's a joke between my friend Sam and me. You met her, when you were moving in."

"Oh, yeah, the energetic blond. I do remember meeting her."

"Well, she gave him to me for my birthday...you know, my own Prince Charming? If I have one of my own, then I don't have to go looking for him."

"Smart woman...I think." He stared at her, baffled by her comment.

"It works for me. With my job and everything, there isn't much time to search." She laughed. "Anyway, in this day and time, he doesn't exist. There's no such person."

"Oh. Why do you say that?" He was surprised at her answer. She seemed to have a different outlook on the dating scene.

"Well, we're living in the new millennium. Women don't have to have a man to support and care for them. We're independent, make our own money and have our own lives. Years ago, women didn't have a chance to get an education and become independent. They relied on their husbands for everything. Most of them went right from their mother's house to their husband's home. They never had a chance to experience life."

"I never thought of it that way, but you're right. I can see how an uneducated woman could feel dependent on a man." He tucked the thought away for his article.

"In college, I did a paper on women's rights and I say, thank God for the sixties and *Cosmopolitan.* It wasn't all sex, drugs and rock and roll." Across her pale and beautiful face a dim flush raced like a fever as she got excited about the conversation. "It was about being your own person, having rights and choosing to make your own decisions. That was the beginning of women finding themselves."

Jack snorted. "Look how far it's got you." He enjoyed

teasing her.

"Hey, nothing's perfect. You take the good with the bad." A kind of wistfulness stole into her expression for a flicker of a second. "Sometimes I think maybe it's gone too far the other way. I still like to have doors opened for me and some men have forgotten how to treat a woman like a lady, but independence is worth it."

"Then the bottom line is, if you can live without a prince, why bother?" She was too independent for her own good, but he liked a woman who could take care of herself.

"Now, you're being cynical. Women have more choices today. Parents can't dictate who they marry or if they marry. It's a woman's right to choose her future." She straightened herself with dignity. "If she doesn't marry, she can adopt children or go to a sperm bank and have a child that way. She doesn't need a man to be happy. Freedom, that's what it's all about."

"An interesting take on the sexes. So, you're really not looking for Mr. Right?" The woman had many sides to her. She wasn't just a pretty face. He wanted to hear what else she had to say and maybe...just maybe he was wrong about her. As far as he could tell, and he knew the signs, she hadn't been drinking the last few days.

She laughed. "I'm cautious. Most of the guys I've dated are Mr. Worthless." An irresistibly devastating grin softened her features. "If Mr. Right shows up, good, if he doesn't, I'm okay with that, too. Someday, I'll have that child I want, with or without a man by my side. But the point is that I don't have to settle for any guy who walks through my door, because I need a meal ticket."

"Here we are." Jack pulled into the parking lot of the Small Animal Hospital. "Let's get your Prince home and get him settled before you have to go back to work."

An hour later, she followed Jack into his apartment. He carried the pup and placed him in the crate next to his desk. The mutt slept soundly. He had awoken only once to lick Cindy's hand and then fell back asleep.

"He looks innocent while he's sleeping, but I have to warn you, he likes to chew on everything." She reached down and patted his head and rubbed his ears. He whimpered in his sleep and rolled onto his side.

"Don't worry. I have the doctor's instructions and he has his chew toys. I'll take good care of him. Go on, get out of here, or you're going to be late for work."

"Thanks, Jack, I owe you." She headed for the door.

"Nonsense, it's no big deal. Oh, yeah, here's my phone number if you want to check on him." He handed her his card.

"Great, I'll call this afternoon." She held the card in her hand and to his surprise, turned back. Her breath quickened and she leaned against his shoulder and kissed him, before she dashed out the door.

His thoughts raced dangerously as he stood there with the subtle hint of her perfume hanging in the air and heat rushing through his veins. It was only a thank you kiss. He was almost embarrassed at how happy it made him. *Stop it. She's looking for more than a one night stand and she's the last person you need to be involved with.*

CHAPTER EIGHT

A few days later, Prince moaned in his sleep. Jack reached down to comfort the pup and patted his side. "Okay, Prince, you're not so bad. Rest and heal old boy." He stood and ran a hand through his hair and glanced from Prince to the computer screen. Today was one of those days when the words refused to come. He had always believed he couldn't wait for inspiration that he had to put himself in the chair and write. Today, it was difficult.

Thoughts of Cindy's luscious body, her quiet demeanor, gentle smile and the kiss from the other day had him in a tizzy. An unexpected warmth had surged through him at the touch of her lips. *Damn.* He had to change this way of thinking...fast. He sighed. Time to get back to work.

He fell into his chair and glared at the screen. Sometimes all it took was a short distraction and when he went back to writing, the words would spill out. He'd check his e-mail. Maybe Snow White had sent something. Nothing. What had she been up to? He would send her an e-mail.

From: JPrince

To: Snowhite

Hi Snow White. How's it going? Haven't heard from you. Did you find Prince Charming? JPrince

He hit send and went over to comfort the pup. He did like

the little rascal, especially when he snuggled next to him on the couch watching *Family Guy.*

A week later, Jack sat on Cindy's sofa, sniffing the air. "Something sure smells good." He grinned. "It's been a long time since I've had a home cooked meal."

A big pot of homemade chicken and dumplings simmered on the stove while a peach cobbler cooled on the pie rack. "It's nice of you to invite me over for dinner." He looked around the condo. "I thought your friend, Sam, was going to be here."

"She was, but she's feeling a little under the weather and decided to stay in today. So we've got lots of extra food." She smiled. "After all you've done for me and Prince this past week, it's the least I could do." She stirred the dumplings, checked the rolls and put the salad on the table. "It'll just be a few more minutes. Would you like some more coffee?"

"No, I'm good." He watched Prince sleeping on the rug in front of the fireplace and leaned down to rub his belly. The pup grunted in approval. He held his hands to the warmth of the fire. "This feels good."

"Since I was a child, I've always liked a fireplace. That's what sold me on this unit. How do you like your place?" She began setting the table for two.

"Oh, I do. It's working out better than I thought." He grinned. "Tell me why did you move to the big city?" He watched her as she moved around the open kitchen preparing the meal and setting dishes of food on the table. Would she tell him the truth?

"Many reasons."

"Oh, come on. Tell me, I'm curious. You're different from the women I've met."

"Go ahead, serve yourself, while it's hot." She sat across the table from him and started putting food on her plate. "I guess the main reason was I just got tired of living in a small town."

"I bet there's a man involved." He grinned. "With a good looking woman, like you, there has to be. Tell me. You can trust me." He took a bite of his food. "Oh, wow. This is great. I'm going to savor every bite."

"Sure, you are. Well, there was a guy, actually an ex-husband that kept showing up with his twenty-year-old bimbo all over town. And one day, I just got tired of having it shoved in my face."

"He was a fool." Jack frowned, not understanding why any man would leave a gorgeous woman like Cindy...and she could cook.

"Thanks, but actually, it's worked out for the best. We were only married a short time. It would've been much harder if we'd been together longer." She loaded up his plate with more and handed it back to him.

He took another bite. "I think I'm in love." He gazed into her eyes. "If I'd known you could cook like this, I'd have been begging at your door every night this past week."

She laughed. "Okay, don't lay it on too thick." A blush covered her cheeks.

"Really, I can't thank you enough. I don't get to eat like this very often."

"Jack, really, that's enough." A smile lit up her face.

He realized as he watched her that he was having a good time just being here with her and Prince...and the food was great.

She grinned. "Okay, I've told you my dark secrets. More coffee?" she asked.

He nodded and she refilled his cup.

"It's your turn to be on the hot seat. Do you have a girlfriend?

He laughed. "No, I'm a widower. I live alone and I plan on staying that way. Nothing against marriage, it's just I'm set in my ways. I don't need anyone." As he spoke the words, he knew he lied.

"Oh, Jack, I'm sorry for your loss." She spoke calmly with a tender expression in her eyes. "I had no idea. How long has it been?"

"It's okay. A little over five years now. I've dealt with all that in the past." He sighed. The only thing left were the raw sores of an aching heart and she didn't need to hear about that. "I've moved on." The words sounded empty to Jack's ears...kind of like his life. "Hey, what's new with you?"

"Me, nothing but the same old day to day routine, work, eat and sleep. You know the drill." She sipped her coffee.

Prince walked over to the table and nudged his head against Jack's leg. "Prince, old boy, you're doing great." Prince licked his hand. "You know, he's healing faster than I thought he would."

"Yes, thank goodness. We won't have to bother you anymore. I owe you so much for helping me with him."

"That reminds me." He grinned at her. "I have a favor to ask of you. From time to time, I have to work double shifts. Would you consider feeding my fish when that happens? At my other place I had a teenager come in and do it." He had ulterior motives. This way, he could see her more often.

"Sure, just show me how. I wouldn't mind at all."

"If you'd like, I could look in on Prince during the day for you."

"Really, that would be nice. Maybe if you stopped by, he wouldn't wreck the place. He does have his moments." She smiled at the memory of Prince chewing one of her favorite shoes.

"After dinner, I'll show you where everything is. Saltwater fish are temperamental, but well worth the extra work."

"Sure. Are you ready for dessert?"

"Oh, yeah, I've been drooling over that peach cobbler all evening. You wouldn't happen to have ice cream with that, would you?"

She laughed. "Of course, I may be from the sticks, but we eat ice cream with peach cobbler, too."

As he ate, Jack realized he was getting in deeper than he should, but couldn't stop himself. It would be easy to fall for a woman like Cindy. She was nice, cared about kids and animals and she didn't seem as desperate as most of the dates he'd been on lately.

That reminded him. He had to get to work. "This has been great, but I have to go get ready for work." He rose from the table.

"Oh, is it that time, already? I'm glad you came over. We'll have to do it again, sometime." She walked him to the door and handed him a container with extra peach cobbler in it. "Just in case, you need a snack later." She laughed.

"Thanks again for dinner. The guys at the station will probably try to fight me for this."

"Well, I have just the thing to prevent that. Today, I made a huge batch of fudge brownies for the pot luck at the beauty school and there's extra if you'd like to take some with you."

"Oh, yeah, I would never turn down brownies. Murph, my partner will be in hog heaven."

She put several wrapped brownies in a basket and handed them to him.

"Thanks, the guys will go crazy over these. You know, you probably won't believe this, but I'm looking forward to seeing Prince during the day. He's good company." He grinned. "I'll see you around." He wanted to pull her in his arms and never let go, instead he kissed her on the cheek and walked out the door.

Later that night, while looking at his schedule, he realized he had a date with Lola Brent the following evening. Damn, the last thing he wanted to do was go on another phony date. But, meeting her in the singles chat room had been interesting. She said she worked as a professional artist. She definitely had a knack for casual conversation. If her picture was up to date, she was a knock-out. She had a body to die for and long beautiful honey-colored hair. The woman must work out at least a couple hours a day. Hell, he'd have dinner with her just to see if she looked like the picture in her bio. After the human octopus, with his luck, the picture would probably be several years old.

Earlier this evening, he had a nice time at Cindy's place. The woman could really cook and Prince had grown on him. The guys had devoured the brownies and asked him to get more. The fact glaring him in the face—he was attracted to the pup's mistress.

The attraction was natural. He was a healthy man and she a beautiful woman. It'd been a long time since he'd been with anyone. He'd made the choice there would be no permanent relationships—he only dated a certain kind of woman. By having short-term, one night stands he'd always be his own man. With this type of woman, nobody got hurt. *Cindy wasn't that type of woman. She wanted marriage, kids and the white picket fence. Damn.*

He sighed. When there's a wife, girlfriend or significant other, there are commands—sit, lie down, roll over. Since his wife died, he had grown up to be an old dog and could leave his chew toys anywhere he pleased without confrontation. He didn't want commitment. He couldn't stand to ever go through that kind of pain again.

He liked it this way. Remaining pretty much celibate and still pining for his family, he didn't need anyone, certainly not Cindy Dawson. She was a distraction, probably because he hadn't had a good lay in months. That's all it could be.

Sure, there was chemistry, but he could fight chemistry. And with her being his neighbor, any involvement, other than being a friend, could get messy. He liked his new condo and didn't need those kind of complications. Maybe, he could do something about his needs tonight and then he would be able to stop thinking sexually about Cindy. In his conversations with the beautiful Lola, she had seemed more than willing.

Later the next evening, Jack watched Lola unlock the door to her home. Dinner with her had been an experience. Surprisingly, she looked as good as her picture and had been blatantly clear with her sexy innuendoes. The meal had only been a prelude to what she had in mind. In her way, she had let him know there would be fun and games with no strings attached. Knowing what she had in mind, he'd agreed to come back to her place for coffee and whatever the night would bring.

If anything, he kept telling himself, he had to do this to get Cindy off his mind. Earlier this evening, her throat had looked warm and shapely above a low-cut bodice when they'd exchanged keys. It had taken much resistance to keep from kissing Cindy senseless and tumbling her into the bedroom.

When he and Lola entered her living room, he gave a low whistle. "What a showplace." He glanced out at the million dollar view of Coors Field and the lights twinkling in the towering skyscrapers of downtown.

She smiled and tossed her coat on the couch. "Thanks, my grandmother left it to me. She was an interior decorator. She liked to call it casual elegance." She smiled. "I like the feeling of being away from the city, yet living right in the heart of things."

"This place does that." Jack shook his head as he looked through the wall of glass to see a seven by seven-foot hot tub gurgling, sunken into the end of a redwood deck on the rooftop, surrounded by trees and potted plants. "You have a hot tub?"

"Yeah, it's built into the deck for privacy." She moved over to him and gently caressed the front of his jacket, giving him the look of a hungry she-wolf drooling over its last morsel of food. "I have Merlot. How about a glass to loosen you up?"

"Loosen me up?" He laughed. The slim wild beauty rubbed her jutting breasts against his chest. He wouldn't be doing any drinking, but what the hell...he'd be a fool not to go for it.

"Let's get comfortable." Her fingers roamed along his shoulders as she removed his coat and threw it on the low sofa next to hers. "Come on, Jack. Let's try the hot tub. I'd love the company."

The woman was determined to have her way with him. Who was he to resist? Jack hesitated for a beat. "Sure, that would feel great. Do you have trunks?"

Her eyes slid over his body. "You don't need them, but there are some in the guest bathroom, top shelf, end of the hallway." She pointed toward the back of the loft. "I'll meet you there."

He watched her curvaceous body sway down the hall, as her voice died away. *Man, this babe was loaded...in more ways than one.* Real art work hung on the walls. He reached his fingers out to touch the golden frame of a floral landscape. Not a print...this was the real thing. *Monet.*

It showed in Lola's home that the lady had taste. As he snooped around, it hit him like a ton of rocks. The artwork and the fancy chrome and glass furniture were beautiful, but something was missing. It left him feeling cold. He shrugged and proceeded to the bathroom to find the trunks. After a soak in the hot tub and a little poke and tickle, he'd hit the road.

Easing himself into the tub, the hot water and bubbles tumbled around him, soothing his aching back. He had tweaked a muscle while moving Prince in his crate back to Cindy's condo. Something about Cindy's things made her home feel warm and inviting. Maybe it was the overstuffed furniture, the fireplace, or her books and plants scattered around her living room. It was homey—something he sorely missed. *Damn, woman, get out of my head!* Since he'd been taking care of Prince, she popped in there several times a day—not a good thing. *I don't need anyone.*

At a sound, he turned his head to see Lola wearing a red string bikini. Her nipples were taut against the thin fabric. She bent forward and sat a tray of drinks and snacks on a table, giving him a great view. "These are for later."

Her eyes sparkled as she slowly stood and untied the top of her bikini and let it fall to the floor. "This is for now." She leaned toward him and stepped into the churning water.

The very air around them seemed electrified. His feelings for her had nothing to do with love. This was pure lust. She wanted to party. Well, he was in the mood to accommodate her wishes...or was he? An image of Cindy kissing him and the warmth he had felt scampered across his mind. *Oh, man, I can't do this.* His sensuous thoughts deflated. *I must be losing it...here she is, a beautiful woman, ready, willing and able...and I don't want her.*

Lola eased into the hot tub with her breasts floating in the water, sitting next to him. She had one thing on her mind and that was getting busy with him.

He swallowed hard. "Lola, I...I'm sorry, but I'm going to have to disappoint you." His stammering voice echoed in his ears not believing what he was saying. He wiped beaded moisture from his face. *Apparently, I've lost my mind.* "All of a sudden, I'm not feeling too well." Stepping from the tub, he grabbed a towel and wrapped it around himself.

"Baby, that's okay...you do look a little green." She continued to sit there with the water rocking her body, giving him that come on look. "You can make it up to me." She licked her lips. "Tomorrow night I have to go to this private party downtown. Would you be my date?" There was a slight challenge in the tone of her voice.

"Sure, sure." At this moment in time, he'd agree to just about anything to get out of there. He ran.

The next evening Cindy sat in front of her fireplace with her laptop and yawned. It had been a roller coaster couple of weeks. The highs were high and the lows were the pits. She had thought Prince would die after he had been hit by Jack's car. Thank God for Jack's quick thinking. Now, Prince was peacefully asleep by her side and getting better every day.

And surprise of surprises, along the way, she had discovered she had been wrong about Jack Riley. He had turned out to be one of the good guys—a nice neighbor.

The man had been gentle and caring with Prince. For some strange reason, she trusted him. And let's face it friends of the male gender you could trust were hard to come by. With his standoffish attitude toward her, there wouldn't be any danger of them becoming anything else. As for now, he had helped her care for Prince and that was special...something a friend would do.

Tonight, a melancholy mood overwhelmed her with memories of what might have been. If things would've worked out between her and her husband, perhaps she'd have a family of her own by now. Like Grace, she wanted to have kids, but not with someone she couldn't respect.

The day they were married, she had taken those solemn words to heart. Love, honor and trust, till death do us part. Then only seven months later, she'd found him making love to another woman—in her bed. So much for love, honor and trust, she sighed. Life was too short to live with that kind of betrayal.

Shaking her head, she'd see if JPrince was on-line. He always seemed to be able to pick up her spirits. She needed them lifted. At this point in time, she was about ready to give up on finding love. Some days it just wasn't worth the effort. She'd try to catch him on instant messaging.

Snowhite: *Are you there?*

JPrince: *I'm here, What's up?*

Snowhite: *Not much.*

JPrince: *Have you been on any more fun dates?*

Snowhite: *Fun dates... LOL. What's that? Not yet. I have a date tomorrow night. Who knows how this one will turn out. Sometimes, I wonder why I bother.*

JPrince: *Hey now. That's not the attitude you're supposed to have. The love of your life is out there. You just have to find him. Think of it as an adventure. He might be the one.*

Snowhite: *That sounds like an old military commercial. Join the Navy and have an adventure. The one, huh? I've almost given up on that idea.*

JPrince: *Listen, if he's not the one, he might be the one that will do till Mr. Right comes along.*

Snowhite: *Maybe. I do need to change my attitude about this dating stuff.*

JPrince: *Good girl. That's what I wanted to hear.*

Snowhite: *Thanks for being there. You've helped me see things in a different light. I'll talk to you later.*

This was crazy, but after she chatted on-line with JPrince she always felt better. He had a good outlook on life. To be so wise, he must be a lot older. She wondered why he hadn't posted a picture with his bio. Maybe he was disfigured. But then again, she hadn't posted her picture either. In her mind's eye, she pictured him as a gorgeous honey living in a cabin in the mountains in a secluded remote area, just him and his computer. Knowing he lived in the city didn't make any difference. It was her fantasy. He was her mentor in the dating game and she had come to rely on him for advice.

Cindy snuggled next to Prince. He was sound asleep. She reached over and brushed his soft furry ears. "You'll always be my baby." A pang in her heart stopped her dead in her tracks. It was true she wanted a baby—with or without—a man in her life.

Getting ready for her date the next night, Cindy glanced at Prince. He lay on the floor trying to scratch his leg. "Don't do that. It'll only make it worse, little guy." Poor puppy was tired of the healing process. She didn't blame him. "At least you're on the mend."

After talking with JPrince, she realized he had been right. She did need to be more open about her dates. Sure, this was a long shot, but she could meet someone interesting. Tonight, she had a date with Todd Chandler. He was a cameraman who filmed sports events and traveled across the country with the athletes.

What to wear? She was supposed to meet him for a drink at the ESPN Zone. Humm...black slacks and a forest green cashmere sweater. That would be comfortable and she could dress it up with gold jewelry.

Glancing in the mirror, she liked what she saw. A good hair day. Her long curly dark hair tumbled around her shoulders as she shook her head. She grabbed her purse and left the condo with her mind open to whatever happened on this date. At this phase of the game, she didn't expect fireworks, but a slight sizzle would be a nice change.

Getting off the Mall shuttle, she saw Todd standing by the entrance. He wore gray slacks and a black turtleneck sweater. His hair was a wavy brown with natural blond streaks on the sides. Wearing gold wire rim glasses over his gorgeous blue eyes, he smiled in recognition with a cute dimple appearing on his cheek.

"Hi, Cindy. You look great."

She laughed. "Thank you."

"Tonight is a private party and I have to make an appearance. I hope you don't mind. If we don't like it, we can go somewhere else."

"Oh, okay." She hadn't realized it was going to be a private party. ***Cool,*** *maybe she'd get to meet some celebrities.*

They walked through the gift shop at the entrance and glanced around as they stood on the escalator rising to the top floor. Loud music greeted them when they stepped off and went into the restaurant-bar area where the party was being held.

A waitress escorted them to a table. "What would you like to drink?" Todd asked.

She had cut back on her alcohol and found she didn't miss it. If he thought she was a ditz if she didn't order something with alcohol, then he wasn't worth her time. "I would love some hot tea, Celestial Seasonings, Apple Cinnamon if you have it."

Todd placed the order for their drinks without comment. Crowds of people milled around the bar and the edges of the room. The place was packed with some of Denver's most famous athletes and arduous sports fans. "There's John Elway." He pointed to a man across the room surrounded by people. "I'd heard he was going to be here."

"This is the first time I've ever seen him this close."

"Would you like to meet him?"

"You could do that?"

"Sure, when he's not busy. I've spoken several times with John. He's a nice guy."

She couldn't help but be impressed. "I bet you get to meet a lot of interesting people in your business." Their drinks arrived. Cindy took the warm mug and held it in her hands. Todd was okay. She liked listening to him talk.

"Yeah, it has its perks."

"What's it like to be around celebrity athletes?"

"Most of them are okay, but every now and then they get funny."

"In what way?"

"Now, that would be telling stories out of school." He teased her. "But, for you, without giving names, I'll break my silence. One thing happened a couple weeks ago, when I had to fly out on a baseball team plane. A certain player had a hissy fit, because his usual seat had been assigned to someone else. I mean he threw things around the plane and demanded he sit in his seat number seventeen or he wouldn't go." He grinned. "And if you're wondering, it wasn't the Rockies."

"That's strange."

"Not with these guys. Most of them are extremely superstitious about what it takes to win. When they get on a streak, they do the strangest things. They have these rituals when they go to bat, doing the exact same thing each time. One player refused to change his socks or wash them as long as they were winning."

"Did they get smelly." She laughed.

"Yeah." He grinned. "Nobody wanted to sit next to him in the dugout."

"You know a lot of secret interesting things about the players."

"Some, but what you have to remember is they're only people with hopes and dreams and idiosyncrasies like the rest of us."

She sipped her tea and listened to Todd. He was fun to be with and nice to look at. He didn't seem stuck on himself and wasn't overly pushy....the problem...he wasn't Jack. That chemistry thing just wasn’t there. She smiled, trying to push Jack to the back of her mind.

"You have a great smile."

She blushed.

"Now, that's something for the books. It's been sometime since I've seen a lady blush." He grinned at her.

"I bet you go out with lots of women." The words slipped out before she could catch them.

He laughed. "Not as many as you'd think."

She glanced around the room and tried to compose herself. One whole wall was covered with several, large, square TV screens, tuned to different sports events. Todd was good company. She sighed. Somehow, she must learn to curb her involuntary reactions to Jack's gentle loving look of concern toward Prince. He had as much as told her at dinner, he was a loner and planned on staying that way. What a waste.

Damn, Jack. Leave me alone. Here she was, having a good time and there he was, intruding in her thoughts. Across the restaurant, as if she had conjured him up, he stood in a circle of guys, with his arm casually thrown around a buxom blond in a slinky red dress. Seeming to sense her presence, he turned his head toward her and their eyes met.

Her heart did a tumble. When she ran into him earlier, he had been kind of quiet and hadn't said anything about having a date, but then again, neither had she. The woman looked like she'd stepped off the cover of *Cosmopolitan.* Sexy as hell. She wondered where Jack had met a woman like that. Not at the police station, but then again...maybe. Just her luck, the woman had reported something stolen or some such thing and Jack had asked her out.

Jack's eyes darkened as he held Cindy's gaze. They stared at each other across the packed room. Fighting the dynamic vitality he exuded, she was too surprised to do more than nod. A rush of feelings assailed her and the butterflies in her stomach turned to batwings. The man was an ever changing mystery. Then again, maybe Jack had picked the blond up for solicitation. Maybe he was only averse to drunks not hookers. The woman didn't look like a hooker. The woman was way out of Cindy's league with her designer fashion and that well kept toned up body, obvious she had a private trainer. She shook her head at her jealous meandering.

CHAPTER NINE

Cindy sipped her tea, masking her inner turmoil with a deceptive calmness and shifted her attention back to Todd.

"You look like you've seen a ghost." He hesitated. "Are you all right?"

"Yeah, I'm fine." She couldn't resist another peek at Jack and glanced at him out of the corner of her eye. He was in deep conversation with the woman. She sighed. "No, not a ghost, it's only my neighbor."

Todd nodded toward Jack and the blond bombshell. "Flashy woman, is she your neighbor?" From the tone of his voice, she could tell that Todd had an obvious appreciation for the opposite sex.

"No, I've never met the lady. Actually, it's the guy...he's my next door neighbor."

"Would you like to leave?"

She watched his eyes widen with concern. "No, that isn't necessary. He's the reclusive type and I'm just surprised to see him out."

"Oh." Todd gave the blond another appreciative glance, which made Cindy green with envy. A melancholy frown flitted across his features. "She's quite the looker. Not my type, but you know what I mean."

She knew exactly what he meant. "Yes, she's pretty." *An understatement, the woman was gorgeous.* And why wouldn't Jack go out with someone like her? He'd be crazy to turn that woman down. Anyway, why should it bother her? They were only friends.

She realized by sitting here making goo goo eyes at Jack, she was insulting her date. She cringed. She should pay more attention to Todd. *Get it together.* She leaned forward and gave him her full attention. "We were talking about your work. How long have you been a camera man?"

He put the matter aside with good humor. The beginning of a smile tipped the corners of his mouth. "About six years. I love sports and that's what drew me into the field. Hey, I have an idea." His blue eyes sparkled with excitement. "Let's go check out my new autographed John Elway jersey. I had it framed and need to pick it up from *The Big Picture.* Would you like to go with me to get it?" He said the words tentatively as if testing the idea. He squinted and removed his glasses for a minute, then put them back on. "It's getting crowded in here. I think I need some fresh air."

He had given her the perfect excuse to leave. How sweet. And yes, she couldn't stand to watch Jack with another woman. She didn't want him, because he didn't want her, but that didn't mean she wanted anyone else to have him. This was just too painful. "Okay, where is it?"

"Not far. We can catch the Mall shuttle. It's at the end of the line. Are you ready?"

"Sure." She pushed herself to a standing position and glanced at Jack one more time. He nodded in recognition as they left the ESPN Zone. It hurt, but she had needed to see Jack with another woman. It clarified the murky waters in which she had been swimming.

"Fresh air." Todd inhaled deeply as they stepped outside into the cool evening with strands of music surrounding them. An older white-haired gentleman sat bundled up in a lawn chair on the corner playing his magical flute. Todd threw a couple of bucks into a box at the man's feet, when they passed the street performer who had taken up residence on the Mall.

"That's Frank," he said. "He's eighty-four and plays outside the Rockies baseball stadium before every home game. He takes in some pretty good money, so I hear. He’s a great old dude."

He smiled at her as a horse and carriage went down the Mall's enclosed street, with a bride and groom sitting in the open back. They cuddled and smiled at each other. The signs of love enveloped them. The clip-clop of the horse's hooves and the slight squeak of the carriage faded away as she wondered what it would be like to be that much in love.

"Have you lived in the city long?" Todd's voice pulled her from her musings. He reached out and caught her hand in his as they walked down the street.

She closed her hand over his, comforted by his presence, but there were no sparks. "Not long, only a few months. I like it here."

"What do you do?" He squeezed her hand lightly.

"Well, right now, I'm teaching Vocational Cosmetology at the University."

"Sounds like fun." He continued the conversation. "Who's your favorite student of all time?"

She glanced at him, appreciating the fact he was showing interest in her profession. "My job isn't as exciting as yours."

"Who says? I bet you have stories to tell. Think about it. Come on. Tell me, who was your favorite student?"

As they walked down the Mall, he squeezed her hand every now and then to just let her know he was there. She liked that, but couldn't help wishing he were Jack. "Well, let me see. A few years ago I taught a young man who was so poor he ate dog biscuits for his lunch every day."

"What? You're making this up."

"No, he did. When the instructors found out we couldn't believe it. The poor kid lived in his car and survived on dog biscuits in order to attend school. Luckily, we were able to get him a scholarship and a part-time job cleaning the school."

"What became of him?"

She smiled in remembrance, as a warm glow of pride flowed through her. She had taught the young man how to do his first haircut. "Today he is a world renowned stylist. He won the Hairstyling Olympics in Europe last year. He owns several of the elite salons in Denver and is doing quite well."

"Who is he? Would I recognize the name?"

"Yes, but I'll keep his secret. He was a good kid who

worked his butt off to make it to the big time in the beauty industry."

"Oh look, we're here. This shouldn't take too long." He let go of her hand and held the door open for her to enter the shop.

"That's okay I'm not in a big hurry." She noted the beautiful framed pictures of landscapes, sports figures and about anything she could think of adorning the walls and displays.

A salesman stepped behind the chrome and glass counter. "Good evening. May I help you?"

"Yes, I'm Todd Chandler. I'm here to pick up the John Elway jersey I had framed."

"Oh, yes, it's ready." The salesman flipped through some invoices. "I'll get it for you. It turned out real nice."

"How did you get John Elway to sign it for you?" Cindy asked when the salesman disappeared into the back room.

"He signed it awhile back at a fund-raiser. I never took the time to have it framed, until now. It's been sitting in thc back of my closet."

"That's terrible. Now that he's retired, I heard those autographed jerseys have been snapped up by sports collectors."

"That's right and one of the reasons why I finally got around to taking it to be framed."

The salesman returned from the back room with the framed Bronco's orange and navy-blue jersey with Elway's name scrawled in black across the top of the white number seven. "Wow, that's something!" She admired the jersey.

"Yeah, it's an authentic game jersey." Todd reached out to touch the glass. "Real special." The black frame was huge, about three feet by four feet.

"As you can see the jersey doesn't touch the glass. No moisture can get inside the frame. It's environmentally protected from the elements." The salesman spoke with awe in his voice and balanced the frame against the counter. "Someone said, he's not signing any more jerseys since the Broncos changed from Nike to Adidas."

"How cool is that?" Todd chuckled.

Cindy watched Todd pay the man. The salesman wrapped the large frame in plain brown paper and handed it over to

Todd.

"It turned out just the way I wanted." He smiled.

"Remember us when you need something else framed."

"Will do." Todd was like a kid in a candy store drooling over the gum balls.

Cindy held the door for him when they left the shop, thinking about boys and their toys. The framed jersey was awesome. "It does look good."

"Yeah, and I have the perfect spot for it in the entry way of my loft. I live down on Blake. Would you like to come over and help me hang it?" He looked at her quickly...hopefully. "It's early, come on...say yes...please."

She couldn't resist his smile. "Oh, I guess. It's not every day I get to see an authentic autographed John Elway jersey hung on the wall." She didn't want to go home yet—she didn't want to run into Jack.

"Done deal. Let's catch the Mall shuttle." He switched the awkward frame from one side to the other. "This thing is kind of heavy. Luckily, the trolley will take us almost to my front door."

"Okay." Cindy stood with Todd at the stop in companionable silence. She supposed, to the passersby, they looked like a happy couple going home for the evening with something new for their place. *It would be nice to have someone to call her own.*

The doors swished open and they stepped inside and sat down. Cindy glanced around. The shuttle was practically empty except for an elderly woman and a couple of teenagers listening to their boom box in the back.

"Here we are." The bus stopped at Blake Street. "My place is right around the corner." Todd braced the frame against his knee. "Can you take my keys?" He held them toward her.

"Yeah." She took them and followed him up some steps to a locked door.

"It's the gold key." He balanced the frame on top of his foot.

She stuck the key in the lock and opened the door.

"The light switch is to the right."

She turned it on. A black and white marble tile entry way

gleamed into view.

He leaned the frame against the hall wall and placed a hand on her arm. "Come into my living room."

She glanced around the spacious room. Black leather furniture and a big screen TV took up most of the space. Glossy black and white photos of everyday people graced one wall. Surprised, she'd expected to see pictures of sport's figures. "Did you take these?"

He pushed his gold wire rim glasses up on his nose and glanced at the pictures. "Yeah, it's a hobby of mine."

"These are good." She was impressed with his work. *A man with hidden talent.*

He waved his hand in dismissal. "I like to think so, but you never know. I'll get us something to drink. Is wine okay with you?" He turned on the stereo as he headed toward the open kitchen and soft classical music filled the room.

"Sure." *One glass of wine wouldn't hurt her.* She continued looking at the photos. There were children laughing and playing in a park, staring into the camera, older people wearing their wrinkles with pride and another of a row of gleaming headstones in a beautiful cemetery. It was like an overview of life from childhood to the grave. Amazing.

Todd came into the room carrying two crystal goblets. Cindy took one. "These pictures are incredible. You've captured so much emotion."

"I was trying to show life in general, that life is for living at all phases of the game."

"Well, you did it. I'm amazed you can do this kind of work with a camera."

"Film doesn't lie. It always tells it the way it is."

"An interesting approach. You should put these in a book or an art gallery. They're too good to just hang on your wall."

He laughed. "I think I like spending time with you. You're good for my ego." Slipping his arm around her, he guided her to his couch.

She sat down and gazed into his blue eyes through his glasses. Before she could say anything, he leaned over and kissed her softly on the lips. He whispered. "You are a very beautiful woman. I was surprised to find you in the singles group. It was my lucky day when I ran into you."

His lips were warm and inviting. It was impossible to steady her erratic pulse, but she shouldn't be doing this. He pulled back and sat their wine glasses down and wrapped his arms around her, kissing her deeply. She seemed to be more afraid of herself than of him. *Good bye to Prudence McPrude and hello to Sluty McFluty.* He placed butterfly kisses across her forehead and nose. She opened her eyes to see a smile on his face.

"I know we've just met, but you're special." He sat back seeming to sense her need to pull away for a moment. "Well, are you going to help me hang John boy?"

Still tingling from his kisses, she wondered if she was "re-virginized." Sam had told her if she didn't have sex for a year she could regain her virginity. She knew that wasn't possible, but Todd's kisses caused sensations she hadn't experienced for a long time...but...something was missing. Actually, she'd felt more from Jack's kiss on the cheek than she did from Todd's kisses. *Damn.* What was wrong with her? Shrugging off these unexpected feelings, she stood and followed him to the entry way. "Yeah, what can I do?"

"Take the wrapping off while I find some tools."

She pulled the brown paper away from the frame. *This loft must've cost a bundle.* Todd appeared to be prosperous and his place was spacious and inviting. The bonus was that he was a genuine nice person.

"Here, hold this." He handed her a hammer while he used the tape measure to mark where the frame would hang. Taking a drill, he put small holes in the wall and added counter sinks. He finished getting the wall ready and reached for the hammer.

"Okay." He placed the frame on the brackets and stood back.

She touched the corner of the picture. Track lighting ran the length of his ceiling, accenting the room. "It's perfect in this light." She smiled.

"I wanted something special to put here and this is it."

"I agree. You've found it."

He reached for her hand and led her back to the couch. "Would you like some more wine?"

"No, I still have some." He snuggled next to her and listened to the music coming from the stereo and rubbed soothing circles on the back of her hand.

"Thanks for your help." He squeezed her fingers. "It was much more fun going to pick it up with you." There was a spark of some indefinable emotion in his eyes.

"I enjoyed it, too." Her voice was shakier than she would have liked, but she wasn't ready for more of his kisses...even though they were nice. "It's getting late and I have to work the early shift tomorrow."

"Oh, I'm sorry. I'm off tomorrow and I didn't think about the time. Come on and I'll take you home." He pulled her up from the couch.

"That's not necessary," she insisted. "You don't have to go back out. I can catch the shuttle. I don't live far from here."

"No way. It's my pleasure to take you home." He held her hand. "Where did you say you live?"

"At Brooks Tower." She brushed a strand of her long hair off the side of her face.

"Oh, yeah, that isn't far. We're practically neighbors." He laughed. "That's a good thing, because I'd like to see you again."

Cindy swallowed hard, lifted her chin, and boldly met his gaze. Caught off guard, she wasn't used to any of her dates wanting to see her a second time. "Okay," she answered, surprised at herself.

He smiled and escorted her out of the building and back to the bus stop. "The temperature has dropped. It's downright chilly tonight." He pulled her close to his side. "You wouldn't believe it's spring time once the sun goes down." Steam hissed out of the street gutters as they stepped on the shuttle.

She snuggled into his warmth. His skin smelled of Aramis Cologne and the subtle scent of soap, a manly aroma.

"Well, here we are," Cindy glanced out the window when the bus stopped at Arapahoe Street. They stepped off the shuttle and walked to the entrance of Brooks Tower.

"You don't have to come up."

"Nonsense, I want to." He waited while she placed her security card in the slot.

A green light flashed and the doors automatically opened. Hand in hand they walked by the security desk. "Hi, Dean. This is my friend, Todd, and he'll be back down in a few minutes."

The man at the desk nodded as they walked by.

"Twenty-four hour security." He glanced at the security cameras. "That's a good thing."

"Yeah, I like it."

"I wish they had it in my building. We haven't had any problems so far, but you never know. And with my schedule, I'm out of town a lot."

"Do you own your place or rent?" Cindy asked.

"I own it, but I'm thinking about putting it up for sale. I want to buy a bigger loft farther uptown."

"I own my condo, but eventually I'd like to buy a loft, too."

"That settles it." Amusement flickered in the eyes that met hers. "You can come loft shopping with me. There's a special candlelight loft tour in Lodo next month. Would you like to go?"

Her heart hammered foolishly as he weighed her with a critical squint, boosting her ego. She smiled. *He thought they'd still be seeing each other next month. Hmmm.* This was nice. "Maybe. It would be fun to see those neat places." She pressed the button for the thirtieth floor, keenly aware of his scrutiny.

He pulled her close to his chest and gazed into her eyes, as they rode the elevator to its destination. "I've enjoyed this evening...."

The elevator door opened and there stood Jack in his uniform, looking disgruntled at the sight of Todd with his arms around her.

A familiar shiver of awareness flowed through her as she noted the questioning gaze that passed between the men. "Uh, uh, good evening, Jack." She backed away from Todd. "I thought you were off tonight. This is Todd Chandler, a friend of mine." Jack's cold stare seemed to accuse her of something.

Jack nodded at Todd. "I got called in." He shook Todd's hand. "Pleased to meet you."

"Yeah." Todd met his glare with one of his own.

"I checked on Prince and he's fine." Jack appraised her with more than mild interest. "See you around." He stepped onto the elevator and the doors closed.

"Your neighbor is a police officer. Isn't that the guy who was at the ESPN Zone?" Todd growled.

She was halted by the tone of his voice. "Yes. My neighbor is a policeman."

"Who's Prince?" His voice was filled with suspicion.

Distrust seemed to chill his eyes and an oddly primitive warning sounded in her brain. "My dog. Jack helps me watch him sometimes." Tired of this type of interrogation, she sheathed her inner feelings and stepped to the door. It reminded her of the bad times with her jealous ex-husband. She chewed her lower lip and stole a glance at Todd.

Her reaction seemed to amuse him as his blue eyes met her green ones. He smiled, easing the tension. "Anyway, before we ran into your neighbor, I was going to ask you if you'd like to go to dinner with me when I get back in town in a few weeks. I'm on the road, a lot." He waited for an answer.

The look on his face mingled eagerness and tenderness. She must have imagined the angry tone. The thought of her ex-husband and his abusive outbursts had fogged her brain. "Let's do it."

"Great." He reached for her hands. "I'll call you soon as I get back." He pushed the down elevator button and leaned against the wall and kissed her, lingering over her lips. The elevator door opened. "Until then."

She tried to hide her confusion as the elevator doors closed. Unlocking the door, she entered her condo. Todd was cute, but she suspected something deeper was going on underneath his smile. She kept rehashing the scene in her head. Jack had been a jerk for glaring at Todd. Why would he act that way? Could he be jealous? And why had she agreed to go out with Todd? The chemistry just wasn't there. Was it to make Jack jealous?

CHAPTER TEN

From the coffee shop window across the street, Jack watched Todd leave the front entrance of Brooks Tower. Something about the guy had warning bells going off in his head. Who was he and why was Cindy with him? Of course, she hadn't bothered to tell him she had a date tonight. But then again, why would she? He'd made it abundantly clear that theirs was a purely platonic relationship.

Later, at the station, Jack caught up on his paperwork and ran a background check on Todd Chandler. The man's record was squeaky clean—not so much as a parking ticket. Yet, Jack couldn't shake the uneasy feeling in his gut about this man. His instincts never steered him wrong.

"Hey, Jack. Guess who I was out with last night?" Murph stood by Jack's desk with a smug look on his face.

Jack laid his pen down. "Now, Murph, with you, I'd never be able to guess. There are entirely too many women in your little black book." He noted the gleam in his buddy's eyes. He was excited about something. "Why don't you come clean and spit it out. You know you're dying to tell me."

Murph smiled and pulled up a chair. "Jack, you missed the boat. You had the chance of a lifetime and you blew it." He laughed with a mischievous twinkle in his eyes.

"What are you talking about?" Jack asked.

"Let me see.... She's blond, trim and loaded. Stands about knee high to a grasshopper and sweet as molasses."

"Okay, Murph, out with it. Who in the world are you talking about?" He shrugged and reached for his Bronco coffee mug. "I don't have a clue. Enlighten me."

"Rhonda, it's Rhonda. She and I have been dating for the past few weeks." A kind of awe filled his voice. "She's the butter on my biscuit...wonderful woman."

Jack glanced over the rim of his cup at Murph, glad he didn't choke on his coffee. Murph was serious. He could see it in his eyes and hear it in the tone of his voice. *Rhonda, the human octopus, had captured Murph's heart.* Could it be? Well, being fair, they were about the same age, but God, what could they possibly have in common? "Rhonda, you're dating Rhonda?" he asked in disbelief. Jack had a hard time wrapping his mind around the concept. Sure, as a joke, he had given Murph the information on Rhonda, but he never dreamed he'd actually follow up on it and go out with her. And now he's saying he's been going with her for weeks. He was stunned.

"I thought you might take it that way." He shrugged. "She said you two didn't hit it off, you were too young and inexperienced for her."

Jack laughed. "Yeah, that's me." *Too young and inexperienced.*

"She's the best thing that's ever happened to me." Murph grinned like a Cheshire cat. "We really hit it off."

"Murph, you be careful. She's way out of our league. What on earth could you have in common?"

"Come on now, Jack. Give me a little credit. I'm good where it counts."

Jack snorted in disgust. "She'll devour you like the black widow, chew you up and bite your head off."

Murph shook his head and frowned at Jack. "Not so. You're mistaken. She's not like that. When you take away her millions, we have lots of things in common. She loves fishing and hamburgers. She's tired of caviar." He looked like he had a secret. "We went to the lake last weekend, camped out and she had a ball getting dirty and messed up."

Surprised, Jack scratched his head. He couldn't picture it. The woman he had met would be in a three alarm panic if she broke a nail. "I can't see the Rhonda I know roughing it. You must mean somebody else."

"I know she's loaded, but she likes the simple things, like roasting marshmallows over the campfire, sitting by the lake and watching the sunset." There was a faint tremor in his voice as though some emotion had touched him. "Says she's missed those kind of things, and I'm the man to show them to her."

It didn't sound like the woman Jack had spent the evening with, but that was okay. If Murph was enamored with the woman, there had to be something worthwhile about her. Murph was a good judge of character. "Well, Murph, you go for it. I'll just have to take the backseat to you in the love department."

"Oh, your day will come. Some little girl will come along...ah, wait a minute, I think she's already with you. I seem to remember you chasing a long-haired mannequin head down the middle of Colfax Avenue. That was Ms. Right, wasn't it?" He was barely able to keep the laughter from his voice. "You keep her in the closet and pull her out whenever you want." He pushed the chair back and roared with laughter.

"Get out of here, you old goat. I have work to do and so do you. The Captain wants our paperwork caught up by morning. You better get to it." Murph's laugh broke off as he walked back to his desk, still grinning at Jack.

Murph and Rhonda, what a rush, they were two lonely people who had found each other. One for the books and his article.

Jack's hand clicked on his mouse. He'd check his e-mail first. An unexpected smile spread across his face when he noticed a message from Snow White.

From: Snowhite
To: JPrince

Hi. It's such a beautiful day. Don't you love Denver in the spring time? Just the smell of freshness in the warm sunshine and the flowers. I miss my mom this time of year. She loved the flowers.

How's the dating game for you? Have you decided to see anyone, yet? I met someone last night who seems nice. There's no bells or whistles going off, but who knows. He's working out of town for a while, but I'm supposed to go on a second date with him in a couple of weeks. I'll let you know. Wish me luck ~ Snow White

To: Snowhite
From: JPrince

Good for you! You're out there playing the field. Go for it! Where's your mom? Maybe she can come see you. JPrince

He clicked send. He didn't want to tell her about his experience with Lola. Snow White searched for the real thing and his date had been meaningless. Lola had been an interesting woman, but she had the heart of an animal. She told him she wanted sex from him—no strings attached and meant it. After two dates with the woman, which had been a mistake, he'd had enough. Time to back off. She was emotionally twisted, trying to replace her lack of feelings with sex. It would only be an exercise for her, no emotion, just action and reaction. The woman acted like a robot. He shook his head and thought that there sure are some strange people in this world.

He could tell Snow White and Cindy cared about things, even if it was a dog or flowers. Lola didn't. She was self-absorbed and cold. He had escaped having sex with her and didn't plan on ever calling her again.

"Jack. Ben called for backup," Murph shouted. "There's a robbery in progress at a jewelry store on Colfax."

"Let's roll." Jack and Murph rushed out the door in unison.

Cindy stood at the reception desk going over the appointments for the evening class. For the third time, she wished she didn't have to work, that she could take the time off and play with Prince. The weeks had flown by and Prince's leg was healing nicely. Jack had become her friend. Things were right in her world, but spring fever had hit hard. She was thinking about how she planned to transplant some flowers for her balcony when Sam rushed by. "Hey, where's the fire? Slow down, you shouldn't be rushing around like that. You might fall."

Sam stood there and sighed deeply. "I have so much to do, I don't know if I'm coming or going."

"Later. You can do it later. Come on, it's break time." She glanced at her friend. Sam didn't look well. "You're flushed. Are you feeling okay?" Sam's face was blotchy and as she took a closer look, she noticed a rash on Sam's hands. "What's going on?"

"Listen, I know you mean well, but I have to take care of the store room inventory."

Cindy took her friend by the elbow and gently guided her to the break room. "Come on. We need to talk." Concerned for Sam in her condition, she helped her into a chair.

Sam frowned at her friend. "Why can't I get caught up? I've never been so disorganized." She sighed. "I'm used to being free, independent and in control of my life. Ever since I decided to keep the baby, everything is falling apart all around me." She sat there looking disillusioned.

"Hey, it's natural to feel this way. It's your hormones. They are out of sync with your body going through these changes. In time, it'll level out and you'll feel more like yourself." She tried to act as if she knew what she was talking about.

"I hope so. I can't take much more of this. Look at me...I'm a wreck." Sam glanced into the mirror and frowned. "I'm spacey and I spend most of my free time in the bathroom or rechecking things I've already done."

"You look fine, but are you feeling ill? What caused that rash on your hands?"

She glanced at her hands. "Oh, God. What now? I don't know. I didn't notice." She touched the back of her hand. "It itches."

"Try not to scratch it. Call your doctor and see if he can work you in for an appointment." She gave Sam a hug. "Calm down. Everything is going to be okay. Go. Call him from the back office."

"Yeah, I will. I'm a mess." Sam rubbed her hand. "I must be having a reaction to something in the school." She frowned. "What next?"

"Don't ask. Things can always get worse. Go. Make the call. I'll cover for you." She didn't miss the look of appreciation shining in Sam's eyes.

"Thanks, I'll be right back." A student came up to them as Sam hurried to the back office.

"Miss Cindy, can you check my haircut?"

"Sure, Brenda." Cindy ran the comb through the customer's hair and snipped it in a couple places Brenda had missed. "Looks good, you did a nice job."

"Thanks, Miss Cindy."

"Anytime." Cindy walked back to the reception desk to check if any new appointments had been added. It looked like it was going to be a slow evening. Of course, everybody was outside enjoying the beautiful weather. Out of the corner of her eye, she saw Sam coming from the office.

"He said he could work me in as his last appointment, if I get there right now. I need to leave." Sam glanced around the styling area and watched the students doing hair. "There's twenty-four students working on the floor, four perms and three colors in process. Are you sure you'll be okay, by yourself?"

"Yeah, there's nothing to worry about. I've watched it when there were a lot more chemicals being processed. If I get in a bind, I can pull Miss Dotty out of the classroom and Miss Bonnie will be here soon." She motioned her hand to sweep Sam out the door. "Go. Get out of here."

"I'll be back soon as I can." Sam scooted toward the door.

"Go." She went over to check another haircut.

Miss Dotty slithered up to the reception desk as she returned. "Where's Mary Sunshine going?"

Cindy bristled. The old biddy took another unscheduled break. "Sam has a doctor's appointment. She'll be back shortly."

"Oh, I know about the baby. The whole school knows about it." Miss Dotty snickered.

Cindy would've liked to punch her. "So? Having babies is a natural thing," she said, surprised word had leaked out about Sam's situation this quickly.

"Well, you know she shouldn't be here in her condition."

She glanced around the room. "It might cause the kid to come out deformed or something." Her big cow eyes behind her black framed glasses looked sneaky and mean, widening in astonishment. "She needs to resign."

Cindy could barely hold her anger in check. "You know that isn't true. Women have worked around these chemicals for years and there's never been any proof of such nonsense." *The woman was a pain in the rear.*

"I wouldn't take the risk," she added with a smug smile. "When I had my children, I took time off from work."

"I'm sure you did. You had a husband." Triumph flooded through Cindy when Miss Dotty winced at her words. "Things are different for Miss Sam. You know that."

"Yes, well, that's how most people do it. Miss Sam played the game, so now she has to pay for being promiscuous," Miss Dotty answered in a rush of words.

Shocked at Miss Dotty's self-righteousness, Cindy held back what she really wanted to say and changed the subject. "I thought you were teaching a class on roller sets."

"I figured you might need some help and gave them a fifteen minute break."

"Everything is fine out here. Besides, Miss Bonnie will arrive any minute. She's coming in early to get ready for the night class. If I get too many chemicals going before she gets here I'll send for you." She moved with unhurried purpose to walk away from the obnoxious woman. Sam had been right. The woman was downright mean. Cindy hoped Sam would be okay. With a baby on the way, she needed her job.

"Miss Cindy, you have a phone call from a policeman."

"Oh, it must be my neighbor, Jack." Her heart did a quick flip-flop. "He watches my dog for me. I'll take it at the front desk." She hurried through the styling stations to see if anyone needed her help, before she headed to the front of the school. It seemed everything was under control. If anyone needed her attention, they'd see her at the reception desk. *Cool. Jack was calling her.* Happiness swelled in her heart. *Was there a chance for them?*

"Hello, Jack, this is Cindy."

"Hi there," a strange man's voice came over the line. "Who

is this?"

"I'm Tom Murphy, Jack's partner."

"Oh, yeah, he's mentioned you. What's up?"

He hesitated. "I'm calling about Jack."

"Oh, okay. If he has to work another double, I can feed his fish."

"I know. That's one reason why I'm calling." He stopped speaking for a second. "I'm sorry to have to tell you this but Jack was in an accident." She hadn't noticed the strained tone of his voice until now.

Cindy gasped and gripped the edge of the desk. "An accident?" She could feel the color drain from her face while she watched the students working on their customers. Momentary panic gripped her mind. "What happened? Is he okay?" She felt an instant's squeezing hurt as she tried to swallow the saliva that seemed to congeal in her throat.

"I'm calling you from the hospital."

"Hospital." The man had avoided answering her questions. Visions of her mother bleeding on the floor gnawed away at her.

"What's happened?" More pain tightened around her heart as a vision of Jack standing naked in her hallway flashed before her eyes. "This sounds serious."

"Jack and I were caught in the crossfire of a botched robbery at a jewelry store. He was shot in the chest with a shotgun."

"Oh, God." She couldn't get close to a cop...cops die. The thought came rushing back like a roller coaster on the downhill slide. Fear knotted inside her as sheer black fright swept through her. "Is...is he dead?"

CHAPTER ELEVEN

Much later that night, Cindy watched the hands on the hospital clock. The time seemed to crawl. Another six hours had passed and Jack was still in surgery. *He's my friend and a really good person. God, please don't let him die.* She drew in a ragged breath. "I wish they would tell us something," she mumbled to herself. Murph sat beside her. Several other policemen drifted in and out. Some sat while others stood around the hospital waiting room lost within their own thoughts.

Murph was a cop's cop. Tall and muscular where it counted. A bit older than the rest, streaks of silver shot through his dark hair. The kind blue eyes that had seen too much softened Murph's hardened face. Tired bags underneath them, gave him the distinct look of a man who wanted to retire yesterday.

"Soon as they know something, they'll tell us." He threw a worn magazine on the coffee table and glanced into her eyes. "Policemen live to help others live." He ran a hand through his hair in frustration. "Heroes aren't born...they just happen. Jack is a hero." He winced as if he were in terrible pain. "He took the blast for me."

"What?" Cindy swallowed the bile in her throat and tried to push down the memory of her mother being shot. She could never forget all that blood. She listened to Murph, not quite understanding. From the stricken look on his face, it was apparent he needed to talk through the experience. "What do you mean?"

"He shoved me out of the way." A streak of pain flashed in his eyes when he spoke. "I didn't see it coming...he did." With moisture in his eyes, Murph glanced down at the floor. "Jack is a good man."

Listening to him speak, she gripped the arms of the chrome chair until her knuckles turned white. She wanted to give Jack's partner her support. The man was going through his own personal hell. "He's going to be okay."

"Yeah." Murph glanced around the room and nodded at another cop.

"What happened to the burglar?" she asked, trying to help Murph open up and get it out of his system.

A strange look appeared on Murph's face. "He's in custody at juvenile hall. A kid. Just seventeen years old. That's why Jack didn't fire against him." He sighed. "After he shot Jack and saw the hole in Jack's stomach the size of a watch face, he threw down the gun and ran. I caught him."

"What a waste." Her heart ached for Jack, Murph and the kid.

"Yeah. We see kids getting into serious trouble all the time and there's not a damn thing we can do about it." Murph shook his head and stared back at the floor as if there were some secret message written there for only him to decipher.

An hour or so later, doors opened from the operating area when a doctor dressed in green scrubs hurried out. Murph went to meet him in the middle of the room.

Cindy hung back and listened to the conversation. When she had arrived at the hospital, Murph told her because of the blood Jack had lost, the first step would be for him to survive the surgery. She shivered and waited to hear the verdict.

"He's alive." The doctor spoke to Murph and the other men in blue who surrounded him. A sigh of relief filled the room. "Thanks to everyone who donated blood to the hospital. He's had ten units—roughly the equivalent of his body's entire blood volume."

Alive. Jack was alive. At the thought of that much blood, she covered her mouth to keep her stomach's contents where they belonged.

The doctor continued, "We have a machine helping him breathe."

Murph asked, "Will he make it?"

"It's touch and go. His injuries were massive. The blast blew away his spleen and his left kidney, shattered three ribs, took out the tip of his pancreas, and he has some swelling of the spinal cord." He hesitated for a heartbeat and glanced at the policemen's stern expression.

"You have to understand there's an eight-inch hole inside his abdomen. His diaphragm was ripped from his chest wall, but the good news is the surgery has stopped the internal bleeding."

As she listened, her whole body trembled. Silent tears streaked down her cheeks. *Oh, Jack.*

"...don't use the word, 'miracle,' often, but it's a sheer miracle he's survived this far," the doctor continued. If the shot had gone in a little to the right, it would have hit his heart. A little higher, it would have destroyed his aorta and killed him instantly."

"Is there anything else you can do?" Murph pleaded to the doctor.

"We're doing what we can at this point. He's weak and will have to grow stronger before we can proceed. The next few hours are critical."

"Is he conscious?" Murph asked.

"No, which is normal for these types of traumatic injuries." He turned toward the operating room. "I have to get back in there to prepare him for the move to Intensive Care. He'll be on the fifth floor." He hesitated. "Everybody can wait up there. If anything changes, I'll let you know. Right now, there's nothing for you to do but pray."

Cindy dried her eyes and wiped her face with a tissue. She must stop blubbering and stay strong for Jack. *He's alive. That's the most important thing.*

The doctor went back behind the closed doors. Murph said the doctor was the best in the five state region for this type of trauma and he sure sounded like he knew what he was talking about.

Murph came back and sat beside her. "Do you want to come up to the fifth floor with us? We're not going anywhere until we know Jack is going to make it."

"Yes, but I think I'll go to the chapel first. If you hear anything, will you send someone for me?"

"Of course," Murph squeezed her hand for a second and released it. "I'm glad you're here for Jack."

She made the walk slowly down the hall and pushed open the door to the chapel. Silence filled the room. The pews were empty, but a small altar on the back wall welcomed her into the quiet sanctuary. Several burning candles sat along the shelf in front of it, glittering in the soft pale light. She reached down and lit a candle for Jack, praying. *Please, God. Give Jack the strength he needs to pull through this.* She made the sign of the cross and returned to the Intensive Care Unit.

After several hours and many Styrofoam cups of black coffee later, she glanced up when the doctor finally came to the ICU waiting room. "He's turned a corner and seems to be stabilized. From the looks of all of you, I suggest you go home and get some rest. If you don't, none of you will be any good to him when he really needs you."

Murph gave a long sigh of relief. "Thank God and thank you, doctor." He grasped the surgeon's hand and shook it firmly.

"No thanks necessary. He's stable, but he has a long way to go. So far, he has shown great strength and a will to live."

Jack was going to make it. Cindy's heart leapt with pure joy that he had made it this far.

"When will he regain consciousness?" Murph asked.

"Not for awhile. His injuries are extensive. We have to keep him in an induced coma so he'll get the rest his body so badly needs."

"I see. Thank you for everything you've done. Will we be able to see him tomorrow?"

"Possibly, we'll have to wait and see. Check with the Intensive Care Unit around noon."

Murph turned toward her as the doctor went back to his business. "He's right, we need to take a break. We've all been through the wringer. Thank God. Jack's stabilized." He glanced at the other policemen. "You guys go home." He turned toward her as she yawned and glanced at the wall clock.

"You, too."

Cindy didn't want to leave, but there was nothing more she could do for Jack. "Will you call me if anything changes? Here's my cell and work number." She handed a business card to Murph. "I'm off tomorrow, so you can reach me on my cell."

"I'll keep you informed. I'm the closest thing to a family that Jack has so I'm here around the clock till things are under control." He frowned. "They're getting me a room down the ward from him."

"You're a good friend." She hugged him. "I'll call in a few hours and check on him."

"Call me. I'll let you know what's going on." Murph scratched a number on a piece of paper he tore off a magazine and put it in her hand. "Here's my cell number. You go home and sleep." He glanced toward another officer. "Johnson, give Cindy a ride home." He nodded toward her. "We'll talk later."

"Okay." She hugged him one more time before leaving the hospital with Officer Johnson. She and Jack weren't lovers or anything near that, but he was a good man, her friend, someone she cared for...deeply. She'd be there to help him through this, like he'd been there for her during Prince's recovery.

A fine misty rain fell as they headed toward the parking lot in the early gray dawn. The gloomy weather matched the inner turmoil churning in her aching heart. Why did such terrible things happen to good people?

Cindy listened to Sam in a daze. At the early morning hour she was so tired she could barely keep her eyes open but she had to touch base with the school.

"I'll come and wake you when I get off work and bring you dinner." Sam insisted. "Afterward, I'll go with you to the hospital."

"Okay, I appreciate it."

"Yes, you're in no shape to go there alone. We'll go together. Who knows? Maybe I'll meet a nice cop," a wistful tone had crept into Sam's voice, "just kidding, but I am here for you and Jack."

"Okay, I'll talk to you later," Cindy said and hung up the

phone. She dragged herself toward her bed and oblivion.

What seemed like only minutes later, she rolled over and tried to ignore the pounding in her head. Rubbing her eyes, she realized someone was knocking at her door. Prince's barking brought her fully awake. "It's okay, boy. Just someone at the door." Cindy grabbed a robe off the foot of her bed and stumbled to the front entrance and looked through the peep hole. Prince followed behind favoring his sore leg.

Sam stood on the other side of the door carrying a large brown paper bag. "Hey, wake up sleeping beauty. Are you in there?"

Cindy unlocked the dead bolt. "Yeah, I'm here." She held the door open.

"Look, what I have. Comfort food from Rock Bottom Brewery, a juicy bone for Prince and Swiss mushroom burgers with fries for us, it’s a sure cure for an empty tummy." Sam waved the bag in front of her nose. "You have to be starving."

The tantalizing aroma of French fries and burgers filled the air. Cindy licked her lips and couldn't think of the last time she sat down to eat anything. "Yes, I am. Come in and share the wealth."

Sam followed her to the kitchen and laid the burgers and fries on plates and gave Prince his treat. He took it over to his cushion and lay in the corner and gnawed away.

Cindy pulled glasses from the cupboard. "Do you want milk?" she asked as she poured a glass for herself. Her stomach rumbled in anticipation of the feast to come.

"Yes. It's good for the little bambino." She grinned. "At least that's what I hear."

Cindy sat in companionable silence munching on her burger. The food was a slice of heaven. She bit into a mushroom, savoring the unique flavor. "This is so good. Thanks for bringing it to me."

"Oh, honey, you're welcome. I was craving Swiss mushroom burgers and ran by on my way home from work...not a big deal."

Sam was a true friend whom Cindy appreciated more and more with each passing day. "How are you feeling and what did the doctor say about the rash?" With all that had happened to Jack, she had forgotten to ask Sam about the rash. Although it had only been yesterday, it seemed like years.

"Would you believe, after all this time, I've developed an allergic reaction to frosting bleach? I'm okay, long as I don't touch it. He gave me a lotion to put on and it's almost cleared up." She glanced at Cindy. "I know what you're thinking, and no it won't hurt the baby. That was my first question."

"Thank goodness. I only wanted to make sure you're both doing okay."

"Thanks honey. We're fine. The question is how are you dealing with this stuff with Jack? Have you heard anything else?"

"I talked to Murph a few hours ago and there was no change. Jack is holding his own."

"He's tough. He's gonna make it." Sam took a sip of her milk and tenderly rubbed her rounded stomach caressing her unborn child. "You know I read our horoscope today at work. Yours said, 'Will an old friendship turn into something spicier as Mercury glides into Capricorn?"

"Sam, you're incorrigible. Jack is in the hospital, barely alive and this is what you're thinking about."

"I checked his horoscope, too. The stars say Jack will make it and you know how much I believe in the stars. Anyway, listen to mine." She plucked a piece of paper from her jacket pocket.

"Sunday's planetary shift of Mercury into Capricorn signals that an older, experienced lover is waiting on the horizon. This is wonderful news for those in need of the romantic tenderness that only comes from hard-won life knowledge." She grinned. "That's me, for sure. And it says, to keep my eyes, ears and heart open to unlikely suitors this week, as mighty little Mercury teaches me age sometimes comes before beauty."

Cindy laughed. "That sounds right up your alley. Do you think it's talking about Larry coming back into your life?"

Sam frowned for an instant. "Oh heavens no, he's out of the picture, but it makes me feel good to know someone else might be out there on the horizon." She sighed. "That's where my Mr. Right will have to stay for a while. You can find me at seven o'clock on a Saturday night fast asleep these days." She sighed more deeply this time. "I'm pregnant." She placed the back of her hand over her forehead with a dramatic gesture. "The dating world will have to go on without me. I'm a lost cause."

Cindy smiled, knowing Sam was trying her best to cheer her up. "I doubt that. Every time you enter a room you turn heads."

Sam smiled. "You think I still got it?"

"Of course you do. That'll never change, no matter how many babies you have."

"Hold on there. One baby at a time." She glanced down at the remains of their meal. "I'll clean up. You get yourself together, then we'll go see how Jack is doing."

After she and Sam rose from the table, she turned and gave Sam a hug. "Thanks for everything."

Sam hugged her and patted her on the back. "Jack will be okay. You'll see. The stars never lie."

Cindy hoped with all her heart Sam was right, that the stars were on their side. Only time would tell....

CHAPTER TWELVE

The antiseptic smells hit Cindy soon as she stepped off the elevator onto the fifth floor. Sam walked down the hospital corridor with her toward the waiting room. She was grateful for having Sam at her side. She had been a good friend in the last few months. "I'm glad you came with me."

"Hey, it's okay. I want to be here, too, but these smells are making me nauseated."

Murph and another older man came around the corner and practically ran into them. "Hi, I didn't expect you back here so soon. Did you get any rest?" Murph asked with concern in his voice.

"Yeah, I did. She glanced at Sam. "This is my good friend, Sam, also Jack's friend."

"Hello, Sam. Thanks for coming. Jack needs all the support we can give him."

"I'm glad to be here." She turned to Cindy, and held her hand. "That's what friends do in these trying times."

"How's he doing?" Cindy asked.

"Good as can be expected. He's still out of it." Murph smiled at her. "There are lots of machines and tubes, but he's going to be okay."

"What else did the doctor say? The last time we spoke, you mentioned you were meeting with him later today for an update on Jack's condition."

"Just that he is stabilized and has a long way to go." He

hesitated for a moment. "He might not be able to walk." He swallowed hard. "It will take another surgery to repair the damage. And it'll take a long time and a lot of rehabilitation."

"Jack is going to need a lot of help." Sam glanced around the waiting room. "Does he have family to help him through this?"

"No, just us and the guys at the station, we're his family. His folks died when he was a kid." Murph looked sad.

"Well, he has good friends so we'll be there for him. I'm up to the task." Cindy meant what she said. She couldn't imagine Jack not being able to walk. If there was anything she could do to help him, she'd do it.

"Are you sure?" Murph quizzed her. "I know you mean well, but we're talking more surgery and lots of physical therapy. This could go on for a long time."

"Yeah, I can imagine what's in store for him. I'll be there if he'll let me."

Murph gave her a hug. "That's my girl. I knew you were made of the right stuff. Jack is lucky to have you in his corner."

"I'll help, too." The other man spoke up.

"Thanks, Briggs. Ladies, this is Tim Briggs, another close friend of Jacks."

"Hello." Cindy shook the hand of a gentle giant. Standing about six feet, the muscular man's dark hair was beginning to gray around the temples. It added a distinguished look to his face, but most of all she liked the twinkle in his dark eyes.

"Pleased to meet you both." Briggs reached for Sam's hand.

Cindy noticed Sam had turned a slight shade of green. Sam reached for Briggs' outstretched hand, missed it and suddenly barffed her dinner all over the man's shoes. Mortified, Sam covered her mouth and ran for the nearest restroom.

When she dashed out of sight, Cindy glanced from one man to the other. They backed away a few feet. "I'm sorry, she hasn't been feeling well."

In surprise, Briggs glanced down at his shoes and frowned. "I'm sure the lady couldn't help it. Hospitals make me queasy, too. Excuse me." He left her and Murph standing alone in the hospital hallway and proceeded to the nearest men's room.

"That's one way to thin out a crowd." Murph said. "Do you

need to check on your friend?"

"Yes, I'll be back." She dashed into the ladies room to find Sam sprawled on the floor with her head hanging over the toilet bowl. "Are you okay?"

She wiped her mouth with toilet paper and stammered something.

"What did you say?" Cindy leaned down with a damp paper towel and handed it to her. "Here, this might help."

Sam pressed the towel against her face. "I'm so embarrassed." She moaned. "I can't believe I tossed my dinner on that poor guy's shoes."

"Don't worry about it. He's a big man who took it graciously. He knew it couldn't be helped."

"Thank goodness. But why me? This morning sickness, actually twenty-four-seven sickness is getting old. It's about to do me in."

"It'll pass in a few weeks."

"From your lips to God's ears." She wiped her mouth one more time and stood up, tossed the paper towel into the commode and flushed it away. "One can only hope. I can't take much more of this."

Standing in front of the mirror, Sam brushed herself off and frowned at her reflection. "How will I ever face that man?"

"It's okay. After you left, he was nice about the whole thing. Women who look like you can get away with murder. What's a little nausea between friends? Smile and everything will be fine." She handed her a breath mint.

"Famous last words." They exited the ladies room together."Are you feeling better?" Briggs asked, with a look of concern on his face. He had been standing outside the ladies room.

"Yeah. I...I'm sorry." A sheepish Sam glanced at the man's big bare feet.

Cindy watched her friend squirm, knowing she was dying to say something about men with big feet. He carried a plastic hospital bag, probably with his ruined socks and shoes in it.

"Don't you worry about a thing, I know you couldn't help it." He spoke to Sam in a soothing manner.

When Sam looked up into his handsome face and saw him

grin, Cindy knew her friend was lost. What a sweetheart. She was sure from Sam's reaction she didn't mind the goofy grin splashed across his face.

Turning back to Murph, Cindy asked, "Can I see Jack?"

"Yes, I put you on the list. We can take turns and go in for ten minutes at a time." Murph hesitated. "Are you sure you're up to this? He isn't a pretty sight."

She swallowed hard and stood taller when she faced Murph. "Yes. I want to see him and tell him his fish are doing fine. I know how much he cares for his salt water aquarium." She bit her lip to keep from crying. "He's probably worried about someone taking care of it while he's laid up."

"Okay, I don't know if he can hear us, but I'll set it up. You wait here." Murph went over to the nurse's station.

"Do you need to go home?" Cindy glanced at Sam, who seemed content to sit next to Briggs.

"No, the worst has passed. I'll wait here for you. Go. See him, if you can."

A few minutes later, full of trepidation, she entered Jack's room in the Intensive Care Unit. Her heart beat nearly twice the normal rate. Murph had been right. There were tubes and machines everywhere. *Machines kept Jack alive.* His skin was pale against the blue hospital sheets. He lay there unmoving, still as death. She swallowed the bile in her throat, trying not to think of death.

She brushed a lock of hair off his forehead and reached for his hand, held it and rubbed the back gently with her fingertips. She tried to will some of her warmth into his body. Because of the ventilator tube in his throat, even if Jack were to wake up, he wouldn't be able to talk. She sat there and held his hand. The beep of the monitors echoed the rhythm of his heart beat.

She continued to rub the back of his cold hand. Then she leaned over and kissed his forehead. "It's going to be all right, Jack. We're here for you. Murph, Sam, Briggs and me and lots of guys from the police station." She blinked back the tears to keep from crying. "You're not going to get out of taking me and Prince to Washington Park this easy." Swallowing hard, she continued to talk to him. "I fed your fish and they're doing fine." She rambled on about his fish tank and condo. "I'm taking care of things for you. Don't worry about anything at home."

He opened his eyes for a split second. Recognition began to dawn on his features when sleep tugged at him and quickly pulled him back under.

"Jack, it's me, Cindy. I'm here for you. Wake up." Too late, he was already out of it. She laid his hand down and kissed him once again on the forehead. "Sleep, sweet prince, it's the best thing for you. I'll come back and see you tomorrow."

With unshed tears she walked away. A sinking sensation hit her in the pit of her stomach when she realized just how hard Jack would have to fight to survive this injury.

"Honey, come sit down." Sam waited for her by the door and led her to a chair in the waiting room. "You're white as a sheet." She handed her a cup of water. "Here, drink this."

Cindy sipped the cool water. "I'm okay. It's Jack." She sniffled to keep from crying and pushed down the pain squeezing her chest. "He looks so fragile."

"He's going to be okay." Sam sat beside her. "We have to keep that in mind and take it one day at a time." She sighed. "Healing is a slow process and Jack's recovery has just begun."

"Yes, of course, you're right...one day at a time."

Murph returned from down the hall. "Are you all right?"

"Yes." She twisted a tissue between her fingers.

"I talked with the doctor and he told me Jack is holding his own. He's doing better today."

"He opened his eyes for a minute," Cindy said. I...I think he knew me."

"I'm sure he did." Murph sat next to the girls. "The doctor said he's able to hear and understand everything we say to him. It's the medication that's making him sleep. His body needs a chance to start the healing process."

"I've never seen so many tubes going into a person." Cindy shuddered as if a chill passed over her body.

Murph frowned. "I'm sorry. I should've prepared you better."

"Oh, no, you did fine. I just don't like hospitals and machines." She remembered the day they took her mom off of life support. A shiver crawled up her spine.

"The doctor said they'll remove some of them later tonight, but he'll still have to be kept on the ventilator for a while longer. When he wakes up, he can write notes to us."

"Notes?"

"Yeah, that's the only way he'll be able to communicate with us. He sighed. "I expect it will be a while, yet."

Sam stood and reached for her hand. "Come on, honey, let's get you home for a good night's sleep." She glanced at Murph. "There's nothing more we can do here tonight. Murph and Briggs have things covered."

Cindy rose. "Yeah. Life goes on for the rest of us, doesn't it?" She turned toward Murph. "If there's anything you need, call me."

"I'll do that, little lady. But your friend is right. There's not much we can do for Jack, except pray for him to have a speedy recovery. He's in good hands." He glanced around the waiting area toward the doors to the Intensive Care Unit. "Go home and come back tomorrow." He stood between them. "I'll call you if anything changes and you know you can call me, anytime."

"Okay, I'll see you later." Her stomach churned with anxiety.

Sam hovered by her when they stepped into the elevator. "Did he really look that bad?"

"Yes. He looked pale and broken. Not at all like the strong muscular Jack, I'm used to seeing running in and out of the building."

"At least the doctors are optimistic he'll have a complete recovery."

"Yes, good news, but to see him now, a person would never believe it." She pressed the first floor button. "When he recovers, I wonder if he'll want to, or be able to stay on the police force. Can you imagine going through something like that?"

"Not in my wildest dreams. Who knows. Men are different from women. It must be the macho thing. Knowing Jack, he'll probably be chomping at the bit to get back to busting bad guys."

"Yeah, that's Jack all right." She smiled. *Macho to the end.*

Why do men have to be so stubborn when it comes to this sort of thing? One is not to reason why the good men die. She gritted her teeth and pushed the negative thought out of her head. *Jack will not die. He's going to make it.*

CHAPTER THIRTEEN

Sleep, sweet prince. Confused, disjointed images tumbled around in Jack's head. Prince? Why was Cindy's dog here? That couldn't be. *Where am I?* When he tried to crack open his eyelids a blinding white light hit him between the eyes.

Right before the excruciating pain sucked him back under, he caught a whiff of Cindy's perfume as her lips grazed his forehead. Through a haze, he thought he heard her talking about his aquarium. *Am I dreaming?*

His eyelids weighed a ton. No matter how hard he tried, he couldn't open them. Why? He tried to move and a sharp pain radiated across his abdomen and chest. Wanting to speak, he realized there was something in his throat preventing him from talking. Waves of pain rushed through his body. *Must be in hospital.* Considering the way his body hurt...*must be in bad shape.*

Colors of purple and gold swirled behind his heavy lids. Like the lure of a siren song nobody could resist he could feel himself being sucked back under—*drugs, must be heavy duty drugs*—carried him away on the colors. The pain was still there, but something had taken the edge off of it.

All of a sudden, the pretty colors were gone and he was somewhere else—inside a white shrouded room. Bright light seemed to radiate from the far corner of the space, turning into a narrow tunnel bathed in gold as Jack's eyes adjusted to the spectacle. Something came toward him through the tunnel, getting bigger as it got closer. He didn't feel frightened, just stunned. He couldn't believe what he saw. He had to be dreaming, but it didn't feel like a dream.

He shook his head, but the vision remained. His dead wife appeared before him. Clothed in cream colored robes, her image was surrounded by a warm white light.

"You must go back." She didn't speak, but somehow he understood her. The words were inside his head.

Transfixed, he continued to stare at the angelic image. Bathed in the soft golden light, she radiated goodness and health. He didn't know how to explain it, but an overwhelming feeling of peace soothed his aching body.

Am I dead? He wasn't afraid and he desperately wanted to tell her how sorry he was for everything he'd done in the past, but the words wouldn't come out of his mouth.

A smile filled with warmth and forgiveness shone on her face. "No, you’re in the between."

Peace and contentment filled Jack's soul while he watched her literally feeling her words...his pain disappeared.

"It's not your time," she said.

Warm healing vibrations flowed from her into his body.

Jack held his hand out, trying to touch her. She hovered slightly out of his reach. She looked like she was trying to persuade him of something. What did she mean?

"Jack. Forgive yourself. You have a full life ahead of you. I see you with another woman and children." She smiled at him. "It's a good thing." She hesitated. "Go back with peace and love in your heart."

He blinked and she was gone, but he couldn't shake her image and what she had said. They must have him on some mighty powerful drugs. As the thought passed through his mind, something tugged him back toward the dark end of the tunnel. A pulling sensation he couldn't resist persisted. Faintly, he heard someone calling his name.

"Jack. Jack. Come on Jack. Wake up. You've had enough beauty rest."

He opened his eyes to see Murph standing over him. The black circles under Murph's eyes gave him the appearance of a tired raccoon.

"Jack. You're gonna be okay."

He desperately tried to keep his eyes open, but they wouldn't work. Murph was alive and squeezing his hand. *So glad to see Murph.* A single tear slipped down his cheek. He squeezed Murph's hand in return.

His eyelids were too heavy. *Can't stay awake. The colors were back. Thank God, Murph was alive.*

Then a jumble of images flooded his mind. He still gripped Murph's hand and started to drift away with the colors floating behind his eyelids.

In a daze, everything happened in slow motion. He remembered a kid with a gun hiding behind a display case. The young boy aimed the gun at Murph, ready to fire. Jack's heart raced in his chest while he relived the scene in his mind.

Murph didn't see the gun. Jack didn't have a clear shot. Running fast, he shoved Murph out of the way. An incredible burning sensation spread throughout his stomach. Everything went black. That must be it. He had been shot.

Murph said he was going to make it. Hold on to the thought. The swirling colors pulled him back down into the dark recesses of sleep with Murph's reassuring voice echoing he was going to make it. *Going to make it...*blackness engulfed him.

Cindy sat at her laptop checking to see if there was an e-mail from JPrince. Nothing. Only one from Grace and Jenna. She had called them both but it was always nice to hear from them. And with everything that was going on she really needed to talk to JPrince. Where was he? She clicked on the e-mail from Grace.

From: Gracetaylor
To: Snowhite

Hi Cindy,

It was great talking with you the other day. Prince sounds like a sweet puppy, I can't wait to see him. I bet he's great company.

Sorry to hear about Jack. I hope he's doing better. From all you've told me about him, he sounds like he's tough. He'll make it through.

Summer sure has gone by fast, but not with many changes here in Cedar Falls. They did add the new rehabilitation wing to the hospital. We went to the grand opening. Since Seth and I donated the most money for it we were asked to be the guest speakers. I never in a hundred years thought I could speak in front of people like that but with Seth at my side it was a piece of cake. That has been our big news for the year. It's up and running and everyone says it's going well and from what I'm told they are helping a lot of injured people.

We just moved the cattle down from the high meadow. The kids are all growing up so fast. The twins are getting into everything and Jamie has a crush on a boy. Can you believe Seth is teaching Joey to drive out on the open range. Seth says it's never too young to start the process. They are having a blast driving Seth's old pickup around the place.

Nana says to tell you hello and to come and see us. Travis and Gloria seem to be working out. I'm so glad you're not bothered by that.

Tell Sam I'm getting a bunch of baby stuff ready to bring to her. It's all practically brand new, just I got so much at the baby shower and the twins outgrew most of it really fast. Nana, Jenna and I have been talking about coming to town to do some shopping. I'll let you know when it's definite. Since you won't come see us, we're coming to see you.

Have you been dating anyone new? Have a great week. You know you're in my thoughts. Later ~ Grace

From: Jennamyers
To: Snowhite

Hey Cindy,

It was great talking to you the other day. I just mailed your book order and wanted to let you know the order is on the way. We sure do miss having you around. When Grace and I get a girls night out and go to Charlie's place for dinner Grace always makes a toast to you and your new adventure. I sure do envy you. Your dates sound like a hoot.

Charlie and I are still friends so that makes seeing him easy enough but I'm feeling I need a change. I'm thinking of putting the bookstore up for sale and moving to Denver, just not sure when that will happen. It would be fun to be in the same town again. Well, a customer just came in the store so have to run. Jenna

The phone rang pulling her away from her e-mail. "Hello."

"Hi, Cindy, how are you doing today?" At first she didn't recognize the voice, then she realized Todd was on the other end of the line. Todd. With everything that had happened in the last few weeks, she had nearly forgotten about him. Guilt pressed against her chest. This was the guy she agreed to go out to dinner with and she had totally spaced him.

"I'm okay, how about you?" She didn't know what to say. She had been so concerned about Jack she'd put everything else on hold. Why had she done it? She and Jack were friends and she would help care for him because he was hurt, but she still had to go on with her own life. She brought her attention back to the conversation and listened to Todd.

"Doing good. I'm going to be out of town for a few more weeks, but I wanted to check to see if we're still on when I get back."

"Yes...I guess so. Things have been kind of crazy around here. I'll look forward to it."

"What's going on?"

"Well, you remember my neighbor, Jack, the policeman?"

"Yeah. The guy at the elevator?"

"He was shot during a robbery. I've been feeding his fish and taking care of his place for him."

"That was your neighbor? I remember hearing about it on the news. Too bad, how's he doing?"

"He's in pretty bad shape. He's in and out of consciousness. They're hopeful and are telling us it looks like he's going to make it."

"That's great news."

"Yeah. He's one of the good guys. He saved his partner's life."

"A real hero. I can't imagine what it's like being a cop and facing life and death situations every day."

She shivered. "Me either. Thank goodness there are people who feel differently than us, but it sure couldn't be me. I'm too much of a chicken."

"I bet you'd be brave if you had to, but who wants to put themselves in that position if you don't have to. Not me."

"I guess we'll have to rely on those who do, if we ever get into trouble." Cindy shuddered at the thought.

"Yeah, let's hope it never happens." Todd hesitated for a heartbeat. "Well, I have to get back to work. I'll give you a call when I get back in town to firm things up. Be thinking of where you'd like to go. Let's get dressed up and go to a really nice place. Your pick."

"Oh, okay, if that's what you want."

"Have a good couple weeks. I'll be in touch."

"Bye." She heard the dial tone in her ear, thinking about Jack. She wished it were Jack she was planning to go to dinner with, instead of Todd. Stop that. Negative Nelly rides again. Todd was a perfect gentleman. It wasn't his fault that he didn't have the same chemistry as when she was with Jack. Why couldn't she be content with what she had, instead of always daydreaming of what she couldn't have?

A couple of weeks later, Cindy stood in Sam's guest room doorway and watched her smile. "You're going to do what?"

"I'm having a paint party. The guest room is going to be the baby's room. I'm turning it into a nursery." She laughed. "You know I can't be around those paint fumes so I have to get somebody to do it for me."

"What a good idea. Who are you going to ask?"

"Not sure, yet, but I'm going to stuff my helpers with junk food. Fill them up with potato salad, chips, Kentucky Fried Chicken, cheesecake, pies—you know all that kind of good stuff." She laughed. "This is the only time in my life I can eat and not worry about gaining weight. The doctor says I need to eat more. Anyway, how can they refuse me if I feed them?"

"I'm sure nobody will turn you down."

"I'm not so sure. You'd be surprised. Now the baby is

showing, men run and hide to avoid me when they see me coming." Sam looked down at the floor and frowned.

"Oh, I don't believe that for a minute. There are lots of men who find pregnant women attractive and they're right."

"It's true—for me. Well, maybe it's not quite that bad. It's probably me being self-conscious."

"You, self-conscious? Never. What color are you going to paint the baby's room?" Cindy asked.

"Antique Lace, sort of a light cream color, and I have these pretty pink and blue borders with teddy bears on them to match the crib set." She motioned to Cindy to follow her into the room. "Come in here and I'll show you."

She couldn't resist looking into what would be the baby's room. There on the bed lay the borders, stuffed animals and a huge pile of baby clothes. "Where'd you get all this stuff?"

"Last night after my doctor's appointment, I went on a baby binge." She licked her lips. "The reason I asked you to come over is because I have some great news I wanted to share with you and I didn't want to tell you at work." She seemed about to burst with the news. "You're the first to know. My doctor did an ultrasound and I know what I'm having."

"Oh, my goodness, how exciting. Tell me. Tell me," Cindy begged.

A grin spread across Sam's face. "A girl and everything looks good."

Cindy hugged her. "That's wonderful news. She's going to look just like you. Cool. It'll be fun shopping for a baby girl. I can't wait till she gets here."

"You think you can't wait." Sam rubbed her rounded tummy. "I'm starting to feel like the Goodyear Blimp."

"You're not that big. You look great. You're glowing."

"Yeah, sure, that's from the energy it takes for me to move this weight from one place to another." She laughed.

"It's going to be worth it when that little person arrives." She smiled. "Have you thought of a name yet?"

"I'm thinking about Jennifer Rose, after my favorite soap opera character."

"What a pretty name. I like it. She's on *Days of Our Lives,* isn't she?"

"Yes." She patted her stomach. "Little Jennie, I can't wait till you come out and see me."

At the sight of the love on Sam's face for her unborn child, a pang of regret punched at Cindy's heart. She wanted a baby so badly. Someday...she'd have a child of her own. "You're going to be a great mom."

"Thanks. I'm going to do my best. But you know it's kind of scary. I'm responsible for a new life and I'm alone."

"Yeah, alone until the pizza guy delivers and I hear he delivers big time." She laughed, trying to lighten Sam's mood. "You know Sam, I look up to you. You're an independent, free thinker, a beautiful woman. Honey, you'll do fine. As long as there's love, everything else will work itself out."

"Yeah, but sometimes I'm not grown up in here." She placed her hand over her heart. "But this child will be loved beyond its wildest dreams—and I might find a father for her."

Sam's eyes held a gleam she'd seen before. "What do you mean?" asked Cindy.

"Every child needs a daddy. And since her real daddy doesn't want anything to do with us, I'll have to look elsewhere. He isn't interested in any part of raising a child. He signed over full custody to me so there won't be any problems from him in the future and that's fine with me."

"As I've said before, you're better off without him in your life. Do you have anybody in mind?" Cindy could tell from the tone of her voice, Sam was in lust.

"I'll never tell, but I may have experienced love at first barf."

"Briggs...you're interested in Briggs?" She should've known.

"I haven't decided yet, maybe... He was so sweet to me while you were in with Jack. Of course, I wouldn't pursue anything but friendship until after the baby arrives." She snickered. "You did see his big feet...didn't you?"

Cindy shook her head, not believing this conversation. "Am I understanding you right? You think Briggs would be good father material?" She stammered. "You don't know the man. He might be a psycho."

"I do know him. I've slept with men when all I wanted was

affection. This time I want a man who'll stroke my hair when I'm sleeping. Who'll show me affection without me asking for it. Briggs is like that. We've talked on the phone several times since then. He's taking me to lunch tomorrow."

"On the phone? Lunch? You move fast, but what do you really know about him?" She felt very protective about Sam and baby Jennie.

"For one thing, he's Jack's good friend and he owns a very successful magazine company. Besides, Jack wouldn't have a psycho for a friend."

"Well, you have me there. Maybe he's okay, but you have to be careful. It isn't just you. You have the baby to think of."

"Hey, now you're sounding like a mom."

She was right. "Oh, Sam, I'm sorry. It's none of my business. I shouldn't have said anything."

Sam laughed. "I don't mind. I kind of like having someone look out for me." She hesitated. "So, do you want to come to my paint party in a couple of weeks? Briggs is coming."

"Of course, I can swing a paint brush right along with the best of them. I wouldn't miss it." This way, she would get a chance to check out Briggs interacting with Sam.

Jack opened his eyes...actually was able to open his eyes and keep them open. A giant tube filled his throat as he looked around the room and saw machines and monitors beeping softly to his heart beat.

"It's about time you woke up." Murph sat in the chair next to his bedside.

Jack blinked to clear the cobwebs from his head. Murph leaned closer to his bed. "How do you feel?"

Jack rolled his eyes.

"Just as I thought." He handed Jack a notepad and pencil. "Here. The doctor said you have to keep the tube in for a while longer. Write what you want."

With a trembling hand, Jack scribbled something on it and handed it back.

"How long?" Murph glanced at it. "You've been here for a little over a month, getting your beauty rest, while the rest of us have been working." He patted Jack's arm. "The doctor says you're gonna mend just fine."

Jack took the notepad and wrote something else.

"Was Cindy here?"

Murph read it and smiled. "Yes, I called her. She stayed the whole first night, along with the guys from the station. Briggs and some of your other neighbors came by, too. Everybody is pulling for you, especially Cindy. She comes here every day."

So she had been there. He hadn't imagined it. Why was she wasting her time sitting around the hospital? When he moved his arm away from the notepad, a sharp pain shot across his chest. One of the last things he heard were machines beeping loudly as he slipped into darkness.

"Jack? What is it?" Murph checked for a pulse and couldn't find one. “Jack, don’t do this to me. Wake up. Wake up you son of a gun, we need you here with us.” A doctor and a couple of nurses rushed into the room with a crash cart and pushed him out of the way.

CHAPTER FOURTEEN

Cindy stretched her arms. It seemed like deja vu. Once again, she sat in the hospital waiting room. Jack had been in surgery for several hours and was now in recovery. The doctor had said there were complications.

"He's sure had a tough time of it," Murph spoke to the group in general and shook his head. "Doc says since he's gone in and closed the last hole the shotgun blast made in his belly, now it'll be just healing time. He took him off the ventilator. That's a good sign. Jack will be back to his old self before we know it."

Briggs sat next to Sam, glancing at the recovery room doors. "The man owes me a magazine article and he knows I'll take it out of his hide if he doesn't deliver."

So that's why Jack had such a nice computer system. Cindy listened carefully. "Jack writes for your magazine? I didn't know he was an author."

"Oh, yeah, he does freelance writing on the side. He's one of my best reporters."

"Really?"

"Yes. It wouldn't surprise me to see his name on the *New York Times* bestseller list, someday. I know he's been working on a novel."

Jack was an author? Cindy realized Jack was a complicated man and she didn't know him as well as she'd like to. When he recovered, cop or not, she'd have to do something about that.

"How long have you known him?" She asked.

Briggs glanced at her. "Since he graduated from college. His late wife was my cousin. We go way back."

"It's good he has you. Real friends are hard to come by these days."

"Yeah, he's one of my best friends. He's gone through some rough stuff in his life and came out the other side okay. Where it would've ruined other folks, Jack survived, and he'll do it again."

"Really," she said, her interest peaked. Much to her relief, Briggs continued.

"When his wife and son died, we thought he was going to drink himself to death, but he surprised us and turned it around."

Drink himself to death. Jack had a drinking problem. Oh, my God. She'd found Jack's closet and there was a skeleton in it. That explained why he was so angry when they first met. He must've thought she had a drinking problem, too. His wife and son were dead. "How did they die?"

"A car accident, they were hit head on by a drunk driver. Both died at the scene while Jack was passed out in the back seat." Briggs ran a hand through his hair. "He always said if he hadn't been drunk and passed out, his family wouldn't have been in that car."

"How horrible." She had lost her mom, but couldn't imagine how traumatic it would be to lose your spouse and your child at the same time and feel responsible for it. *Poor Jack.*

"Yeah, he went through it. He knows pain and suffering from every end of the spectrum, his own and others he sees on the job. That's why he's such a good author. He has lots of life experience."

She was stunned. Jack had experienced such loss. No wonder he always seemed distant. He had good reason to be mad at the world. She admired the man he had become in spite of what he had gone through. *How can I help him?*

The doors to the recovery room opened and a nurse came

out. "Mr. Murphy. He's asking for you."

Murph glanced at the others. "I'll tell him you're here. I'm sure he'll appreciate it."

With a lump the size of a bowling bowl lodged in his throat, Murph followed the nurse into the recovery area.

"We'll be moving him back to his room shortly. Don't stay too long. He needs his rest," the nurse said.

"Yes, Ma'am." Murph stood beside Jack's bed. Most of the machines and monitors had been removed. He almost looked normal, except for being pale. He opened his eyes.

"Murph," he croaked.

"Yeah, Jack. I'm here."

"What happened?" his voice sounded scratchy.

"You gave us a scare. Doc said you had a reaction to some medication and he finally had to go back in and plug the last holes the gunshot made inside you. He even saved you a souvenir."

Jack stared at Murph. "Huh?"

Murph pulled a clear plastic pill bottle from inside his jacket and shook it. He sat it on the bedside table, next to a pitcher of ice water. "The twelve shotgun pellets he plucked out of you."

Jack reached for the bottle. "These suckers are what's caused me this excruciating pain?"

"That's about the size of it." Murph pulled a chair next to the bed and sat, wishing he could take Jack's pain away. "Don't you think you should keep them to remind you not to jump in front of flying bullets?"

Jack glanced back at Murph. "Yeah, you might be right."

The lump in Murph's throat grew bigger. "Listen, Jack." He swallowed hard. "I...I owe you. You saved my life. Thanks."

"No thanks necessary." Jack closed his eyes.

"Are you all right?" Had Jack passed out, again? Murph's heart hammered in double time. "Jack. Do you need the nurse?"

Jack settled back against the pillows, his eyes still closed. "No, you old coot, I need sleep."

Murph gave a loud sigh of relief. "Well, you've slept for weeks, pretty boy, but if that's the way you feel. I do have to tell you Briggs, Cindy and Sam are outside." At the mention of

Cindy, Jack opened his eyes.

"Cindy?"

"Yeah, and the others. You have some good friends in these people. We're all here to help you."

A frown appeared on Jack's face. "I don't need anyone to look over me. Tell them to go home."

Surprised at Jack's reaction, Murph stepped closer to the bed. "Don't be like that. These people care about you. Don't be a jerk. Let them in."

"I have to sleep." Jack closed his eyes.

"Well...you stubborn mule, at least, let Cindy in. I'll check on you later." Murph left the room thinking Jack was going to be a pain in the rear through his recovery, but with the help of his friends, they'd get him through it.

A few days later, Cindy came into Jack's room with a large calendar and posted it on the wall in front of his bed, next to a bulletin board covered with get well cards. "Hi there, you've had so many visitors I thought it would be cool to keep a record of the people who've been to see you," she said in a cheerful voice.

Actually, Jack had been depressed and withdrawn since he found out he couldn't walk. She wanted him to see with his own eyes how many people were there for him, hoping it would lift his spirits. During the past few days there were countless MRI's and X-rays, a steady stream of antibiotics to fight infection and many visitors.

"Whatever." Jack lay in his bed and frowned at her handiwork. She gave him a new bundle of cards that had arrived in the mail at his apartment.

"My, aren't you in a good mood?" she teased, wanting Jack to react. He'd been sullen and distant the last few times she had visited.

"If you were laying in this bed, having to have people wait on you, then you wouldn't be in a great mood either."

"Jack. You know it's not going to be forever."

"Cindy...always the optimistic one. I've been around. I know how the world turns. Everything isn't as rosy a picture as you try to paint."

"Hey. You've been hurt, but you're healing. Look around. You'll find somebody worse off than you."

He sighed. "Yeah, but this is my life." He hesitated and waved his arm, indicating the room. "The Captain was here. Because of my injuries, I'll end up in a damn wheelchair. I won't be able to go back on the force, unless I work permanent desk duty." He cringed. "My other choice is to take an early medical retirement. My career is done for."

"Oh." That was what was eating him. "No matter how bad this moment feels, there's something better around the corner. When God closes a door, he opens a window."

"Easy for you to say, my damned window is stuck." He sighed. "How's my fish? Have you fed them to Prince yet?"

"No. He prefers beef. Your fish are doing great. They grow on a person." She laughed. "You know, I've come to really like them."

"You don't say. Maybe, after I get out of here, with all my free time, I'll help you set up a tank of your own."

"Knock, knock. Hello, Jack." They both turned to see Lola Brent standing in the open doorway wearing a tight low cut black dress.

Cindy glanced at Jack. He looked like he'd swallowed his tongue. *Damn, it was that woman again.* "I'll step out so you can have some privacy." Cindy glanced at Jack once more. "Hopefully, he'll be nicer to you," she spoke to Lola.

Lola gave her a smile when she left them together. *That woman.* Seemed a little stuck up at first, but at least after she read about the incident in the paper she had visited Jack, which had put Cindy in her proper place—a caring neighbor.

Jack was a hard man to figure. Most of the time since his last surgery, he was cool, calm and collected. It seemed he hid his pain tucked deep inside. She recognized the wall he had built around himself. *But where did Lola fit in...and was Jack as distant with Lola as he had been with her?*

The days slipped into weeks, weeks into months, passing like a blur for Cindy. She kept busy with work, daily visits to the hospital and taking care of Jack's apartment. Today she was at Sam's house for the paint party. Somehow Sam had managed to con several people into coming to help.

"Come on. It's time." Sam yelled through the open doorway.

"Okay, I'm ready. What's the rush?" Just then, Cindy's phone rang. "I have to answer that." Grabbing the receiver, she said, "hello."

"Hi, I'm finally back in town. I thought I'd see if you wanted to do something today."

"Todd. Oh, I'm sorry I'm at a paint party to help a friend get a room ready for the imminent arrival of my God-child." She returned Sam's grin.

"Need any more help? I'm available."

Should she say yes? Sam had three or four people coming, but another pair of hands might be nice...and it would take her mind off Jack and Lola. "Are you sure you want to do something like that?"

"Well, of course, if it means getting to see you. You helped me hang my John Elway picture. I owe you. Anyway, it sounds like fun and I'd like to meet your friends. What do you say?"

"Oh...okay. She lives in the Barkley on the Sixteenth Street Mall, right down the street from me in unit 2207. I'll let the front desk know you'll be coming over."

"I should be there in about an hour."

She hung up and glanced back at Sam holding plastic paint cover sheets in her hands.

"So, I finally get to meet Todd."

"Yeah, I hope you don't mind."

"Not at all, the more the merrier and the more work I'll get done." She winked at Cindy. "Did I tell you, Briggs is going to put the new crib together tonight?"

"No, when did you get him to agree to do it?" Cindy said.

"Last night. He brought the paint over for me and we talked most of the night. He stayed over."

"What?" She frowned at Sam.

"Don't be that way. It's not like a truck load of single guys turned over on the expressway. And if I hurry, I might be able to pick one up while he's still stunned. Anyway, he slept on my couch." She sighed. "You shouldn't be such a prude. We have to do something about that." She laughed. "Maybe, this Todd guy can help."

"Shame on you, I'm not a prude. I'm picky and I haven't made up my mind about Todd. Besides, you said nothing was going to happen while you're pregnant." She stammered, not wanting to offend her friend. "I'm confused."

"Nothing happened and you know what...it's nice. I'm getting to know Briggs and nothing sexual is going on. Now, that's a change for me." A twinkle appeared in her eyes. "He said he likes me as a person and thinks I'm brave for having the baby by myself."

"Honey, you are brave. And, of course, he likes you. He'd be a fool not to. You're a great woman."

"Well, this is the first time a guy has told me that without expecting something—like sex, in return."

"Then you've been going out with the wrong guys."

"That's what Briggs said. You know we watched movies and talked almost all night. He wanted to know my plans for the future. He was actually interested in me and my baby and what my hopes and dreams are for the future—not sex."

"Yes, he's interested in you, but don't kid yourself, he's interested in sex, too. They all are."

"Oh, I know, but the thing is, he isn't pushing it." She looked dreamily down the hallway. "In a way, I wish he would."

"Hmmm." It seemed Sam was falling for this guy. "He does seem like a nice person, but you know what they say about nice guys. They finish last."

"Then, *they* are not very smart. I'm beginning to think we could have something together. And you know what? He shared his feelings with me last night. He said he'd always wanted a family to call his own, but with establishing the magazine, he hadn't found the time. He says he's ready to delegate some of his workload to find time for a life. Maybe it can be with me." She appeared to glow with happiness.

"Really. I had no idea things had progressed this far."

"I don't want to jinx anything, but sometimes you just know when something is right. It feels like we've known each other forever. I wish I was carrying Briggs' baby." She sighed. "But anyway, come on. I have to tell everybody what I want done."

"Okay, you're good at bossing people around." Cindy laughed.

"Yes." Sam winked. "It's a great life if you don't weaken."

An hour later, Cindy was taping off windows when Todd came up behind her and placed his hands over her eyes.

"Guess who?"

"Let me think...Todd?" She knew it was Todd, but there was no warmth in his touch...not like Jack.

He stepped around beside her to look into her eyes. "It's good to see you. I met Sam. What a whirlwind. Before I knew what hit me she shoved a paintbrush in my hand." He chuckled.

"Yeah, that's Sam, all right. Are you sure you're up to this?" she asked.

"Sure, I like doing this sort of thing when I get a chance. I like working with my hands."

Would she like him working her with those hands? Where did that come from? *It was Jack she wanted—but Jack had Lola*. Like JPrince had told her, maybe she might have to settle for Mr. Almost Right until Mr. Right came along. *She'd try.* "Well...okay, let's get to work. We can cover this wall." She stuck her roller in the paint pan and began applying the cream color.

"What are your plans for later?" Todd asked.

"I'm helping Sam get the place put back together."

A grin appeared on his clean-shaven face. "You're a good friend."

Paint splashed onto her bare foot as she poured more into the paint pan. "Oh, darn."

"Here, let me get that for you." He cleaned the paint from the top of her foot with his handkerchief. "You have beautiful feet."

"Thanks." She stood back and looked at the room. Briggs finished painting the ceiling and stood in the doorway talking to Sam. She had to admit they did look cute together. The looks passing between them warmed her heart. Would anyone ever look at her that way? She glanced at Todd. He grinned and kept on painting. Maybe her happiness was right here in the present...closer than she thought. Damn, she wished he were Jack?

CHAPTER FIFTEEN

Home at last. Jack sat in a wheelchair in his living room...brooding. After eighty-seven long days in the hospital and the loss of summer, thanks to Cindy's help, he was finally back in his condo. "Hey, Prince. Your leg looks good." He leaned down and rubbed the back of the puppy's head. With a silly grin on his face, the dog sat there and let Jack scratch him.

He rolled over to his desk, touching the keyboard with his fingers. His friends had made his condo handicap accessible, but God, he didn't want to spend the rest of his life in this chair. *Why did this happen to me?*

"I think that's the last of it." Cindy came through the open door carrying a couple of plants and some get well cards. Even her walk had a sunny cheerfulness. "Where do you want me to put these?"

"Anywhere, I don't care," he growled.

The amused look left her eyes as he watched her. She'd brought him home from the hospital and unloaded the stuff they always gave patients to take home with them. After all she'd done for him he shouldn't be so hard on her.

"Hey, I'm sorry. I don't know what's wrong with me today." He sighed.

"Yeah, sure." Her smile broadened in approval. She sat one plant and the cards on the coffee table and the other in the dining room. "They look nice."

He glanced at the plants and noticed his fish tank. The fish swam peacefully in the salt water aquarium. "Have you fed them today?" He had missed his fish.

"No. I thought you might want to do it."

He wheeled to the aquarium and reached for the fish food. Realizing he couldn't get it, he sat back and glared out the window. *Damn.*

"Here." Cindy handed it to him. "Keep it on the side where you can reach it next time."

"Easy for you to say." He felt an acute sense of loss. Then he grabbed the fish food and sprinkled it into the tank, watching the fish come to the surface and nibble the flakes.

"Are you hungry?" Cindy asked.

He knew she was trying to take his mind off the situation, but she tried too damn hard. It was getting to him. "No." He ran his fingers through his hair. "Look, I'm just not good company today. I shouldn't be taking this out on you. You've been great."

"Jack. It's all right. Your life has been turned upside down. I'd be angry, too." She sat on the sofa and pulled a throw pillow onto her lap and played with the fringe. A look of sadness passed over her features before she continued. "You don't have to stay an angry, bitter person about what's happened. You're a strong man. I know you can overcome this."

"Overcome it? Look at me. Everybody feels sorry for me," he lashed out at her. "For God's sake, woman, I'm in a frigging wheelchair...possibly for life." His misery was like a steel cloak as he waited for her reaction.

"Get over it," she said firmly. The doctor said with physical therapy and rehabilitation, in time you might be able to walk again." She sighed. "It's up to you."

"Yeah...maybe." But he didn't believe it for a minute.

"I know you can do it." She said, softly, her eyes narrowing as if she could look inside his soul. "Don't give up. Look how far you've already come."

"I'm alive. That's about all I can say," his voice broke miserably.

"Untrue. You should be ashamed of yourself. You can still get around in your motorized wheelchair. I see people in them on the Mall scooting around all over the place. It hasn't stopped them." She sighed. "There are a lot of people worse off than you."

Unable to pull himself together, he let his anger take over. "Enough." He growled. "Don't preach to me!"

Sudden anger lit her eyes. "I wouldn't dream of it, but you, of all people, must realize there's more to life than crying in your beer."

He glowered at her. She'd gone too far—struck a nerve. "What do you mean by that?"

"Nothing." He hadn't missed her glancing away, as if she knew something she didn't want him to know. Did she know about his past?

"Right." His temper flared. "Who've you been talking to?"

"Nobody. Why are you being so defensive?" For an instant her green eyes clawed him like talons. "Seems to me like you need to spend some time by yourself to get your head clear. I made up a bunch of microwave meals for you. They're labeled and in the refrigerator on the lower shelf."

She came to him and placed an arm on each side of his chair and stared him down. Her eyes were like polished jade. "Jack Riley." She lowered her voice, purposely getting his full attention. "You're angry at your own demons, not me. I refuse to fight with you. Call me, if you need anything." She kissed him on the cheek, turned on her heel and walked out the door, taking Prince with her.

He touched his face as if she had slapped him. She should have been yelling and screaming at him...and she kissed him. He couldn't get over it. The woman was an enigma. *Way to go, jerk.* She had gone out of her way to take care of his home and him...this was the thanks he gave her. *What a schmuck.*

His mind congested with doubts and fears. *I'm such a fool. And she was right. There are a lot of people worse off than me. Damn. I need to get off my pity pot and get on with it.*

The next morning Cindy stood by the reception desk at work, talking with Sam. She glanced at the appointment book. "It looks like it's going to be a slow day."

"Good, I'm tired. The baby is kicking like crazy."

"You're doing okay, aren't you?"

"Yeah, I'm doing great. No more morning sickness. Thank goodness." Sam tapped a pen against the desk. "How's Jack doing, now that he's home?"

"Not too good. I think he's on a downhill slide, trapped in the self-pity phase of healing." she sighed. "I don't know what to do to help him out of it."

"I'm sure he'll pull out of it. I'll talk to Briggs. Maybe he can think of something." She smiled. "The baby's room is finished. You'll have to come over and see it. I think I'm ready for little Jennie to get here." She rubbed her rounded tummy.

"That's great." She wished she had a baby on the way, and wondered what it would be like to have a child growing in her body.

"Hey, don't worry so much. Briggs will think of a way to turn Jack around."

"You know, I wonder if anyone can help him. He needs to decide to help himself, but how does he get strong enough to make that decision?

"Miss Sam, Miss Cindy. Come quick," a student shouted. Miss Dotty cut a man's ear off. There's blood everywhere."

"Where is she," asked Sam.

"In the back classroom. She was teaching haircutting. The student spoke with a shaky voice.

"We'll talk more after I take care of this," Sam said. "Darn, ears bleed worse than anything. Cindy, bring the first aid kit. I'll see if I can get the bleeding stopped. Meet me there."

"Okay." Sam nodded toward the man's reflection in the mirror. "It's about stopped." She glanced at Cindy. "It was just a nip. Give me the styptic pencil."

She handed it over and watched her work on the pale customer.

"Does it hurt?" Sam asked.

"No. Stings a little," the man said. "It's not a big deal." He looked into the mirror above the styling station. "Looks like its stopped bleeding."

"Thanks." He glanced at Miss Dotty and the students hovering around him.

"You shouldn't have moved and this wouldn't have happened." Miss Dotty's voice was filled with anger and she looked as if she was ready to argue with the man. Cindy couldn't believe she said that.

Sam turned the styling chair so the man faced her. "I'm terribly sorry this happened. We'd like to make it up to you." She pulled a card out of her smock pocket and wrote on it. "I'm going to give you your next five haircuts for free."

"Cool." He grinned at Sam and glared at Miss Dotty. "But I want you to supervise them."

Sam grinned. "I'd be happy to do that for you. Next time you come in, show this card to the student at the reception desk."

"Okay." He rose from the chair. "I'll see you next time." He grinned at Cindy.

After he walked away, Cindy glanced between Sam and Dotty. You could almost feel the tension in the air.

"Miss Dotty. Come into my office. We need to talk," Sam demanded.

"I have nothing to say to you. The man moved."

"Do you really want to discuss this here?" Sam asked. Students crowded around them, hanging on every word.

"Oh. All right." Miss Dotty threw the bloody towel she held on the styling counter and stomped off toward Sam's office, Sam close on her heels.

"Man. I wouldn't want to be in her shoes. Miss Sam looked upset," a student whispered to her friend.

Cindy overheard the students. She had to get the classroom under control. The last thing they needed was more grist for the rumor mill.

"Listen up, everyone. It's over. Continue working on your models. And for your own information, know it looked worse than it was. Accidents happen. Learn from this and always be careful when cutting around ears."

One by one, the students went back to work on their friends. Cindy returned to the front desk and saw Sam coming from her office. "How did it go?"

"Very well. Thank you for asking. It's nice to finally have something solid on the old bat." She smiled. "Now, where were we, before Miss Dotty caused a scene? Oh, yeah, I was thinking. Why don't you and Jack come to my house for Thanksgiving dinner with me and Briggs?"

"He does need to leave his apartment." Cindy hesitated. "He's kind of upset with me. But if he says yes, I'll come."

"Well, whether he comes or not, I want you to be there. Briggs and I have a surprise. I suspect Briggs will get him to say yes. Hey, what about this Lola? What's the deal with her?"

"She's a hard one to figure. I guess Jack likes her."

"Jack's not smitten with her. I can tell. She's not the one for Jack," Sam said.

"Then, why does she keep coming around?"

"Give it time. Jack is the man for you."

Cindy's heart leapt into her throat. "Why do you keep saying that? Sure, I like the guy and worry about him, but it's strictly one-sided. Anyway, Jack has Lola." She frowned. "Why are we having this conversation?"

"The cards never lie. They said you would meet your soul mate a few months ago and you did...Jack. It's something I know, like I know the sun will come up tomorrow. Just accept it and go for it." She walked away to check a haircut.

Jack. Her soul mate. Too bad, he didn't know it. She took a deep breath. She'd been distracted throughout the day with thoughts of Jack. He couldn't possibly be her soul mate...could he? Her heart thumped dangerously in her chest. Regardless, even if the man didn't know she was alive, he wasn't doing well and she wanted to be there for him. The phone rang. The student on desk duty answered it, pulling Cindy back to reality.

"Miss Cindy, it's for you."

Cindy reached across the appointment book for the cordless phone. *Please, God, don't let anything else be wrong with Jack.* "Hello."

"Hi, Cindy, this is Todd. I'm sorry to call you at work, but I needed to speak to you."

"It's okay I'm not busy at the moment." Todd, the last person she wanted to talk with, was on the other end of the conversation. A cold knot formed in her stomach while she listened. Sometime in the near future, she was going to have to tell him their relationship wasn't headed anywhere. The sooner, the better. Sure, he was nice, but... After the paint party, she had discovered there just wasn't enough there for it to go any further. The bottom line—he wasn't Jack.

"What's happening pretty lady? Do you have plans for tomorrow afternoon? I know it's short notice, but I just got back in town and I have free tickets to the Bronco game if you're interested."

Half in anticipation, she did love the Broncos and half in dread, she answered. "No, no plans. Sure, I'd like to go to the game with you." This would be their third date, if she counted the paint party, and a chance for her to let him down easy. Todd was sweet. If possible, she wanted to stay his friend. Who knew what would happen, but no matter, honesty was the best policy. She wouldn't lead him on she'd tell him during the game. Maybe it would be easier with lots of people around.

"I'll pick you up at your place at about noon so we can hit some tailgate parties. I hear the food is really good. The game starts at two-fifteen so we'll just grab something to eat there."

"Okay, see you at my place." She hung up the phone and turned back to watching the students on the styling floor when Sam came up to her.

"You're not going to believe what I just heard from home office." Joy bubbled in her voice and shone in her eyes.

"What?" she only half-listened as she struggled with her conscience. What was she going to do about her feelings for Jack?

"You know the guy who Miss Dotty injured?" She smiled, barely able to keep the laughter from her voice. "Well, it turns out he was our secret shopper for this month."

Cindy blinked and refocused her gaze. "You have to be kidding." She laughed.

"No, Miss Dotty is in deep trouble with the home office." Her whole face spread into a grin. "It's about time."

"My thoughts exactly. What's going to happen to her?"

"I'm not sure. They're going to get back with me after they review the incident reports I've sent them over the past months." Sam's quick blue eyes were filled with humor. "With my luck, she'll probably get a slap on the wrist and a gift for sucking up. She's like the ass whisperer."

Cindy laughed. "Maybe, but this is serious. The man bled all over the place and she tried to make it appear to be his fault. Could be tense for her."

"One can only hope. I'll know in a little while."

"We'll keep our fingers crossed."

For an instant, Sam's gaze sharpened as if she could look into her heart. "I talked to Briggs and he's working on Jack. I think he'll make it for Thanksgiving. So plan on coming."

"Okay, okay, I can take a hint, but I haven't spoken to him since he was being ornery." She glanced at the students to make sure nobody needed her help. "He's had enough time to stew in his own juices. Tonight, I'm going to drop by and see how he's doing?"

"Yeah, your timing would be perfect. Briggs said Lola was about to drive him crazy." She grinned. "It's a good time for you to make a move on him. She comes by everyday and insists on babying him. Can you imagine a man like Jack putting up with her?"

"Make a move on him, in his condition?" She threw her hands up in frustration. "Now isn't the time. And anyway, Lola is beautiful. I wouldn't stand a chance against her." She sighed.

"That's what you think. You'd be plenty of competition if you'd put your mind to it. I've seen the way he watches you when you aren't looking." She chewed on her lower lip, deep in thought. "However, sometimes guys put up with anything, if they're getting what they want from a woman."

Cindy's heart sank. She pushed a strand of hair behind her ear. "Sam, do you think they're doing it?" She cringed at the thought. "Do you think it's even possible in Jack's condition? Wish it were me." The words slipped out before she realized she'd said them.

"I knew it. I knew you had a thing for Jack." Sam's features became more animated. "That's cool. At least you are finally able to admit it to yourself. You'd be good for each other."

"Yeah, me, Jack and Lola." She sighed. "What a perfect match."

"Trust me, from what Briggs said, Jack is sick of Lola and her always pushing her chest in his face. Briggs said the doctor told Jack he would heal, a lot of his problems were in his head.

Maybe it's possible for him to get it up and let her do the work. But there's more to a relationship than a fabulous body. Anyway, you have a great body, too."

"Yeah, right. Next to Lola, I look like a flat-chested boy." A shadow crossed her heart as a memory of her ex-husband calling her breasts baby boobs rose to the surface.

"Nonsense, you're a beautiful woman." Sam raised her eyebrows. "It's a fact. You're gorgeous."

"Whatever you say," Cindy sighed and wondered if Jack and Lola were getting it on. Was it possible for Jack? And with the changes Jack was going through, she couldn't imagine him being interested in making love to anyone. But Sam's words had given her a sense of strength and her despair lessened.

"Mark my words, you and Jack are meant to be together." Sam winked at her and went to help a student check a hair color.

Cindy mulled over the conversation while she stood by the reception desk. Was a future with Jack...possible?

CHAPTER SIXTEEN

Cindy walked beside Todd, among the crowd returning from the Broncos football game. It had been a perfect fall afternoon and everyone was excited about the win. Some of Todd's friends showed up and she hadn't gotten the chance to tell him she only wanted to be friends. Somehow, she had to work it into the conversation before the date ended.

"Want to come to my place for a drink, before I take you home?" he asked.

Ah...the perfect opportunity. "Sure." She could break the news to him there. She walked down the street in silence.

"Here we are." He opened the door and escorted her inside. "I have a surprise for you." He led her into the living room.

A soft gasp escaped her. "A surprise?" God, she hoped he didn't have a gift for her. Guilt pulled at her heartstrings. *Damn, why does dating have to be so hard?*

"Come, sit on the sofa and I'll get us some wine." His face brightened when she glanced in his direction.

"That's nice, but don't go to any trouble."

"Trouble, you'd never be any trouble to me." In the open kitchen, he popped the cork on the wine and poured two glasses.

Taking a glass, Cindy wondered what he had on his mind. God forbid! It was the dreaded third date and he was acting strange. Some guys thought on a third date the woman had to put out or get out. Well, if that was the case, she'd leave.

Todd sat down, picked up the remote, and dimmed the lights.

Should she leave? No. She was an adult. Todd was okay. He wouldn't do anything she didn't want him to do. "What's on your mind?"

"I told you I have a surprise for you." Frowning, he continued. "Here, let me make you comfortable. Lean back and enjoy your wine." He set his wine on the glass and chrome table top and slowly slipped off her sandals. "I've been admiring your feet all day."

"Uh...uh my feet?" Uneasy feelings swept through her.

"You have pretty feet. I know we're just getting to know each other, but I'd like to share something with you. I want to massage your beautiful feet."

She took a deep breath and adjusted a smile, trying to figure a graceful way out of the situation. In the meantime, Cindy hoped her feet didn't smell and tried to go with the moment. Todd held one foot in his large hand, gently massaging her toes.

"Relax. It's okay, don't be nervous." He pulled out an electric foot bath with warm water and lotion from under the coffee table. "It's part of the surprise. You've had a hard week, lie back and let me work my magic on those toes." He washed her foot and applied warm lotion in circling motions, making her foot feel wonderful.

Okay, she'd try to relax and talk to him after the foot massage. She closed her eyes and leaned back against the sofa trying not to be a prude. He massaged the other foot. What could it hurt? The man had great hands. He applied more lotion and covered her feet with plastic bags. She opened her eyes.

"Sit here and relax. Let the lotion soak in, it makes the skin feel great. I'll be right back." He clicked the remote and stood. Slow sexy music filled the air and the dim light turned a muted pink color.

"What's happening?" She sat up. "I don't understand."

"Not to worry, my dear. Part of your surprise. I'll be right back." He disappeared into the bedroom.

"Oh, yeah, there's a gift for you beside the couch," he called from the bedroom. "Pull out the big black bag and we'll open it together."

A gift. *Damn.* "Todd, you shouldn't have got me anything." Groaning inward, she pulled the large black suitcase onto the sofa, beside her, wondering what on earth could be in it. A nagging in the back of her mind warned her that this wasn't a good thing. Such a big case, but it wasn't heavy.

All of a sudden, the music changed to an upbeat rhythm and Todd came dancing out of the bedroom dressed in nothing, but a pair of silver sequined speedos. Cindy's mouth fell open. She sat there in shock. He gyrated around the room to the sounds of the music with a strobe light flashing red, white and blue colors. It was a flashback to the sixties. Heaven forbid, he was an Austin Powers wannabe.

Pushing his silver sequined pelvis toward her face, he said, "Baby, this is for you, but first things first." He reached down and removed the wrappings from her feet. Sitting on his knees, he gently took her feet into his hands and massaged them. His expression grew serious when he licked between her toes.

Her hands, hidden from sight, twisted nervously in the sofa. She sat still, with the lights flashing around them as he suckled her big toe. More startled than frightened, she couldn't believe what he was doing to her foot. It was if he were making love to her big toe. He was actually getting turned on by her foot.

Trying to pull her foot away she noticed the bulge in his pants. *Yuck! The man has a foot fetish.* A shadow of alarm skittered across her mind. She'd play along with him until she got a chance to run for it. With an effort she looked at him. "Looks like you have a big package for me?"

"Oh, baby." He gave her a narrowed glinting glance. "And I deliver on time." He continued to worship her toe as if he were about to have an orgasm. She couldn't stand it any longer. This wasn't sexy. It was sick. When she tried to pull her foot away, she accidentally bumped the latch on the suitcase. The lid flew open. Out popped a female blow up doll. She couldn't believe her eyes when it bounced around the sofa.

All her nervousness slipped back as she read the label written around a large hole in the doll's vagina, 'Pleasure Zone.' It was an obscene flesh colored, red-headed doll with bare breasts the size of melons with huge red nipples. In stunned disbelief, she read the label on another box in the case as she tried to tug her foot away from Todd. Twelve strategic positions for exciting love play, compatible with Doc Johnson's patented tie up system. Comes with repair kit and twenty-five feet of extra black rope and attaches easily to a door for vertical pleasure. Every fiber in her body warned her against him. *What had she gotten herself into? The man was a raving sex maniac.*

He held her foot, but stopped suckling her toe. "Oh, wonderful, you've found the rest of your surprise. That's Dolly." His eyes gleamed with excitement when he glanced up at her for a second and then proceeded to suck her toes, pulling almost her whole foot into his mouth. He seemed harmless, but she wanted nothing to do with this kind of surprise. She looked at him with amused wonder. If she wasn't so disgusted, she'd laugh at the sight of a grown man sucking her foot. She decided the best way to get out of this situation would be to make a clean break for it.

She shook her head, and glanced down to see Todd with her foot in his mouth, rubbing his sequined penis with his other hand. This was the last straw. She'd be damned if she let a guy get off on her foot. Her stomach churned as she pulled her toes out of his mouth and pushed him back. "I'm sorry, honey, but you're going to have to deliver your own package without my help." She grabbed her sandals and with long purposeful strides ran for the door.

Glancing back she shouted, "Sorry, Todd, this isn't for me." She slammed the door with the vision of Todd sitting on his knees in the strobe lights, rubbing his engorged sequined penis, looking at her as if she'd lost her mind for leaving him in his condition.

Her heart beat faster while she rushed down the hallway. Thank God, he wasn't following her. Out of breath, she stopped to put on her sandals and burst out in uncontrollable laughter. Maybe she didn't have a man in her life, but she still had a sense of humor. This rated right up there to when she'd gone on a blind date with a mortician and he asked to touch up her makeup. *I've had it. No more dating. Lord just take me now.*

Jack rubbed his eyes. He had been working on his novel all morning, a rewarding, but mentally draining experience. It had felt good to get lost in his writing. When he was in that other world he didn't have to think about what had happened to his life. He could be any man he wanted to be—one without physical problems. Ideas had flowed through him, like water down a stream, but now it was time to face reality. *Damn, he didn't like feeling sorry for himself.* He pushed his wheelchair away from the computer.

Someone knocked at the door. Earlier, he had clicked the deadbolt into place. Jack wheeled over to the lower peephole to see Briggs standing on the other side. "Great, he's here for the magazine article." Jack sighed when he opened the door.

"Hey, Jack." He looked at him from beneath craggy brows. "How's it going?" Laugh lines crinkled around his eyes as Briggs grinned at him. "I come bearing gifts." He lowered his voice, purposefully mysterious and handed a book to Jack.

"Come in." Jack placed the book on his lap and rolled back into the living room. "What's this?" He measured Briggs with a cool appraising look, knowing the man had something on his mind. Then he turned the book over and read the title. *Living Well With Chronic Pain.* He swallowed hard, lifted his chin, and watched Briggs.

Briggs flopped onto the sofa, making himself at home. He cast an approving glance around Jack's condo. "I like what you've done with it." He boldly met Jack's gaze. "The lady who runs that clinic in Cedar Falls wrote it. Man, she had a lot to deal with and successfully overcame it. You have to read it. I was amazed."

"Maybe later." At odds with himself, he tossed the book on the coffee table. "What brings you here?"

Briggs looked like he'd been caught with his hand in the cookie jar. "I wanted to see how you're doing and I want you to read that book. It's filled with success stories of people going through things similar to what's happened to you."

"Wonderful, thanks." Jack managed to say as he glanced at the book.

"So...how are you really doing? You don't have to give me the sugar-coated version. I know you're about to lose your mind. If I were in your position, I honestly don't know what I would do." He sat very still, his eyes narrowed as if trying to bore into Jack's head. "But I do know I wouldn't give up." Briggs settled into the deep green cushions and looked him in the eyes.

"You don't know what you're talking about," Jack growled. "If I want to give up, it's my own damn business."

"No. That's where you're wrong." Leaning forward, in a controlled voice, he continued. "In the past few months, you've touched a lot of people's lives and they're concerned with what happens to you. For some Godforsaken reason, they care about you." He steepled his fingers on his lap and growled right back at Jack. "It's time to take the gloves off, Jack. Time for you to get on with it."

Gazing at Briggs, Jack realized the man had an air of authority and the appearance of one who demanded instant obedience. But it wouldn't work this time. "I don't want anyone to care about me." Jack gripped the arms of his wheelchair, wanting to throw Briggs out the window. Never mind it was thirty stories up and Briggs weighed about two-hundred and thirty pounds.

Briggs sighed and his expression grew serious. "Get off that same old song and dance routine. Frankly, I'm tired of hearing it and I think the others are, too." He had Jack's full attention. "Jack, it's time for you to make some changes. It's time to get some help."

"Sure, easy for you to say." Somehow he managed to face the bear of a man. "I've had help and look where it's got me." He waved his arms at the wheelchair.

"Yes, let's take a look at where it's gotten you. You are alive and mean as a snake. You've come a long way since the hospital. You're home, doing physical therapy and living on your own terms. You should be thanking your lucky stars you're doing as well as you are."

His eyebrows flared in a frown. "Actually, this isn't easy for me to say, but I've known you forever and someone has to say it. You're my best friend. It's killing me to watch you hide away in this condo." He shook his head. "Sure, I know you can stay here and write. Probably be a success with it, but you deserve more out of life. My God, Jack, you've given up and accepted things the way they are, without trying to make them better." He looked as if he'd lost his best friend and frowned, again. "That's not like you. Since when did you become a quitter?"

"I'm not a quitter." In anger, Jack gripped the arms of his wheelchair, his eyes level with Briggs' stare, not liking what he was hearing.

"When was the last time you were out of this condo?" In a lightning-fast motion the huge man shot off the couch and paced the room. He stared out at the skyscrapers across the way.

Jack cringed. It was true he hadn't been out of the place since he returned home from the hospital, a couple of months ago. He had his groceries delivered and the maid service come in to take care of stuff he wasn't able to manage. "I don't feel like going out. It's not a crime." He stubbornly glanced away from Briggs and watched his colorful fish swim in and out of the lighthouse.

"Yes. It is. It's a crime against yourself. You deserve better." He stood motionless in the middle of the room. "And you have choices to make. You can work at the police station if you do desk duty, or you can retire from the department and write. You'll have a good life. But I never thought I'd see the day you'd give up without a fight and hide away. Think about it, Jack. At least read this book and consider going to the clinic."

"You and Murph have gotten together on this, haven't you? You're like two old dogs with a bone. You won't let it go. Like I told Murph I don't want to go to some place and let people mess with me. I've had enough of it to last me a lifetime."

Briggs moved closer to Jack until he left no room at all, towering over him. "If you don't do this, Jack, you will be the biggest fool I know. And I know you aren't a fool. Don't answer me now. Read the book and think about it. In a few days, I'll talk to you again and get your final answer." He backed away and sighed. "I didn't come here to argue and fight with you." His black eyes sharpened. "I want to know what's happening with that article. Are you going to be able to finish it?"

"Yeah," he muttered. "I'm about done." At this point, he was beyond intimidation. "Give me a couple of days and I can flesh it out. It's not exactly what I had in mind, but it'll work."

"Good to hear. I want it in the Christmas issue." He looked around the condo. "Looks like you've been doing okay. You say the maid service comes in to help you out? I thought Cindy was doing that?"

"She did, for awhile. Then I told her I didn't need her anymore. I don't want to be beholden to anyone."

"I'm sure she didn't mind. She's a great lady. You could do worse."

"You and Murph." He shrugged his shoulders in mock resignation and shook his head. "I've been alone for the past five years and you guys left me by myself. Why all this interest in me and Cindy?" he asked in a hard edged voice. "My God, I haven't even taken the woman out. Have you guys lost it? There's nothing between us, except friendship."

Briggs sat back down on the sofa. "Okay, you asked. Maybe, we see things the two of you can't," he said, talking with his hands. "She stood by you when a lot of folks turned their backs on you, after a few short weeks. There's more to it than a platonic friendship...or let me say, there could be, if you weren't such a damned ass."

"I think you and Murph have had one too many. Cindy is a good person, but she deserves more than an invalid in a wheelchair. She's a nice woman with a big heart. She feels like she has to help care for me because I helped her with her dog. That's all it is." He ran a hand through his hair in frustration. "I don't know why you and Murph keep trying to read things into it when there's nothing there." He sighed. "Anyway, like I told Murph, even if I was interested, I couldn't do anything about it." He wheeled into the kitchen. "Want a bottled water?"

"Sure, I'll take one."

Jack rolled back into the living room, tossing a bottle to Briggs, sitting on the couch. "Good catch."

"You have a strong arm, there. Do you work out for your upper body?"

"I have a series of strength building exercises they showed me in the hospital." He grinned. "Look, I can move my leg." He slightly lifted one leg.

"Wow, that's great, Jack. Now, I am impressed. See, you can get through this. I know you won't be in that chair for long."

Jack stared back at Briggs. *Could he be right*? "I don't know. It's not much after all this time."

"But it's something. It's a start. I know you can get better if you give yourself a chance. Hell, what do you have to lose? Nothing. But you also have lots to gain if those people can help you. Think about it and we'll talk more later."

"Okay, I'll think about it." That was a quick and disturbing thought, but maybe Briggs was onto something. Maybe there was help for him.

"Great, it's what I wanted to hear. Now, I'll come by to get you around four for an early Thanksgiving dinner. I hear the girls are going to get dolled up and go to a lot of trouble fixing us a candlelight dinner." His smile broadened in approval. "I suppose we should send them some flowers for their trouble."

"I don't want to go. I can't face Cindy right now. I have a lot of stuff going on in my head and I can't afford to be distracted."

"Jack, I've never known you to be a coward, and you have to eat. Of course, you'll go. For Pete's sake, it's Thanksgiving, and you have a lot to be thankful for." He grinned from ear to ear. "I didn't say you had to marry the woman—unless you want to."

"Why should I put myself through this?" Jack tried to maintain his curtness. "I have nothing to offer her."

"Well, I didn't expect you to offer her anything right now, but maybe you should stop being selfish. Think about the stuff she's done for you, purely out of the goodness of her heart, expecting nothing. Anyway, Sam told me she broke up with that other guy and needs an evening with friends."

"What a fool, I've been. I forgot about Todd. It's like I am trapped in this useless body and life goes on around me and I don't see what's happening. I have feelings and yearnings, but I can't do anything about them. Anyway, Todd is better for her. He's a complete man. I'm not. They'll probably get back together."

"Get off your butt and do something. It's your choice. You can sit in that chair and feel sorry for yourself or you can at least try to do something about it. Don't come crying to me, when you haven't tried. Now, as I said, I'll be here at four. Be ready. I'll send flowers from both of us."

"Don't bother. I can send my own damn flowers." He was so tired of this conversation, his nerves throbbed.

Briggs threw back his head and laughed. "That's the Jack we know and love. The stubborn asshole."

"You and Murph need to take a flying leap and let me deal with my problems. Butt out. Do you hear me? I'll decide what's best for me." Briggs seemed to enjoy his struggle to capture his composure.

"Sounds like a personal problem to me." Briggs stood and shuffled his way to the door. "Take your time with the article. I won't need it for another week or so. However, I do want to read your novel, soon as it's finished." He grinned. "I have a friend in publishing who wants to take a look at it."

"Sure, when cows fly." He felt a strange numbed comfort at Briggs' intervention in his life while he glared at the book on the coffee table.

"I happened to see a couple flying by on my way over here. Seems like you have some reading to do. I'll see you on Thanksgiving." His laughter boomed into the room when he went out the door, clicking the lock into place behind him.

Jack picked up the book and opened the cover. *My friends are driving me crazy with their good intentions. Why can't they just leave me be?*

CHAPTER SEVENTEEN

Early the next evening, Jack sat at his computer rereading his messages from Snow White. It had been several months since he'd written to her. She had probably forgotten him by now. However, there were several messages from her over that time. All saying basically the same thing. "Where are you? I miss you."

Should he answer her? So much had happened. But he did owe Briggs the article and now with him in the wheelchair, there was no way he could go on dates to get more information. He could ask her about her latest dates. Besides, he had missed her, too.

From: JPrince
To: Snowhite

Hey, Snow White, how have you been? I'm sorry I haven't been on-line. I've been away from home. How did your date with the prospective prince go? I'd like to hear from you.
Your friend ~ JPrince

Hell, he didn't actually lie to her. He had been away from home—in the hospital. A lot of time had passed. She could be married by now, not that it should bother him, but life had passed him by while he lay in that hospital bed. He sighed and pushed delete. Snow White didn't need his problems, he'd make the article work without her.

Briggs had come by nearly every day and Murph had always been there for him. Cindy and Sam had turned into good friends, putting up with his bull and always looking the other way when he was being an ass. But the question on his mind was why did Lola keep showing up? They really weren't friends. Even as much as she'd pushed it, he'd never had sex with her. Tired of the woman, he'd dropped enough hints. He decided he'd have to come out and just tell her not to come by anymore. Maybe then, she'd get the idea.

A knock sounded at the door. "Yeah, who is it?" he growled, not in the mood for company, realizing too late, the door was unlocked.

"Just little old me." Lola opened the door and walked in carrying a large grocery bag. "I've come to make you a home-cooked meal. You have to be tired of those microwave meals I saw in your fridge." She started unpacking things in the kitchen while he watched.

"Lola, we need to talk." He rolled away from the computer toward her. "I think we need to get some things out in the open."

"Why, Jack, whatever do you have on your mind?" She leaned on the counter, exposing a full expanse of cleavage.

He took a deep breath. "You know I like you as a friend, but you can't keep coming here every day. I have work to do and I can't do it when you're around."

Suddenly, her face went grim. "Work, what kind of work can you do?" She snorted. "Every day, because I care about you, I come here to make sure you're eating right and taking care of yourself. Look around you. Those so called friends of yours have deserted you. Honey, I'm all you have left. You'd better be nice to me."

The conversation had taken a turn Jack hadn't expected. "I have friends. They prefer not to come by when you're here." He paused, trying to make this easy on her. "Lola, you don't need me."

"That's right, and don't you forget it. I don't need you or anybody. Think about that, while I make dinner. Now go back to the work you have to do. I'll let you know when it's ready."

He'd be damned if he'd let her boss him around in his own home. He'd had enough of her attitude. "I don't think so. Lola, it's over. Whatever it was we had, is way over." He couldn't bear the sight of her. Take your food and get out. I don't want, or need you to come here anymore."

"My, aren't we in a snit today. Where are you going with this? You can't do anything for yourself." She smirked. "You need me. I take time out of my busy day to come and check on you and this is how you thank me. Shame on you." She shook her finger at Jack.

"I appreciate what you've done for me, but I can take care of myself. I think we should call it quits." He rolled toward her.

"Out of the goodness of my heart I come here to help you and this is how you treat me. You're a bad boy, Jack."

"The goodness of your heart. You don't have a heart." He'd had enough of this woman to last him a lifetime. He didn't want to hurt her feelings, but needed to rid himself of her. "You are the coldest woman I've ever known. You need therapy."

She glared daggers at him. "If that's true, so do you. You, the man in the chair who can't get it up." She snarled and turned her nose up in disgust. "Why won't you let me make you happy? I know I can help you."

He backed up in his chair. He didn't want her to touch him. She made his skin crawl. "See what I mean? Sex is the only thing on your mind. If I wanted a blow job, I'd hire a hooker. Now get out of my house."

She threw a bunch of carrots at him and stomped toward him, placing her arms on each side of his wheelchair. "All I have to do is tip you over and you will lie on the floor the rest of the night. Is that what you want?"

"Don't do it, Lola," his voice took on a hard edge. "That's not what you want to do."

A large grin split across her face. "You're right about that. I know what you have in those jeans and that's what I'm after." She tugged at the zipper on his pants.

He clamped onto her wrist. "Don't go there. Sex isn't the answer to everything. Now, while you still can, get out of my house."

She stood, rubbing her wrist. "You've never been man

enough for me. And now you are a worthless invalid." She stormed around the kitchen, as she ranted and raved, pushing everything from the counters onto the floor. "Let's see you clean that up." A gleam of pure evil shone in her eyes.

She picked up a butcher knife. He stiffened, as though she had struck him and prepared himself for the inevitable. The woman just might be crazy enough to try something.

"You're right. I don't need you." She kept playing with the knife, waving it in slow circles toward Jack. "Nobody does—in your condition."

Just then, Cindy came through the door with the pup on her heels. "I heard a noise." Prince barked and growled at Lola. "Jack, are you okay?" She took in the scene. "Lola, what's going on here?"

"Stay back, Cindy. It's none of your goddamned business."

"It's okay, Prince. Come to me, boy," Jack said. The pup went immediately to his side. Jack spoke to Cindy, but never took his eyes off Lola. "Lola is leaving."

Lola touched the edge of the knife and continued to glare at him, slowly running her finger down the edge of the blade, not acknowledging Cindy or the dog's presence.

"Lola, put the knife down. You could hurt yourself." Jack spoke softly, never taking his eyes off the woman or the knife. Cindy stood as if rooted to the spot in the living room. He didn't think Cindy could overpower Lola. If it came to that they would both be in trouble. "Lola, I don't want you to hurt yourself, please put the knife down." He continued speaking in a mellow, singsong voice.

Lola glanced from the knife to him. "Yes, you do. You want to hurt me. You told me I was cold. You're like all the rest." She blinked and seemed to come back to her senses.

"Screw you, Jack Riley. You're a useless invalid that can't get it up. You're right. I don't need you." With a moan of distress, she threw the knife on the floor and stalked out of the apartment.

Cindy ran after her and locked the door. She rushed to Jack and hugged him to her side. He felt her shudder as he drew in a deep breath. He hugged her back.

"Are you okay? What was that about?" she asked. Then she

held up her hands. "No, never mind, it's none of my business. But you need to rest. That couldn't have been good for you. Do you want me to get you a pain pill?"

Jack's head was about to burst open from the tension. The woman could have killed them. "Ye...yes, two, please, they're on the counter." He glanced at her and Prince. "Thanks for coming over. I don't know what would've happened if you hadn't showed up." An inner torment began to gnaw at him. He hated this helpless feeling. "When I told her I didn't want to see her anymore, she went berserk."

Cindy gave him a glass of water and a couple of pain pills. "Maybe you should lie down and rest while I clean up this mess. That woman is nuts."

With his hand still trembling, Jack handed her the glass. "I do think I need to lie down for a bit. Would you stay long enough to call a locksmith. I want those locks changed."

"Sure, Prince and I will be here when you wake up. Do you want me to help you?"

"No. I can manage by myself." A bitter cold despair dwelt in the caves of his lonely soul as he rolled his way through the debris, across the living room and toward the bedroom with Prince following at his side. "I need to be alone for awhile." He turned his head toward her. "Thanks for coming to my rescue."

She was saddened by the tone of his voice. "Anytime." It was like he had given up. Didn't he realize she didn't rescue him? It was the way he had talked to Lola that brought the crazy woman under control. All she did was come through the door with Prince. The kitchen was a mess. She had her work cut out for her when she started wiping up spilled flour and a carton of broken eggs splattered across the floor.

She stopped in mid-swipe and washed her hands, went over and double checked the locked door, hoping the loony woman wouldn't return with a key. Picking up the phone, she called the front desk. "Hello, Dean. This is Cindy Dawson. I'm in Jack Riley's condo, 30-H. His friend, Lola Brent just trashed the place. He doesn't want her in the building and he wants his locks changed immediately. Can you help me find a locksmith?"

"The woman just left the building. She looked angry."

"Believe me, she was more than angry. Will you help me?"

"Yes. I'll get hold of the locksmith and put a rush on it. Are you staying with Jack or should I send someone up?"

"He took a couple of pain pills and is resting, but I'll stay here till things get under control. I'm trying to put his place back together before he wakes up. Have the locksmith knock softly and I'll hear him. Jack needs his rest."

"Okay, I'll send him up soon as he gets here. Good luck."

Luck. It was going to take some old fashioned elbow grease and hard work to clean up this mess. The woman had thrown food and everything that sat on the counters all over the place. "Yuck." Coffee grounds, eggshells, flour, sugar and broken glass lay scattered across the kitchen floor. "Jack, you owe me for this one," she whispered under her breath.

After she had swept up the large stuff and mopped the floor, she washed her hands and tiptoed to the bedroom door. Peeking around the door frame, she saw Jack sleeping soundly with Prince curled against his side. A lump formed in her throat. She continued to watch them. Her dog was a traitor, but they did look cute together. A soft knock sounded from the living room. Must be the locksmith. She glanced at them one more time. Jack's gruff exterior was merely a smokescreen to his true feelings. He cares for Prince...does he care for me?

Cindy had replaced the locks and the kitchen had been restored to order, minus a few canisters and glasses. A spaghetti chicken casserole was slow cooking in the oven and the delicious aroma wafted through the condo as she sat on the sofa trying to read a magazine. She felt a warm glow flow through her when she imagined what it would be like to cook for Jack everyday. *Dangerous thoughts.*

She sighed. Those pills had knocked him out big time. Under the circumstances the sleep he was getting was a good thing. He shouldn't have to deal with a lunatic. She had talked to Murph and he told her he would be over soon as he could to check on Jack. Said the woman might be dangerous. She shivered at the image of Lola standing over Jack with that big knife.

Another soft knock came from the door. Peering through the peephole, she was relieved to see Murph standing there.

"Hi, come in. Jack's still sleeping."

"Is he okay?" Concern shimmered in the light blue of his eyes.

"Yeah, I think her reaction took him by surprise. He was shook up and in some pain when he lay down, but I'm sure he'll be okay."

"What's the whispering about?" Jack's gruff voice caught them off guard. "Murph, what the hell are you doing here?" He sat in his wheelchair in the open bedroom door, glaring at the two of them, accusing her. "Did you call Murph?"

"Now, don't go getting on your high horse, old son. When a nut goes after my partner, I want to know about it." Murph glared right back at him.

Jack wheeled into the living room with Prince by his side. "I'm fine. The woman didn't take the news very well that I didn't want her around here." He glanced around the room and into the kitchen and nodded toward Cindy. "Thanks for cleaning up."

"Don't worry about it. The locks were changed. New keys are on the table. There's a casserole in the oven and salad chilling in the fridge. It'll be ready in about twenty minutes."

"You didn't have to do all this. I could've called housekeeping."

She looked at him and shook her head. The man was an ass—a cute one, but still an ass. "Yeah, you could have. Prince and I are going for a walk. If you need anything, you know my number." She forced an ease she didn't necessarily feel as Prince glanced back at Jack and whined when they left the condo.

Soon as Cindy was out the door, Murph sighed in frustration. "You are some kind of fool. That woman is the real thing. She cares about you."

"Are you blind? Can't you see? I don't want anyone to care about me." He gestured with his hand. "Look at me." His voice grew quiet. "Take a long hard look. I'm in a damn wheelchair—half a man. I couldn't even defend myself against

Lola. I thought she was going to stab me until Cindy and Prince came through the door." He ran a hand through his hair, sighing in frustration.

Murph listened and let Jack talk. He needed to get it out of his system and out into the open.

"For the first time in my life, I...I was afraid—afraid for Cindy and Prince. I couldn't have protected them if Lola had turned on us." He dropped his head in his hands.

Murph hesitated, measuring Jack for a moment, then squeezed his shoulder. "Jack, you're going to pull through this, like everything else you've done in your life. A reaction like this is normal under the circumstances. Now tell me. Did this woman threaten you? Do you want me to bring her in?"

Jack glanced at Murph. "No. Don't pick her up. She's flaky and was just pissed off, reacting to the heat of the moment. She won't be back."

"Jack, don't be macho." Murph chose his words carefully. "If you need help, dammit, ask for it."

"I don't need help from you or anyone else." His voice rose in anger. "I need to keep the psychos out of my home and be by myself. Which is what I intend to do from now on."

"That's a good place to start. What are you going to do about Cindy?"

"Cindy? What about Cindy?"

Once again, Murph was the victim of Jack's glare.

"Why should I do anything about Cindy?" He spoke with quiet, but desperate firmness. "She's just here."

"Have you asked yourself *why* she's here? Why she's always willing to take your crap and shrug it off? You have to realize she cares about what happens to you. Don't go messing up a good thing. You need to be nicer to her or you're going to scare her off."

"Scare her off. That's exactly what I want to do." Loneliness and confusion welded together in the tone of his voice. "Clean your ears out, old man. Didn't you hear a word I said? I don't want anyone. I want to be by myself."

"Yeah, yeah, I hear you mouthing the words, but I see the look on your face when she's around. You're attracted to her."

"I can't be attracted to anyone. Now, leave it alone."

Murph knew when he had pushed Jack to the limit. He needed more time to erase the pain of what had happened to him. He'd let it go for now. "That casserole should be done. It sure smells good. Are you hungry?"

"Yeah, dish it up and don't talk." Misery cloaked him like a glove as he wheeled over to the kitchen table in a dark funk.

They sat there and ate in silence until Jack finally spoke. "She is a good cook, isn't she?"

"Yeah. This tastes mighty good." Apparently, Jack had managed to get his foul mood under control.

"Maybe I should send her some flowers for cleaning up the place." He sighed as a ball of guilt lay buried in his chest. "It was a mess."

"Now you're talking. That's the least you could do. An excellent idea." Murph took another bite.

"Don't go getting the wrong idea. I didn't say I was getting involved with the woman. Hell, I don't have anything to get involved with." He glanced down at his waist. "I'm sending her some flowers to say thank you. I do appreciate what she's done for me."

"It's a start." Murph laid his fork down, pleased to hear Jack admit he had a problem. That was the first step toward healing. "The doctor said with hard work, physical therapy and time, you would have a chance for a complete recovery."

"Yeah...time. I have a lot of it lately."

"You know, after meeting Rhonda, I've learned that love, not time, heals all wounds. Let yourself feel something for Cindy. She can help you. You won't be sorry."

"Murph, why do you keep pushing this woman on me? Don't you realize she probably has a drinking problem?" His expression was one of mute wretchedness. "You know I can't be around anyone who drinks."

"I've never seen her drinking." He hesitated, deep in thought. "Oh, you're talking about the night you arrested her on her birthday. It's a common mistake. Have you seen her drink anything since then?"

Jack stared at Murph with a glint of wonder in his eyes. "No. Actually, I haven't. The night we saw her in front of the college, she said someone spilled beer on her." He pushed back in his chair as though thunderstruck. "How could I have been such a narrow-minded bigot?" he said with a faint tremor in his voice.

"Yeah. You could, and are. The many days and nights she came by the hospital, I never saw her drink anything other than coffee. And I would know if she had been drinking before she showed up." A satanic smile spread across his thin lips. "Sounds like you've been a narrow-minded bigot to me."

She didn't have a drinking problem. His admission was dredged from a place beyond logic and reason. He just knew it. His mind had been cluttered with his own past, not hers. He had superimposed his problems on her. "Don't rub it in, you old coot." His voice was low and smooth. "But this doesn't change anything." He threw his hands in the air. "I have nothing to offer. I couldn't even make love to her."

"Ah, ha, you do feel something for her. About time you realized it and admitted it to yourself." He smiled. "How do you know you couldn't make love? You haven't tried. Now, don't be a bigot and stupid." He spoke softly, his eyes narrowing. "The doctor said you could go to that clinic and get the help you need. Why don't you consider it?"

"Man, I don't want to go some place with a bunch of doctors pawing all over me. I'm sick of doctors and needles." He winced, his head was puzzled by new thoughts.

"This place isn't like that. Of course, they have doctors, but it's in the mountains and they treat you with physical therapy and counseling. You can even go horseback riding. It would be good for you to get out of town for awhile to clear your head." Murph glanced out the window. "Maybe in time, you'll change your mind. The clinic isn't going anywhere."

"And neither am I. I don't want someone digging around in my head." Jack sighed, realizing he had his own battles to fight.

"Don't be so damned stubborn. It could be good for you. I think you should at least check it out. And it's only Cedar Falls, Colorado, not the ends of the earth. Briggs and I'd come see you. I hear they've helped a lot of people."

"Yeah, maybe," answered a small voice inside his head.

A couple of hours later, Cindy sat on the sofa, talking on the phone while she rubbed Prince behind his ears. "Sam, the woman had this insane look in her eyes." She began to shake as the fearful image built in her mind's eye. "I thought she was going to kill Jack or me."

"Is Jack okay?"

"Yeah, but he was torn up about the whole thing and in a lot of pain from the drama of the situation. I would've liked to kick her butt for making him go through such turmoil, but she's nuts and bigger than me." The fact she didn't do anything gnawed away at Cindy's confidence and a sense of inadequacy swept over her.

"Don't be silly. You did the right thing by staying away from her. If you would have attacked her, you could have made it worse. How horrible. You know, you may have saved Jack's life, by showing up. No telling what she would have done if you hadn't gone to his place when you heard the noise."

"That's for sure. I hadn't thought about it like that. She threw everything from his counters onto the floor and stomped around in it. It was a mess."

"What did Jack say?"

"Not much. Just to give him some pain pills and change the locks. He's stubborn, but I stayed after he fell asleep and cleaned up the place. There was no way Jack could do it."

"You did the right thing."

"I thought so. Murph was there when he woke up and I think Jack was pissed at me because I called him. But I don't care. I thought he needed to know what Jack's crazy girlfriend had done. What if she tries something else? What could Jack do?"

"Hey, now, Jack isn't helpless. I imagine he still has his gun and will keep it close until this blows over. He's not a fool. He'll take care of himself and if he had the locks changed, there's no way she can get back in the condo or through the security at the front desk. He's safe."

"I hope you're right. It was the look in her eyes, as if she were somewhere else in an evil place I wouldn't want to be."

"Well, you don't have to worry about it. Now, she's out of your lives for good. That opens the door for you to go after Jack."

"Me? I don't think so. He's always upset with me. No matter what I do, I can feel his disapproval. The anger is there. He tries to hide it, but it's there, right beneath the surface."

"You should know what that's about. It's the old theory about the guy subconsciously knowing you are the woman for him and he's fighting it because he doesn't want to lose his freedom."

"Oh, Sam, you have such a way with words. I've come to the decision I'm an independent woman who doesn't need a man. Sure, it would be nice to have someone to lean on, but all the grief you have to go through to find Mr. Right makes me wonder if it's worth it."

"Worth it? Of course it's worth it?" Sam gave an anxious little cough to clear her throat. "Have you lost your mind?"

"No. I think I may have come to my senses. I'm getting older with every passing day and my clock is ticking. I want a child of my own. I don't need a man to raise a child. I have money and a good job. I need a sperm donor. Look at you. You're doing fine without a man."

"Where has Cindy gone? Wh...who's this pod person?" She practically stuttered. "Where is this coming from?" Sam didn't speak for a short time. "Well, something has changed your mind. What happened with you and Todd?"

"Nothing much, he's not what I'm looking for and I broke it off with him." She wasn't ready to tell Sam about the foot fetish, not yet—it was too sick. "I'm through playing the game. No more dating. And as for Jack, sure I like him, but he's too stubborn to do anything about it. I'm tired of waiting for love. It's time for me to get on with my life. I'm going to check into artificial insemination or adoption. I want a child of my own."

"You're serious about this? I...I'm surprised. But if that's your decision, I'll stand by you. Look at me. I'm the living, breathing example of what you're going to get yourself into. But promise me one thing. You will take the time to think this through. It's not going to be easy raising a child by yourself. I lay awake at night worrying about how my child will feel about not having a father."

"Times have changed. I don't think your child will care about not having a father because she will be loved. And by the time she's old enough to care, well, you might be married. Otherwise, you'll figure it out." She sighed. "I'm tired of waiting and searching for Mr. Right. I'm taking charge of my future."

"Well, think on it. Don't rush to make this decision. It will affect you for the rest of your life. Who knows, maybe Jack will wise up and you won't have to worry about finding a sperm donor."

"Is Jack coming over for Thanksgiving dinner?" Cindy couldn't dull the sound of hope in her voice.

"Yes, he said he'd come, before this happened. Briggs had already talked him into it."

"It will be good for him to get out of his condo. He needs to accept his situation and make the best of it."

"Talk about moving on. He should let go of his anger and accept the changes he's been forced to go through. Maybe then, he could get his life back to some kind of normal."

"Easy for us to say, but it's probably hard to get to the acceptance stage, especially with a macho guy like Jack."

"But even macho men have to face reality sometime." "Yes," She agreed.

"Hey, you were off yesterday and I forgot to tell you the big news. Miss Dotty is no longer with us. Home office told me I could let her go. It did my heart good to tell her the news."

"Oh, really. How did she take it?"

"Like you'd think. She said she'd sue the school for putting her in this position."

"Now, that sounds like the Miss Dotty we know. What do you think will happen with it?"

"Not much. Home office deals with this sort of thing. With over forty schools in the cooperation, they have lawyers out the kazoo. She doesn't have a case. They're willing to let her retire early with a severance package. Better than most places would offer under the circumstances."

"She should retire gracefully and take the money and run."

"If she knows what's good for her, but we know Miss

Dotty."

"I'm glad she's out of our school. That happened fast."

"Home office has been building a file against her with all my reports for some time, and this last incident was the straw that put her on the unemployment line. Couldn't happen to a nastier person." Sam laughed.

"I hate to laugh at anybody's trouble, but you're right. She deserved what she's getting for being so miserable to everyone at work." Cindy yawned. "Listen, I have to go. It's getting late and I still want to check my e-mail. Oh, do you want me to bring anything for Thanksgiving dinner?"

"No, just yourself and wear that little black number your friend gave you. We're going to get dressed up for a candlelight dinner."

"Oh, why do you want me to wear that? I haven't worn it in ages."

"Because you look so pretty in it. Don't ask questions, just do it for me."

"Okay, if you insist. Should be fun. I'll talk to you later."

"See you tomorrow at work."

Cindy put the phone down and yawned. She did have a lot to think about and it was getting late. She'd check her e-mail in the morning. After getting ready for bed, with mixed thoughts of Jack and babies, she fell into a restless sleep.

CHAPTER EIGHTEEN

A few days later, Cindy set Sam's good china on the table and checked on the turkey. "I don't know if this is a good idea or not."

"Of course it is," Sam said. "It's Thanksgiving. Nothing is going to go wrong. We'll have a great time."

"Then why is my stomach in knots?" Cindy laid the dark green napkins next to the white gold rimmed china on top of the flowered place mats and stood back, admiring the table.

"That's normal for a woman who's on a mission. A woman who has decided to go after what she wants." Sam winked at her and turned on the stereo. Strands of soft classical music filled the air. "Come, help me with this centerpiece. I want the vanilla tapers on each side of the flowers. Wasn't it nice of Jack to send flowers to us?"

"Yeah, it was." She touched one of the sunflowers in the centerpiece. "Did I tell you he sent me a dozen yellow roses to thank me for putting his kitchen back together?" Cindy rubbed a water spot off the edge of a fork. "Yellow is for friendship, isn't it?"

"That's what they say, but he wants more than friendship."

"You're wrong. I think he has his own problems to deal with and there isn't room for anything else. And I can't say I blame him. My goodness, the man has been close to death and put through the wringer the last few months."

"Yeah, but he's stronger than you think. I still say you guys would be great together."

"You would." Just thinking of Jack as father material shattered her. He would never want her. It would never happen. It was time to move on. "Did I tell you I picked up some information on sperm donors and artificial insemination? It's very civilized."

Sam frowned in exasperation. "Don't tell me you're still thinking about going that route? Why don't you find someone to sleep with...like Jack and do it that way?"

"Jack. If he would do it, I'd take him in a heartbeat. Like that's going to happen. I've given up on Jack. He doesn't know I'm alive. Anyway, under the circumstances it might be better if the father were anonymous."

"Sure, anonymous, except for Jack. Maybe he would do it for you. Have you talked to him about it?"

"We don't talk about stuff like that. I wouldn't know what to say to him. He'd think I'd lost my mind. I don't even know if he's able to make love. I couldn't do it." Cindy shook her head and finished putting the silverware on the table. "Your table looks beautiful. You have some great place settings."

"Thanks, I've had them for a long time. They don't get much use, but maybe that'll change. This is fun, isn't it? We're going to have a great time." Sam went over and hugged Cindy. "This is going to be a good night." She rubbed her stomach and sat down on the sofa.

"You look a little pale. Are you okay?" Cindy hesitated, concerned about her friend. "Are you sure you're up to this?"

"Of course, I am. I'm a little tired and the baby is restless. I've had some cramps, but there's nothing to worry about. I have another month to go."

"The time sure has gone fast, hasn't it? I can't believe what we've gone through in the past few months."

"In some ways, it feels like I became pregnant yesterday and in others I feel like the elephant that's been carrying her baby for years."

"Well, the good news is, you don't look like the elephant. You look beautiful. You're in your element. I'm happy for you and baby Jennie. I can't wait to hold her."

"You think you can't wait? I haven't been able to sleep very well for the past few nights. She keeps moving around. With the kicking she's been doing, I swear she's going to be a soccer player."

"That's cool. Your wait is almost over. Are you ready for her?"

"Yeah, everything is set. My suitcase is packed for the hospital. All she has to do is come out and see me." She grinned. "Oh, by the way, I bought apple cider for you and Jack since neither of you drink much. Would you like a glass before they get here?"

"Why not? Cider sounds refreshing. You know, I don't miss the alcohol. Sure, I still like a glass of wine now and then, but I'm not drinking much these days. It's just not worth it. It's so easy to slip into a pattern of drinking. A drink with friends after work or a glass of wine in the evening to relax after a hard day's work, and before you realize it, it becomes a habit. I can see how people turn into alcoholics. I think it kind of sneaks up on you."

"Yeah, I've been pretty wild in my day, but now that Jennie is almost here, I'm glad I never had alcohol problems. I had and still have issues I need to deal with, but I was lucky not to get caught in that trap."

The doorbell sounded. "Must be the guys." She squeezed Cindy's hands. "Are you ready for this?"

"Yes, here goes nothing. It's only dinner with friends, but why am I nervous?" Her heart beat with the pulse of the music.

"Don't be. You wait and see everything is going to be wonderful. I predict great things to come of this evening. You have to let yourself go and see what happens." A smile crossed Sam's face. "The fates are on your side." Sam winked at her, before she went to the door.

Jack took a deep breath and sat back in his wheelchair when Briggs rang the doorbell. Briggs had been right. He needed to get out of his condo, even if it was only a few blocks down the street. *Thanksgiving with friends.* It had been a long time since he'd spent Thanksgiving with anyone besides his fish and football on his big screen TV. He looked forward to seeing Cindy. How should he act toward her? Looking back, he realized the last time he had seen her he'd acted like a prickly old bear. He needed to make it up to her for his hateful ways, starting tonight. *Well, here I go.*

"Come in." Sam answered the door. "Come in, we've been waiting for you."

Jack rolled through the open doorway and watched as Sam smiled at Briggs. She was in the full bloom of motherhood. Her long blond hair swirled around her shoulders and she glowed with happiness. From the expression on Briggs' face it was apparent the man was in love. He had fallen for her and the idea of a baby like water going down the wet and wild slide. *Lucky man.* "Good evening, Jack, I'm glad you could make it. It's about time we all got together. Get in here." Sam gave him a kiss on the cheek and switched her attention back to Briggs.

The tantalizing smell of roasting turkey tickled his taste buds. He noticed Cindy sat in an overstuffed chair, in the background watching as he rolled toward her.

"Hi," she said to both of them. Briggs nodded in her direction, but couldn't seem to take his eyes off Sam.

"Hello." Jack gave Cindy the once over. Wearing a slinky soft black dress with a low neckline and her raven hair pushed back in a cluster of curls, she looked like she'd stepped off the cover of *Vogue*. "You look nice." The woman's natural beauty nearly took his breath away.

"Why, thank you. Sam requested I wear it, because it's one of her favorites. She said we have lots to be thankful for and we're celebrating tonight. You look nice, too." He appraised her with more than mild interest.

Jack glanced down at his sport jacket and jeans and frowned. "My tux is at the cleaners." Glancing back at her, he didn't want to tear his attention away from her.

Cindy laughed. "You look fine. And thanks for the beautiful roses."

"You're welcome." She'd done so much for him. He could smell the subtle fragrance of her perfume as he neared her. His mind told him to resist, but his body had other plans as he moved closer.

"How are you?" she asked.

"Doing better. Things are working out." Gazing at her was a purely sensual experience. He grinned as sexual thoughts scampered around in his head. He felt drugged by her clean and womanly scent.

"I'm glad. If there's anything I can do to help, you know I'm only a phone call away." The woman was a saint to put up with him and his lousy moods. She deserved a medal.

Her willingness to be there for him once again touched his heart. He cleared his throat. "I've been meaning to thank you for everything." The words sounded hollow. He was a writer and couldn't find the right words to tell her how much he appreciated what she had done for him. A strange surge of affection rushed through him as she leaned toward his chair and took his hand.

"No thanks necessary. That's what friends do." She squeezed his hand gently and released it. "And Prince and I consider you our friend." Her soft voice held a rasp of excitement, or did he imagine it?

"Friends, yes," he stammered, "it's good to have friends." He had been thinking of what Briggs and Murph had been trying to tell him. It was as if his eyes were finally opened to her. There was some kind of tangible bond between him and Cindy...and even the pooch. Why hadn't he noticed it before? Could it be because he had been so self-absorbed with his situation? Inwardly, he grimaced. It was hard to remain coherent when she was so close to him.

The doorbell sounded. "Oh, that must be Rhonda and Murph," Sam said.

Rhonda and Murph? "I didn't know they were coming," Jack said in surprise. He froze, not quite sure how Rhonda would react to seeing him.

"I didn't either, until I helped Sam set the table. But you know Sam used to be a party animal. The more, the merrier." Cindy laughed.

"Good evening, everyone," Murph said. He entered the condo with Rhonda on his arm. "Something smells good." He handed Sam a box of candy from the Rocky Mountain Chocolate Factory.

"Oh, my favorite, but you didn't have to bring anything." She kissed Murph and Rhonda on the cheek and held the door for the two of them to enter the living room. "You make yourselves comfortable, and Briggs and I'll bring out some drinks. I have wine, beer and hot apple cider." After taking the drink orders, Sam glided into the kitchen with Briggs close on her heels.

"Hello, Jack, it's been a long time," Rhonda spoke to him with a twinkle in her eyes. She reached out her hand to him. He noted the talons had been painted a subtle pink and trimmed to a more normal length when he shook her hand.

"Why, hello, Rhonda, I like your new hairstyle." The woman had gotten rid of that hideous beehive and now wore a short sleek, blond bob. She looked ten years younger and seemed content to be sitting there holding Murph's hand. He identified with the slight flicker in her eyes. She was nervous about how he would react to her. *I'll be damned.*

"Thanks." She and Murph sat across from him. "I was glad to hear you're doing well. You had a tough time of it, didn't you?" Compassion shone in her eyes when she glanced at Murph with a look of love. He still had a hard time with the idea of Murph and Rhonda as a couple, but it looked like they were doing well.

At least the woman was being civil and seemed to be trying to fit in. "Yeah, it wasn't any picnic, but I'm better now." He wouldn't admit to her this was the first time he'd been out of his condo in months. The guys were right. He had turned into some kind of recluse and needed help.

"Sam told us in addition to Thanksgiving, it was a celebration. What's the occasion?" Murph glanced at Jack and Cindy.

"She's being secretive about whatever it is. Usually, she can't wait to tell me everything, but this time, she's not saying," Cindy said.

"Hmmm...Briggs has been the same way," Murph added. "They must be in it together."

"I guess we'll find out when they are good and ready to tell us, and not until," Jack commented. "People with secrets always intrigue me. And from the looks they've been giving each other, I have a feeling this is an interesting one."

At that moment, Briggs came into the cozy living room carrying a tray of drinks and handed them around to everyone as Sam placed a vegetable tray at the center of the coffee table.

Briggs spoke up and stood there holding a mug of apple cider in one hand and Sam's hand in the other. "I would like to make a toast. We have a lot to celebrate this evening." He glanced at Jack. "First, to Jack's full recovery, which is right around the corner." He smiled at the others. "Second, to being with good friends, and last, but definitely not least..."

He kissed Sam on the cheek and turned back to his audience. "We have something special to share with you. I've asked Sam to be my wife and she said yes. We were married this morning." He held up her hand showing them a wide band of gold and a two caret diamond solitaire winking on her finger. "To my wife," he said with the look of love in his eyes and drank to her. Everyone toasted the newlyweds.

"Oh, my God." Cindy jumped up and hugged Sam and Briggs. "Congratulations. Why didn't you tell us?"

Rhonda congratulated the newlyweds and Murph and Jack shook Briggs' hand and kissed Sam on the cheek. "You old rascal. Why did you do this behind our backs?" Jack muttered. He was quickly affected by his friend's enthusiasm. Briggs was the happiest Jack had ever seen him.

Briggs held Sam close to his side and gently caressed her tummy. "Sam and I discussed it and under the circumstances, Sam didn't want to make a big deal out of it, which was fine with me."

Sam chimed in. "We have two homes full of furniture, plenty of baby stuff and don't want a reception or any kind of shower. We wanted to share our happiness with the people who mean the most to us. You guys. This is our wedding party."

Cindy glanced at Jack and smiled. Her nearness kindled feelings he thought were long gone. Her face was full of a quiet strength, shining with a steadfast and serene peace.

Jack wondered what Cindy was thinking. He was happy for Briggs. His wife had once said Briggs should take time away from the magazine and get a life. She'd been right. Briggs was grinning from ear to ear.

"You lucky dog." Jack smiled at Briggs, feeling a pang of jealousy while he watched the happy couple. He envied Briggs the good times ahead—a wife, home and family.

"Hey, you look like you're a million miles away," Cindy said. "A penny for your thoughts."

He glanced at her, wondering if they could have something if he'd let himself try. Maybe the guys were right about her, too. "Most of my thoughts aren't worth a penny."

"Yeah, I bet. You're probably working out some kind of diabolical plot for your next book. Briggs told me you were an author."

Caught off guard, he laughed. "Yes, I try."

"I'd like to read your stuff sometime." She smiled at him. "I bet you're good."

"Good. Who knows, but I'm almost finished with my first novel." He sighed. "When I send it out to the publishing houses in New York, we'll see what they have to say."

"I'm sure you'll go places with your writing."

"If you keep going on like this, you're going to give me a big head." He sipped his cider, trying to remember when the last time was he'd truly enjoyed himself with a woman. *The last dinner with Cindy.* It seemed so long ago. "Tell me about your work. How are things at the school?" He savored the feelings of wanting to get to know Cindy on many other levels.

"Going well, it's a fun place to work." She looked over at Sam and Briggs. "They make a cute couple. I'm happy for them."

"Yeah, they do, don't they. Briggs is excited about the baby. He's always wanted to be a daddy." He remembered when Briggs would come over and chase his young son around the house. The memory didn't hurt as much since he'd had the vision of his wife in the hospital. Now he remembered his family with more love—not so much pain.

"Did he tell you she's having a baby girl?" she asked with a touch of longing in her voice Jack picked up on.

Jack laughed. "Yeah, he called and told me. He about bought out the toy store the day he found out." He snapped his fingers. "I must be slipping, that should have tipped me off to what he had on his mind."

"Give yourself a break. You were preoccupied with other things. And they did a good job of keeping their secret. She's my best friend in the city, but I'm truly amazed she was able to keep her mouth shut."

"Yeah, I've never known Briggs to be this tight lipped about anything. It must be love."

"Yeah, they glow with happiness."

"Okay, everyone, it's time for dinner. Come into the dining room," Sam said.

The meal went smoothly as far as Jack could tell. The food was awesome, and the couples seemed to enjoy the meal and the small talk which flowed around the table. And surprise of surprises, Rhonda seemed to fit in with everyone as she gazed lovingly at Murph. He was pleased for Murph.

Over coffee, Jack watched Cindy with an open mind. What he saw startled him. The woman was beautiful—inside and out. He was the one carrying around the negative baggage—not Cindy. It was an awakening experience which left him reeling.

Sitting next to her with thoughts of holding her in his arms, gave him a quiet ache in his crotch. *Knock me over with a feather, Mr. Happy still works.* All that time when Lola was pushing herself at him, he felt nothing but disgust. One glance at the swell of Cindy's cleavage had turned him on, good and hard. He had always known there was something special about her from the very beginning. His vow not to become involved shattered completely. The woman didn't have a drinking problem. He had built things up in his mind to avoid involvement. Because of past hurts, he was afraid to commit to a real relationship.

Then, a thought flashed through his mind. *Jack, you will remarry and have more children. Go back. It's not your time.* It was the message he had received in the dream from his late wife. He shivered as if he had caught a chill. Could it be true?

"Are you okay?" Cindy was seated at his side and leaned over caressing his arm. Her touch comforted him in many ways.

"Yeah, I pulled a muscle in my upper back earlier today and I felt a twinge from it." He glanced around the table. "Things are winding down. I think it's about time for me to go." He needed to be alone with his thoughts for awhile, but he also wanted to talk more with her.

"I was thinking the same thing. I mean...this is their wedding night." A delightful blush spread across her face.

He hesitated for a heartbeat. "Hey, would you like to come over to my place for a while? I could make some coffee."

A look of confusion crossed her face, but she hid it well. "Sure, but first I have to check on Prince. You know how he can be."

Jack laughed. "Yes. He's a special pup. I'd like to see him. Bring him with you. I've grown fond of him."

"Okay." The lively twinkle in her beautiful green eyes excited him.

Jack tapped the side of his crystal water glass with a spoon, getting everyone's attention. "I'd like to make one last toast before I call it a night." The warmth of love and friendship in the room surrounded him when he held up his glass. "To Briggs, Sam, and the baby. Here's wishing you love and happiness throughout your lives."

Everyone toasted the couple with their drinks. "Now, I need to be rolling out of here." He pushed himself back from the table and glanced at Cindy.

"I think it's time for me to go as well. Jack, I'll give you a ride home." She rose from the table and joined Jack. "I need to take Prince out." Cindy gave Sam a hug and whispered in her ear, "I'm thrilled for you."

"Thanks, sweetie, your time is coming," Sam whispered back and glanced over at Jack. "Remember, he's the one. Go for it." She winked at Cindy and turned to Jack. "We have to do this again, sometime soon."

Jack smiled when she kissed him on his cheek. "Count me in. This was the most fun I've had in a long time." He answered graciously and realized he meant it.

CHAPTER NINETEEN

A short time later, Jack opened his door and let Cindy and Prince into his home and his heart. She'd changed into a pair of comfortable forest green sweats, but to him she looked just as glamorous as she had earlier in the evening. The tap, tap of Prince's toenails on the hardwood floor greeted him when they entered his condo and listened to the soft strands of music surrounding them.

"Oh, I like that sound. What is it?" Cindy asked.

"It's an old Tim Weisberg CD, called, *Listen to the City*." He glanced down at Prince. "How are you doing, boy?" Jack rubbed him behind his ears. Prince had his doggie grin plastered across his wrinkled face while he gazed at Jack with adoration.

"When you do that to him, he's in heaven." Cindy watched the two of them. Her eyes were gentle and contemplative.

"The coffee is on. Would you mind pouring for us?" he asked.

"Not at all." She grinned when she lifted down the coffee mugs she had purchased for Jack after the Lola incident.

He sat in his wheelchair, enjoying the sight of Cindy being domestic in his kitchen and Prince at his side. Lightly, Jack patted Prince on the head. The dog stared up at him with those huge brown eyes as if to ask, "Okay, Bud, now that you've realized we're good stuff, why don't you do something about it?" Jack pulled his hand back like he'd been bitten, thinking somebody must've spiked his cider.

Cindy carried the steaming mugs of coffee into the living room, wondering why Jack had decided to be more friendly with her. She couldn't put her finger on when, but his mood toward her had softened.

Jack took his cup of coffee and tasted it. "Thanks, I'm full from that fabulous dinner Sam prepared, but this tastes good. There's pumpkin pie if you would like some."

"I couldn't eat another bite, but if you want some, I'll get it for you."

He waved her off. "No, sit down and relax."

She leaned against the cushions on the sofa and watched Jack. He winced as if in pain. "What's wrong?"

"Nothing, just that muscle I told you about."

"You know I teach massage therapy at the school. If you would like, maybe I could get that muscle to loosen up with a gentle massage."

"Oh, that would be something." He gave her a hopeful look. "It's been bothering me all day and I don't want to take any more pain pills."

She rose from the sofa and stood behind him. "Let me take your jacket off." Sitting his coffee down, he slipped his arms out of the coat sleeves. The bulging muscles in his upper arms were tight against his dress shirt. She swallowed an intake of breath at the gorgeous sight. "We'll need to remove your shirt, too."

He hesitated for a heartbeat and unbuttoned it. She added it to his jacket on the sofa. "Now, that's better." She began rubbing circular motions across his shoulder blades, trying not to hyperventilate when she glanced over his shoulder at the soft hair on his masculine chest. The scars only endeared him more to her. He was a real hero. He had risked his own life to save Murph.

"Oh, that feels great." Jack hung his head and mumbled, "Don't stop."

Stopping was the last thing she had on her mind. She had noticed at dinner that Jack had been unsuccessfully trying to hide a bulge in his jeans. It was possible. He could make love—or she could make love to him. At this phase of the game, she didn't care.

She had wanted this man since the first day she had set eyes on him. His naked image standing in the hallway had haunted her dreams for months. "You know, it would probably be better if you lie on the bed and let me give you a complete rub down. It would be easier for me to get to those lower back muscles that bunch up and cause you spasms." *And to get you out of those jeans.*

He glanced up, making eye contact with her. "Are you sure you want to do this?" It sounded as if he was asking her for something else. Did he have an ulterior motive, too, or did she imagine it? So what if they used each other for pleasure? She was tired of going to bed alone and he needed to realize even though he was in a wheelchair, he was a "whole man" and the wheelchair didn't matter to her.

"If it makes you feel better, I don't have a problem with giving you a full body massage. The question is," she hesitated for a heartbeat. "Are you up for it?" She leaned down in front of his chair and kissed his lips. An instant shock shot through her. She backed off for her own protection.

"I'm up for anything you want to give me." A look of desire shone from his warm brown eyes. "Shall we go into the bedroom?"

"Yes." That was exactly where she wanted him—on the bed—at her mercy.

One word was all it took. He wheeled toward his room. Now, it was up to her. She knew in her heart she wanted Jack. *For once in my life, don't think. Just do it.*

"I need to run home and get some massage oil. I'll be right back." A thrill of anticipation raced through her. "You get ready." Her heart beat in overtime when she went toward the door.

He turned and glanced at her. "Prince and I'll be waiting." Was his look of longing, mirrored in her face? Prince lay stretched out in the middle of the rug in front of the sofa, sleeping contentedly.

Rushing into her condo, she took a deep breath, looked at

her reflection in the bathroom mirror and started taking pins out of her hair. It tumbled loosely around her shoulders while she thought of consequences. The worst thing that could happen would be tomorrow Jack would realize he didn't want her. But she would have tonight. She could handle it. She had made this decision over months of agonizing about what to do with her life. She wanted Jack. *I'm going for it.*

Now was not the time to chicken out. She clutched the vanilla scented massage oil in her hand and returned to Jack's condo. Glancing through his bedroom door, there he lay on his stomach in the middle of the bed with his eyes closed and a lock of dark curly hair falling across his forehead. His skin glistened in the soft glow of candlelight. Wearing only a skimpy pair of black briefs, he looked like a handsome Greek warrior who had been offered up to the Gods of fertility. *Tonight, she was one lucky woman.*

She sat on the side of the bed with the bottle of massage oil in her hand, warming it with her fingertips. "This might feel a little cold, but it will warm up in a minute."

"That's okay," he said. "All that good food made me sleepy." She rubbed the lotion over his back and began to massage across his shoulders and up and down his arms, not leaving a spot on his upper body untouched.

"Relax." She massaged his tight muscles, amazed at what good shape his body was in. "Let yourself go."

He sighed..."ummm, your hands feel wonderful."

Massaging his lower back, her fingertips touched the waistband of his briefs. She admired his gently rounded tush and continued working the massage oil into her hands and applied it down his inner thigh and on the soles of his feet and back up the other leg. She noted a bulge between his legs and was thrilled she was causing him to react to her administrations.

"Lady, your hands could be lethal weapons." He rolled over on his side looking at her. Gently, she touched the scars on his chest and stomach, kissing them in the candlelight. "Come here," he murmured. "It's my turn to make you feel good."

She tumbled on the bed beside him. Glancing into his eyes, he leaned over and kissed her. Their tongues tussled in a war, with him winning which caused warm sensations to spread throughout her body. He placed butterfly kisses across her face, and down the side of her neck and leaned back and looked into her eyes. "Do you want me to stop?" He waited patiently for her answer with a look of longing in his eyes.

"No." She would explode if he stopped. She returned his kisses and leaned into his arms. When he caressed her breast under her shirt a delightful shiver of wanting ran through her. Gently, he raised her sweatshirt over her head and tossed it across the room to land on a chair. He gave the top of her breasts a feather light tentative touch, causing her to quiver as he leaned down to kiss her skin. He raised his head to gaze into her eyes. "I've wanted to do that all evening."

She was lost in a swarm of feelings when his mouth traced a sensuous path across the swell of her breast. She hadn't expected this much involvement on his part. He gently tugged at her waistband.

Helping him, she removed her sweatpants and lay next to him wearing her special black lace, Victoria's Secret lingerie, hoping she looked appealing to him. He made no attempt to hide the fact he was watching her.

He reached out and pulled her on top of him. "I want you." She straddled him and he reached behind her, unhooking her bra. "You're so beautiful." He pulled her face to his and kissed her gently, almost inhaling her. Emotions swirled in her mind as she felt the fullness of him pressing against her. His arms were like bronzed bands of steel wrapped around her waist when his tongue explored the rosy peeks of her breasts. Glancing down, she realized he wanted her as badly as she wanted him.

He kissed her taut nipples, rousing a melting sweetness within her. Straddled across his chest, she lifted her head and gazed into his eyes when she removed his shorts. His engorged penis shot up in the air as if it had a mind of its own. She grasped the smooth surface with her hand, gently stroking his hardness which aroused her passion.

"Oh, my God, what you do to me?" She glanced at him and saw a bright flare of desire spring into his eyes. "There are condoms in the nightstand," he said.

Should she lie and go for it? She wanted a child, but not this way. No—she couldn't do it this way—he'd never forgive her. "Okay." She pulled the drawer open and clutched a foil package in her hand.

He sighed and ran his fingers through her hair when she trailed kisses down his chest. She lowered her head to his arousal and took him into her mouth. With her entire being she wanted to make Jack a happy man. Wetting her lips she caressed him, listening to his moans of pleasure.

He reached for her shoulder, pulling her up on top of his chest. "I want to be inside you."

She smoothed the shield over his engorged shaft and slid up him. Her bare breasts tingled against the hair on his chest. She pushed his smooth shaft inside her, almost passing out when the surge of ecstasy consumed her body. Tight around him, she continued to raise herself slowly, up and down, up and down.

His lips brushed her nipples when she leaned over him, moving her hips against him, nearly sending herself over the edge. His body rose to meet her in a moment of uncontrolled passion. He nibbled at her breast, causing shudders to spread through her as she rode him high. Pulling her close, he rubbed the bare skin of her back, making the concave hollow of her spine tingle at his touch.

The dormant sexuality of his body had been awakened and he moaned in pleasure. Then she realized she was moaning, too. Her own breath came in long, surrendering sighs, building in intensity. Passion inched through her veins. She wanted to yield to the burning sweetness that seemed captive within her, but waited for Jack. The hysteria of delight rose inside her as a bursting of sensations freed them both.

Electricity arced through her. She clung to him. Her thoughts fragmented while his hands and lips continued their hungry search of her body. The hot tide of his passion swirled around her and she fell across his chest, unable to move.

He rolled her to his side and held her close, caressing her back. His breath was moist against her face. "You were sensational," he whispered and kissed the side of her forehead. She drifted into sleep loving being held in his arms.

Several hours later she awakened to the sounds of cold sleet beating against the window pane. She lay in the drowsy warmth of her bed, snuggled against Prince, closing her eyes against the pale light of a gloomy day. Her eyelids popped open. She became instantly awake, fully aware of her surroundings. This wasn't her bed—she wasn't snuggled against Prince. Jack slept beside her with his arm swung over her chest in a possessive manner. The sheets smelled of vanilla massage oil and sex when she pulled them to her chin.

The events of Thanksgiving evening came rushing back. A turkey day to remember. She impatiently pulled her drifting thoughts together. Jack was a kind and gentle lover, but she couldn't face him right now. Oh, my goodness.

Momentarily, lost in her own reveries, she realized she had slept with a man who was a loner and had *told* her he wanted to stay that way. Why didn't she listen? She had been a push over. Feeling foolish, slowly, she lifted his arm and laid it next to his side and eased her way out of the rumpled bed. *Please, please, please, don't let him wake up.* He grunted and threw his arm out and she tucked the covers around him waiting for him to fall back asleep. His deep breathing assured her. Now was the time to make a break for it.

Prince peeked around the doorway, sniffing the air. "I'm coming. Don't look at me that way," she mouthed at him. Her underwear wasn't anywhere in sight. Damn, she felt like a breathless girl of eighteen.

Pulling on her sweats, she glanced at Jack sleeping peacefully, realizing she couldn't talk to him yet. Her feelings for him were intensifying and it was too easy to get lost in the way he had looked at her last night. She desperately needed time away from him. It would be better if she spoke with him later in the day after she'd had a chance to get her emotions under control. Entirely caught up in her own feelings, she didn't have the guts to do it now. Tiptoeing across the room, she stepped on her bra, picked it up and wadded it in a ball in her hands.

Glancing out Jack's peephole, the coast was clear, nobody was in the hallway. She quickly left his condo and hurried into her place with Prince by her side. Her heart danced with excitement when she realized she had actually done it. She had slept with Jack. Clutching her bra in her hand, she sighed. Now what?

CHAPTER TWENTY

Jack awoke and reached out to find an empty pillow. He had been dreaming of Cindy. Then he smelled the vanilla on the sheets and glanced at the burned out candle realizing it hadn't been a dream. He had made love to her. Reaching under the sheet, he pulled out a black thong. Feeling the sheer silk against his fingertips, he smiled as a vision of a sexy black lace clad Cindy popped into his head. The woman had been awesome. Her skin had been soft to the touch, like velvet. Was she in the bathroom, the kitchen? He listened for the sound of running water, hoping she was still here. Nothing.

His hopes plummeted. Who was he fooling? She had left him. He almost wished he'd kept the wall between himself and the rest of the world. He sighed. Wave after wave of insecurities churned in his gut. She must have realized during the night he wasn't any good for her. It was definitely a black Friday. *Damn. Stop feeling sorry for yourself. Get out of this pit of self-pity you're wallowing in this morning and do something about it.*

He bit down hard on his lower lip and glanced at the clock. It read ten a.m. Grabbing the phone he called Murph. "It's me. I need your help."

"What's wrong? Are you okay?"

"Yeah, but something's come up. I know you and Rhonda are probably spending the day together, but can you come over?" He knew that Murph and Rhonda had moved in together and he hated to disturb them.

"Sure, I'll be right there. Rhonda has been gone for hours hitting the day after Thanksgiving sales for Christmas shopping. Are you alright? Do I need to bring a doctor?"

"I don't need a doctor." He heard a heavy dose of sarcasm in his voice and fought it. "I'm fine. I need to talk to you about some stuff I don't want to talk about over the phone."

"Oh." He exhaled a long sigh of relief. "I'll be there in the next half hour or so."

"You don't have to rush. I have some things to do before you get here. I'll see you." Jack laid the phone on the night stand. He pushed his way to the edge of the bed and pulled his wheelchair toward him. He scooted into it, glancing at the unmade bed. So what if she didn't want to be with him. A pang of hurt stabbed at his heart but she had done him a favor. Now he knew there was hope for him. When they made love, he had felt pain in his legs.

He yanked clean clothes from his dresser and headed for the shower. Heavy thoughts weighed on his mind, but this was a chance for him to grow whole again. He could still smell Cindy on his body, but now wasn't the time to be distracted by romantic notions.

Sitting in the shower chair under the spray eased the pain in his tired muscles. He reminded himself, pain was a good thing. Where there was pain, there was life. The hot water beat against his skin while he lathered his body and made his decision.

After his shower, he dressed and wheeled his way into the bedroom. Pulling the sheets off the bed, a shaft of pain sliced through his heart when he stuffed them in his closet and remade the bed. Tossing the candle into the trash, traces of the night before had been disposed of except for Cindy's thong. He stuffed it in his drawer, next to his framed medal for bravery, trying not to remember when he had taken it off her.

"Damn," he swore softly. He picked up the award and threw it against the wall, shattering it into a thousand pieces. Jack watched it drop with a satisfying thud, then ran a hand through his hair in frustration. He looked away from the mess. It only reminded him of what he had lost. *Damn, get over it. You should be doing something besides throwing things and acting like a spoiled kid.*

A short time later, he sat in the living room drinking strong black coffee when Murph knocked at his door. "Come in. It's open."

Murph rushed into the room. "Hey, you had me worried." He spoke in an odd, yet gentle tone. "What's wrong?"

"Grab yourself a cup of coffee." He tried to lighten his mood, afraid his self-pity would be reflected on his face. "I've been thinking and I need your opinion."

Murph poured the coffee and glanced at Jack. "Since when does my opinion count with you?"

"Since always, you old coot." He took a quick swallow of his drink. "I have a huge favor to ask." He sipped his coffee and watched Murph's expression.

"Whatever you need. I'm here." Pausing, he regarded him with a speculative gaze. "Tell me."

"That's what I hoped you'd say." He ran his finger around the top of the coffee mug, working out his plan as he went. "You and Briggs have been beating on me to get a life. Well, I have come to the conclusion you're right." For an instant, Murph's gaze sharpened. "I guess, I had to work my way through some things, but I've never given up and I'm not giving up now. After reading that book, Briggs brought me I've decided to go to that clinic in Cedar Falls."

Murph almost choked on his coffee. Coughing, he set the cup down and looked at Jack. "That's great. What changed your mind? When do you want to go?"

"I called the clinic this morning and told them what was going on with me. I'm experiencing some pain in my hips and legs. They said I should come today, while I'm feeling something." He took a deep breath, hoping he'd keep feeling something that it wasn't just in his mind. "They said that there's a new surgery that can be done on patients like me. If their tests come out the way they expect them to, then I can have the surgery and possibly walk again." He looked at Murph. "Do you think I should do this?"

"Feeling. You're having feeling in your hips and legs?" He spoke with a bit of disbelief in the tone of his voice. "That's wonderful. And yes, of course, you have to go for it. Have the surgery. It's worth a shot. You have to take a chance," his excitement rose as he continued.

"I can lift both legs. Watch me." Beads of sweat popped out on Jack's skin as he lifted each leg. "This is the first time I've been able to lift both legs since before the incident."

"I knew you'd beat this." Murph slapped him on the back, grinning from ear to ear. "I can't wait to tell everybody."

"Hold on right there. That's part of what I need you to do for me. I don't want you to tell anyone, not even Briggs. He might let it slip to his new wife." The words were playful, but the meaning was not. "I mean nobody. This isn't a sure thing and I don't want anyone to get their hopes up for me."

"I don't understand. Why don't you want anyone to know?" He sighed with exasperation. "They'd all be happy for you, especially Cindy."

"Especially Cindy." Jack could feel his voice simmering with barely checked emotion. "I don't want her to know anything about me. What I'm doing or where I'm at."

"That doesn't make any sense. You guys were getting along so well last night." Murph frowned. "Did something happen between you?"

"Nothing worth talking about," inwardly, he cringed. "Let's drop it. This is the way I want you to handle things." He rigidly held himself together. "Can you keep this secret or not? Otherwise, I can catch a cab and disappear." He sighed heavily, his voice filled with anguish.

"I think it's the wrong thing to do, but if it means that much to you, of course, I can keep your secret. But what do I tell everybody?"

"Act like you don't know anything, be as surprised as they are when they find out I'm gone." He was suddenly overwhelmed by the things that had happened the night before. "That way you don't have to lie to Rhonda. It looks like you have the start of something good going and I wouldn't want you to mess it up over your involvement with me." He sighed. "I guess you can say I went to the mountains to finish my book. I'm going to do that, too."

"Okay, at least that's something, if you're hell-bent on doing it this way. What do you need me to do?"

"I need you to take me to the clinic and load some of my stuff I'll need to take in your car, mainly, my laptop computer, printer and my fish. They said I could bring that stuff with me because I'll be there for awhile. I've already packed my clothes in the duffel bag by the door."

"Great, time to get this show on the road. There won't be much traffic today and I can be back in the city before Rhonda returns home from shopping."

Jack held his hand out to Murph. "Thanks."

Murph slapped his hand away and gave him a hug. "I'm glad you're having feeling in your legs. I know this surgery will work." He pushed away and looked Jack in the eyes. "That's the best news I've ever heard."

"Murph. I know you blame yourself for what happened to me, but it wasn't your fault. Get over it." He wheeled toward the bedroom. "I'll get the rest of my stuff."

"Okay, I'll take the computer and printer out to the car. I'm in the parking garage so nobody should see us leave."

"I'll have the fish ready when you get back. The car is warm, isn't it?" he called from the bedroom.

"Yeah, it's warm." Murph picked up the packed laptop and printer. "I'll be right back," he called to Jack when he left the condo.

Jack looked around the bedroom one last time to make sure he hadn't forgotten anything. He reached into his drawer and pulled out a black strip of lace and stuffed it in his pocket. He sighed heavily, his heart aching with pain. It would remind him of what he would be missing and make him work harder. The next time he saw her—he would be walking.

Cindy punched her pillow. She had taken a shower and laid down to rest for a few minutes and had fallen asleep. Looking at the clock, it was late afternoon. She had slept most of the day away. For some reason, she had turned into a wanton woman last night and was embarrassed to face Jack. Sure, she had always wanted him, but last night, she had believed she would lose her mind if she didn't have him. She had moved out of her comfort zone and wow—it had been worth it. The man was an intense lover. Her heart twisted in her chest. It still felt like he was inside her. She wanted to keep the feeling as long as possible.

Her phone rang, pulling her from her thoughts. "Hello."

"Hi Cindy, what are you doing?"

"Sam. I didn't think you would be calling today." Cindy's heart was bursting with love and anguish, but she couldn't tell Sam. This was her time to be happy. She wouldn't cloud up Sam's sunny day with her problems.

Sam chuckled. "I'm just down the street and I can talk to my friend and be on my honeymoon." She laughed. "Anyway, Briggs is taking a nap."

"Oh, I'm glad you called. Tell me is Briggs as wonderful as you thought he'd be?"

"Even more so. It's divine ecstasy when he kisses me and he makes me happy in every way." She was practically purring as she spoke. "I can't believe I found the love of my life at a hospital."

"Yeah, love at first barf." Cindy sat on her bed and noticed it was snowing outside.

"He's the best. I don't know how I got so lucky, but I thank God for bringing him into my life."

"That's a fact—you're one lucky woman." Cindy glanced out the window. "I didn't know it was snowing."

"Where have you been? It's been snowing on and off all afternoon." Sam hesitated for a second. "Tell me. How did it go last night? I heard him ask you over for coffee."

"Oh, Sam, I think I made a huge mistake." Damn, she wasn't going to tell her, but it slipped out.

"Honey, it's okay. Tell me what happened. I'm sure everything will work out in the end."

"Are you sure you want to hear this?"

"Of course, I do. You're my best friend. Come on spit it out. Right now, tell me."

"Well, okay, if you insist." Cindy hesitated for a second. "I messed things up big time. We were having coffee and he had a muscle ache and I told him I would give him a massage. I don't know what came over me. I had to get him in bed. All I could think of was getting him naked. I've never felt this way."

"Cool. That's not so bad. Well, and did all his parts work?"

"Oh, God, yes," Cindy quivered at the sweet memory of his lovemaking. "He was.... I can't find words for it."

"That's what I hoped you would be telling me. Everything worked. Wonderful."

"But Sam, it was...it was surreal. I have never been so turned on in my life. I don't understand what happened to me. I think I'm in love. It's never been this good with anyone."

"Honey, yes, it's love, that's what happened to you. When you love someone, really love them, it makes all the difference in the world."

"Love? I...I don't know what to say." She couldn't get over how much she had shared with Jack, last night. Even in remembrance, she felt the intimacy of his touch. *Oh, lord, I am in love with him.*

"You don't have to say anything. I know this was what you both wanted. If it wasn't, you wouldn't have done it. The man loves you and you love him."

"I don't know about that..." His lips had been more persuasive than she'd cared to admit. Was this love? "I suppose you're right." She needed time to get used to these new emotions.

"So, it was good?" Sam laughed. "I'm happy for you. At dinner it seemed like you both were about to explode with wanting each other and didn't have enough sense to go for it."

Cindy's memories of Jack were pure and clear. "There was an attraction."

"An attraction," Sam laughed. "You both were shooting off sparks. That's a lot more than just an attraction. Tell me, how was Jack this morning? Was he happy?"

She sighed. "I don't know. I woke up first and I left. I was embarrassed at the way I acted last night. I couldn't face him this morning."

"You knot head. You should have stayed around for seconds."

"Believe me, I had seconds and thirds." She laughed, releasing some of her pent-up emotion.

"That's my girl. I knew you had it in you. The man doesn't

stand a chance. He's yours for the taking."

"Seriously, how do I face him?" Cindy recalled the ecstasy of being held against his warm body.

"The same way you do every day. Only now you both have this delicious bond to share."

"Maybe, you're right. I should go over and see how he's doing." Cindy savored the feeling of satisfaction he left with her. "Maybe, it's not as bad as I think?"

"Honey, it's not bad. Making love is a good thing. I'm sure Jack is on cloud nine, waiting for you to show up."

"Do you think?" She hungered for the touch of his mouth on hers.

"Yes, I know men. You are a gorgeous woman and now he's had a taste of you, he'll want you all to himself. He's the one for you."

"The one for me, that's what you keep telling me and you know what? You're right." Just thinking of him, caused Cindy to feel a warm glow. "I would love to be his."

"This keeps getting better and better. Here's what you do next. Get dressed and take him a plate of home baked cookies. Guys love it when you cook for them."

"Cookies?" Nothing quite like going from the bedroom to the kitchen in a heartbeat.

"Yeah, first you get them through sex and then you cinch the deal with food. That's the way it's been for centuries."

"Where do you come up with this stuff?" Cindy laughed.

"You'd be surprised at what I know about men." Sam giggled. "Hey, the man has been alone long enough. You've got to trust me on this one. Get to baking and go get your man."

"Okay. I'll do it." Cindy sighed, as it really didn't matter, because she loved to bake. "At least that will give me an excuse to see him again. Talk to you later."

"Yeah, call and let me know how it goes. It's all going to work out just the way you want, babies and all. Just you wait and see."

"I will." She put the phone on the charger. "Come on Prince, let's go for a walk in the snow, then we'll bake cookies." Maybe Sam was right with any luck things would be fine. Thinking about Jack laying there on the bed in the candlelight brought a smile to her face, and a warmth throughout her body.

CHAPTER TWENTY-ONE

Jack sat in his wheelchair watching the snow blow across the landscape pitting against the window pane, wondering what Cindy and Prince were doing. Coward that he was, he should have faced her and told her he was leaving. On a heavy sigh, he watched the pine trees in the distance disappear from sight under the white stuff. Murph had headed back to the city. With the department pulling a few strings, he had gotten checked in at the Springs Rehabilitation Center. They would be starting the tests in the next hour or so. He hadn't done much praying lately but if there was a time, this was it. *God. I know you haven't heard from me in a long time but please let the tests show I am a candidate for this surgery and let it work.*

"Mr. Riley, they're ready for you. We're a little short-handed today, because of the holiday weekend, but we have enough of the team on duty to get most of the tests done. Come with me."

"Okay, I'm right behind you, Mrs. Rogers." He grinned, happy to finally be doing something to help himself. "This is a big place. I didn't expect it to be so homey."

"Most of the folks who come here stay with us quite awhile. We try to make it comfortable. Did you get settled in okay?"

"Yeah, the room is great."

The nurse smiled as they went down the corridor. "You will be meeting with Dr. Jones before we start your tests. He's right in here." She held the door open for Jack to enter. "I'll see you later."

"Thanks." Jack read the sign on the man's desk while he wheeled into the room. Dr. Clyde Jones, Ph D, Clinical Director.

"Good afternoon, Mr. Riley, I'm Dr. Jones." He stood and extended his hand across the desk to Jack. The doctor was an older man, about one-hundred-eighty pounds, graying hair around the temples and brown eyes behind silver wire rim glasses. The striking thing about him was an aura of peace that surrounded the man. *Must be nice to feel that way.*

"Hello." Jack shook his hand and glanced around the room to see the doctor's diplomas covering the walls and knickknacks sitting around his desk. He supposed they were gifts from his patients.

Dr. Jones sat behind his desk. "We're glad to have you here with us. As you know, at this treatment facility, we work as a team of doctors. You will be seeing several of us." He smiled. "When you see me, it will be in group therapy, individual therapy, family counseling or biofeedback therapy. Soon, you'll meet the rest of the rehabilitation team. The team includes a physician, nurse, occupational therapist, recreational therapist, physical therapist, and exercise physiologist. Your case manager and specialists are called in when needed. We have a class room, gym, swimming pool and exercise room at your disposal."

"Why so many doctors?" Damn, it was just like he'd thought, and they'd all be poking on him.

"With spinal cord injuries, many of our clients develop a symptom of their illness called chronic pain. That's a pain which never goes away. These people need to have help in every aspect of their life in order to be able to live a pain free productive existence."

"I don't have chronic pain. Why do I need to see these doctors?" He was sick to death of doctors.

"Your case is different, but you will need to see all of us. You went through a traumatic time and whether you believe it or not, you do need our help." He grinned, giving Jack time for the words to sink in. "That's what we're here for—to help you move on from what's happened to you. Most people get stuck somewhere in the recovery phase of healing. They don't know how to move forward."

"How's that?" He suddenly felt ill-equipped to undertake the task ahead of him.

"They aren't the same person they were before the accident and many get stuck in the anger phase and tend to isolate themselves from their families and friends. Turn into some kind of recluse if their friends and family let them. That's where the trouble starts."

"How so?" This was beginning to sound more and more like what he was doing, before he came here.

"They stay by themselves and don't want to see anyone, and they get angry at the world for their predicament. They take this anger out on their loved ones lashing out at the people who care for them. It makes life tough for everyone around them. They get caught in this self-pity hole and can't dig their way out of it without help." He hesitated for a second. "Mr. Riley, have you experienced any of these feelings?"

Jack cringed. It was as if the man could see right through his defenses. *Well, here it comes*. He'd have to bare his soul. When he checked in, he wasn't aware he'd have to talk with a shrink. "I've experienced some of that," an understatement.

"Like what?" The man's gaze bore into him.

Jack looked him in the eyes. "I don't like people looking at me in this wheelchair." He sighed. "It's as if I become the nothing man when I'm in it, or they look at me with pity in their eyes and I can't stand that." He bit his lip. "I haven't been out of my condo in months."

"Those are natural responses. It will take time to work through what has happened to you. Your tests will be completed over the next couple of days, and there's a good chance you'll be starting with the new class on Monday. The orientation will explain what we expect of you. You won't be accepted into the program unless we as a team think you are ready to be helped and that we can help you."

"So, I won't know until Monday if I can start with the group? I thought if I came here, there would be hope for me to walk again." He regarded him quizzically for a moment. Was he on a wild goose chase?

"That's possible, but we won't know for sure until we get

your test results back. We don't want to give you false hope. That's the worst thing a doctor can do with a patient like yourself. The bottom line is before you leave here, you will know, once and for all what your options are. I admire you for coming here. It takes guts."

"I have to do something." Jack hit the wheelchair with his fist. "I...I guess, I'm stuck."

"Another natural response, you'll be taught how to live with your condition, no matter how it turns out. We can help you, but first you have to help yourself. You need to have the tests. Are you ready to proceed?"

"Yes. Let's get on with it. That's why I'm here," an uncertainty crept into Jack's voice.

"Okay, I'll call your case manager, Mrs. Rogers, back to take you to your next appointment. It was a pleasure meeting you. I look forward to working with you." He picked up the phone and paged Mrs. Rogers.

"Well, how did it go?" she asked as they left Dr. Jones' office.

He hadn't had time to digest the fact he'd been speaking with a shrink. "Okay, I guess. I hope these tests show I can be helped."

"Have faith."

Faith, it had been a long time since he'd had faith in anything.

Later in the day, Cindy pulled a batch of chocolate chip cookies out of the oven. Prince sniffed at the air. "Sorry, boy, you know you can't have chocolate." Placing the cookies on the cooling rack, she thought about Jack. She didn't know what to say to him, except the truth—she had fallen in love with him. She sighed and put the cookies on a plate and covered it with *Saran Wrap.* "Come on Prince, time to face the music. Jack is Jack. We'll be able to take whatever he dishes out. Maybe, I'm reading things wrong. Maybe, he'll be glad to see us."

Prince sat on the rug, watching her with his doggy grin spread across his wrinkled face as if to reassure her that she was doing the right thing.

"Okay, boy, here goes everything. As Sam would say, let's go for it."

Cindy stood outside Jack's apartment. She still had an extra key from when she had his locks changed, but she hoped he'd answer the door. If he wasn't home, she'd drop off the cookies with a note. She knocked against his door with her shaking hand. Prince barked.

"Be quiet, boy, you don't need to get the neighbors involved." Still no answer. Odd, last night was the first time he'd been out of his condo in months. Could he be gone again? "Come on, we'll leave the cookies on the kitchen counter for him." She put the key in the lock and pushed the door open. The apartment was plunged in darkness and felt cold. "Something's wrong." She flipped on the light and looked around the place. Now, she knew what it was. Jack's lighted aquarium was gone, along with his computer. She rushed to the bedroom. Broken glass lay on the carpet by the wall. She picked up his award and pushed the glass shards off of it and laid it on the dresser. What had happened here? Everything else was in its place, but Jack was gone.

She checked the other bedroom and ran into the living room and glanced around. Nothing had been disturbed. His papers were on his desk. Everything was in it's place, except his laptop was gone. She glanced at a stack of printed e-mails on the desk. She knew she was being nosy, but they might give her a clue of where Jack had gone. Her heart sank.

"Oh, my God." Some of the e-mails were from Snowhite to JPrince. Jack was JPrince. Her mind spun with bewilderment. She fell into the chair at the desk in total disbelief. The shooting was why she had stopped hearing from JPrince.

Her brain refused to register the significance that she had slept with JPrince. The man who had already experienced the love of a lifetime. The man to whom she had poured her heart out to through e-mail. The man who wasn't ready for a relationship—he couldn't commit—and now he was gone.

In a crazy way, now, things made sense. Did he figure out she was the lonely Snow White? Had he made love to her out of pity? Her heart squeezed in pain. Too many questions and not enough answers. She had to find him.

She ran back into the bedroom and jerked his closet doors open. Sure, enough, his closet was nearly bare. But, where did Jack go...and why now and how? Did he run away from her?

She swallowed a sob building in her throat and turned off the lights. "Come on, Prince, there's nothing left for us here." She left the condo as she had found it. Clutching the plate of cookies, she stumbled back to her place with a dull ache clawing at her chest. She had blown it. Jack Riley, aka JPrince, wasn't ready for a relationship and she had forced him into one.

Prince whined when she let them back into her condo. "I know, boy, I'll miss him, too." She put the cookies on the coffee table and fell on the sofa, crying. Prince jumped up beside her, trying to snuggle and get her attention. Wiping her tears away with a Kleenex, she absent-mindedly rubbed his belly and scratched behind his ears. Then she grabbed the phone and dialed Murph. If anyone knew where Jack was, it would be him.

"Hello," Rhonda said.

"Hi, Rhonda, this is Cindy. May I speak to Murph?" Surely, Jack would've told him where he went. She held the phone tightly in her hand, hoping for the best.

"Of course, dear, just a minute, I'll get him."

She could hear Rhonda calling Murph to the phone. What would she say to him? The truth. She swallowed the huge lump in her throat to keep from crying.

"Hello." Murph's friendly voice came on the line.

"Hi, Murph. The strangest thing has happened. I took some cookies over to Jack and he's gone. I'm worried about him being out in weather like this. Do you know where he is?"

"Oh, he's okay." Murph seemed to hesitate before he answered. "He called earlier today and said he had a ride to a ski resort in the mountains complete with room service. He wanted to finish his book and get his head on straight."

"Did he tell you where?" She bit her lip as she waited for his answer.

He cleared his throat. "He said he didn't want anyone to know where he's gone. He needs this time alone to get the work done with no distractions. Don’t worry, Cindy, I know he'll be back in a few weeks."

"If you hear anything, will you let me know? I need to talk to him." Her throat ached with defeat.

"Sure, it's not a problem." When he spoke again, his voice was full of warmth and concern. "Cindy, don't give up on him. This is something he has to do. He has a lot of personal things he has to work out for himself."

"I know. Thanks, Murph." A few weeks, she shuddered inwardly at the thought. Jack was going to be gone a few weeks and there was nothing she could do about it. Her heart was crushed—empty inside. But whatever she decided to say to Jack would have to wait until he reappeared. Well, the best thing she could do would be to keep busy. "Damn, I have the worst luck with men." She wrapped herself in her favorite throw, a cocoon of anguish and held Prince next to her on the couch and wept.

Some time later, Prince started to whine. "Okay, boy." she blew her nose and washed her face. "Come on, I'll take you out. I could use some fresh air myself."

After returning from walking Prince, Cindy decided to check her e-mail. She grabbed her laptop and sat on the sofa with Prince snuggled next to her. It had been ages since she'd checked it. Since she'd resigned from the singles group, she didn't get much e-mail, but there was one from Grace. Perfect, right now she needed her friends. She clicked open the document.

From: Gracetaylor
To: Snowhite

Hi, Cindy,

I hope you had a great Thanksgiving. You'd never guess what is happening. I have the most marvelous news. Sheriff Thompson asked Nana to marry him and she said yes. I can hardly believe it, myself. He asked her on Thanksgiving and gave her the ring. It's so sweet. They've been friends for as long as I can remember.

I know this would be fine with Papa. He'd want Nana to be happy. And she is. Cindy, I haven't seen her this happy in a long time. They are planning on getting married on Christmas Eve. You just have to come home for the ceremony. Nana wants you and Jenna to be her bridesmaids and me her maid of honor. We're having a small ceremony at the Cactus Rose Ranch. Say you can make it home for the wedding.

Also, Nana, Jenna and I are planning on driving into Denver tomorrow to look for a wedding dress. Can you go shopping with us? We're going to stay the weekend at the Marriott Courtyard, near you, on the Mall. I'll call you later with all the details. Love You Like A Sis ~ Grace

How wonderful. Nana was getting married. At age seventy-two. Nana was always like a mom to Cindy, of course, she'd attend the wedding. The school was closed for the holiday so she could spend the entire weekend with them, which would keep her mind off other things. "See, Prince, things have a way of working out the way they're supposed, too." She scratched behind his ears with her free hand and he grunted in his sleep.

She picked up the phone and called Grace.

"Hello." A child's voice answered the phone.

"Hi, Jamie, it's Cindy. How are you?" In her mind's eye, she could picture the pretty little blond child on the other end of the conversation.

"Okay. Did you know Nana is getting married?" The excitement in her voice made Cindy smile. "I get a new dress to wear to the wedding and I get to be the flower girl."

"Yes, your mom told me about the wedding. Is she there?"

"Yeah, hold on, I'll get Mom." Cindy heard her lay the phone down and yell for her mother. She took a deep breath and tried to keep thoughts of Jack at the back of her mind.

"Hello." Grace spoke softly.

"Hello, yourself." Smiling, Cindy leaned forward and continued. "What's this I hear about Nana getting married?"

"Cool. You received my e-mail. Isn't it great news? I was going to call you after I put the twins down."

"Do I need to call back later?" She knew Grace had her hands full with four children and a husband.

"No, don't worry about it. Seth can watch them while I'm on the phone."

"This is wonderful news. I always thought Frank and Nana were cute together at church." They've known each other forever.

"Amazing, isn't it. I know Nana has been lonely these past few years. Frank is perfect for her. They enjoy the same stuff. He volunteers at the hospital rehabilitation gift shop, too. I think he did it because he knew Nana was working there."

"How cute. What time will you be getting into town? I'm off all weekend and I'm ready to shop." Shopping would take her mind off her recent troubles. "Because of the holidays, the crowds will be terrible, but it'll be a blast and there should be a lot of good sales."

"All right, I can hardly wait. Seth is keeping the kids so it will only be me Jenna and Nana. We plan to do most of our Christmas shopping, along with finding a dress." She paused for a second. "Nana doesn't want the traditional wedding gown, but I'm sure we can find something special."

"I'm glad you're coming to town. You don't have to stay at the Marriott. You can all stay with me. I have plenty of room."

"Nana didn't want to put you out. And besides, she said she needs to have a place to go back to and rest if we wear her out. You know how she is. Don't worry about it. We'll be at your place most of the time, anyway."

"Okay, if that's what you want to do." She pushed a strand of hair behind her ear, just pleased they were coming to town.

"Where are some good places to shop in the downtown area?"

"Let's see. There's the Pavilions and Tabor Center on the Sixteenth Street Mall, Larimer Square, and of course, we can go to Cherry Creek Shopping Center. They have anything and everything you could possibly want." She rubbed Prince's ears as he snuggled next to her on the sofa.

"Sounds great. We're leaving early, so we should get there around ten. Are you sure you're ready for the invasion of your country friends?"

"Are you kidding?" If Grace only knew how much she needed their company. "I can't wait to see you. It's been too long." And she realized it had been too long. She should've gone back to the ranch to visit way before now, but she'd let herself get caught up with Jack's problems. Not that she'd minded, but she should've taken more time for herself.

"Okay, we'll call you when we get to town. See you tomorrow."

"Okay, tomorrow." She hung up the phone. *This is just what I need to take my mind off Jack and the awkward way we left things.* "Damn. If I'd only stayed there until he woke up, my stomach wouldn't be in icy knots." She had walked into the situation with her eyes wide open and look where it has gotten her—hurt. Prince shook his head and jumped off the sofa as if to say I told you so.

"Know-it-all dog, don't give me your attitude," Cindy scolded. Prince sighed and lay down on the rug, closing his eyes. She closed her laptop and stared into the fireplace, mesmerized by the flames. Little by little, warmth crept back into her body.

Jack was JPrince. That still boggled her mind. As much as she cared about Jack, she was happy he was taking control of his life...even if it was without her.

Her head ached with swirling thoughts. Why did Jack leave her without a word? That wasn't like him...or was it? Apparently, she didn't know him as well as she had imagined. Could it be he was as much a coward to face her as she was to face him? Or was it he just didn't want to get involved?

The next morning came in with clear blue skies and lots of sunshine. Colorado winters were always a treat. One day snow and the next it would melt off. Cindy sat sipping her morning coffee, trying to make a Christmas list while waiting to hear from her friends. While they were here, she did want Grace and Jenna to meet Sam.

A knock sounded at the door. "Cool. It must be them," she said to Prince. He lay on the rug watching her go to the door, not bothering to move.

"Hi, we're here," Grace said.

Cindy was so glad to see Grace, the tall blond on the other side of the door grinning at her. And next to her was Jenna with her beautiful auburn hair. Jenna rushed forward to grab Cindy for a hug.

"Oh, Jenna your hair has gotten so long. I love it," Cindy

said. “Looks like the girls at the shop have been taking good care of you all.”

“They have, but we miss you doing our hair,” said Nana with her short white hair. She stood beside Grace smiling.

"Oh, it's so good to see you guys," Cindy said. Before she let them in the doorway, Cindy hugged them all again. They hugged her back. "Come in. This is Prince."

"Oh, he's cute. I've heard about you. You are who she's spending her time with these days." Grace went over and scratched his belly. "Some guard dog, you are." He gave her his doggy grin, that charmed her completely.

"Here, let me take your coats." Cindy hung them in the hall closet, excited they were here. "How was your trip?"

"It was fine. The roads were clear," Nana said. "Sit down, make yourselves comfortable and I'll get you something to drink and then we’ll make our game plan for shopping." Nana sat on the sofa and Grace continued to play with Prince.

"Coffee is on, but I can make tea if you want."

"Don't bother, coffee sounds good to me," said Grace, as she walked over to the sliding glass doors leading to the balcony off the living room. Jenna stood there looking out over the balcony. “Wow, now that’s a long way down.”

"Coffee is good for me, too," Nana echoed.

"You have quite the view from up here, don't you?" Grace added.

"Yeah, I love it." She handed Nana and Grace their coffee.

"I like your condo. It feels real homey,” Jenna said as Cindy gave her a mug.

“And honey, you look wonderful. As much as we miss you at the beauty shop back home, I have to admit it looks like the city agrees with you," Nana said and glanced around the living room.

Hearing it put that way, Cindy smiled. She was happy here, no matter how things worked out with Jack. This was her home, for better or worse. She was lucky to have good friends at work and in the building. A warm glow flowed through her with that realization. No matter what happened. Life was good.

"We sure do miss you at home. Are you sure we can't talk you into coming back?" Grace said with a twinkle in her eyes.

"I know one lonesome cowboy who would like to see you return to the fold."

Cindy smiled at the memory of Travis. They had dated a few times, but it hadn't gone anywhere. He was too much like a brother. "How are Travis and Gloria doing?" There would always be a soft spot in her heart for him.

"He's doing okay. It seems he has an eye for her, but if you came back to stay, that might change," Nana teased.

"That's wonderful. Gloria is perfect for him. Travis is a nice guy and deserves happiness." Powerful relief filled her. She really hadn't meant to hurt him when she moved to the city.

"Well, so do you. Do you have a new man in your life? How is your policeman friend doing?" She hesitated. "From your e-mails, he sounds like a great guy."

Cindy braced herself, gripping her coffee mug. She had been expecting this question. "Jack is doing good. Actually, he left town yesterday to go to the mountains to finish his novel."

"Where did he go?" Grace looked at her as if she suspected something was up.

"I...I'm not sure. Murph said he decided at the last minute he had to get out of town to work on his book." She sighed. "Who knows? He's still working through what's happened to him, I guess." She couldn't tell them she had driven him out of town.

"Well, you can't blame him for that. Life gets pretty tough sometimes. And with what he's been through, maybe he needs this time to decide what he's going to do with the rest of his life." Nana shook her head. "It was a shame that poor boy was hurt so badly. They showed the whole thing on the Denver news. Said they didn't think he would make it at first." The tenderness in Nana's expression touched her heart.

"He's doing a lot better. I'm hoping that he'll be back soon." She was barely able to talk about Jack. Cindy had to change the subject or she'd break down. "But tell me about this wedding." She grinned at Nana. "And of course I wouldn't miss it." She'd go home to the mountains to lick her wounds and attend the ceremony.

"I'm glad you'll be able to come home to the ranch. It means a lot to me." She smiled. "Frank and I decided to tie the knot. We're tired of being alone." Nana grinned and held her hand out to show Cindy the ring.

"It's beautiful." She held Nana's hand for a second, admiring the diamond ring. "I'm happy for you. Look at you, you're glowing." Nana radiated happiness all around her.

"Honey, it's been a long time, but I feel lucky. Frank is a good man."

"Yes, he is. He was always fair with me and Grace growing up. Many times he could have booked us for speeding, but he let us off on a minor offense and community service." She glanced at Grace, wanting to change the subject from men. "Okay, where do you want to go first?"

"Everywhere. Wear your walking shoes, because I mean to shop till we drop." Grace laughed. "At least that's what the kids said to tell you."

"How are Jamie and Joey and the twins? By the way, you look great." She envied her friend having four beautiful children and an adoring husband.

Grace modeled for Cindy. "I'll have you know, I lost my baby weight in six months and I haven't felt better in my life."

"That's wonderful. You look fabulous." She laughed. "I bet Seth loves it and how is he doing with the new babies?"

"He's the best father ever. He dotes on the twins, but makes sure he has time left for Jamie and Joey."

"It's wonderful to see you guys." Tears pressed at the back of Cindy's eyelids. "I have so many things I want to catch up on with you all, but the stores are waiting. We'd better get going." Or she'd start blubbering.

"Okay, girls, let's hit it," said Grace. "Come on, we have to find that special dress." Cindy pulled the door shut behind them, trying to block thoughts of Jack out of her mind. Today, she was going to spend time with her loved ones. Tomorrow was early enough to dwell on Jack. "Look out Denver, here we come."

CHAPTER TWENTY-TWO

"Has Murph or Briggs heard anything from Jack?" Cindy asked Sam as she tossed empty boxes into the store room. She had volunteered to help Sam do the inventory for the beauty school. "It's been two weeks and not a word." She was furious with the man.

"Briggs talked to him on the phone last night, but Jack was pretty tight lipped and wouldn't tell him where he was staying. I'm sorry, honey, I tried."

"It's okay. I should move on and forget it, but I can't." Cindy sat on top of one of the boxes. "I hate this not knowing. One day, I think he hates me and the next, I think maybe there was some kind of misunderstanding. I'm confused. Most days, I just don't know what to think."

Sam waddled up beside her. "It's okay. The man is a jerk not to call you. I think he needs his butt kicked for the way he's acting."

She laughed. "Yeah, right, and who will do the butt kicking. You or Briggs?" She'd like to kick his butt too—and do a few other things to it.

"Whoever sees him first." Sam sat down. "We've done enough. How about we call it a day and take in a movie or something? I could use a break."

"Sure, but let's get something to eat at the food court." Since Jack left, she'd had to force herself to eat. Cindy really wasn't that hungry, but knew Sam was eating for two.

"That works for me. I'm always hungry." Sam rubbed her tummy and pulled her coat around her.

Cindy grinned. "Are you ready for Christmas?" She had finished her shopping with Grace, Jenna, and Nana and just had to wrap her packages. In a moment of insanity, she'd even bought one for Jack.

"Ready as I'm going to be. Briggs and Murph went to the mountains today to cut Christmas trees. Can you believe it? There are trees for sale on every street corner and they insisted they go chop down their own." She smiled. "They're bringing you one, too. Briggs said not to worry, that they might not get back until real late. Men." Sam laughed. "We're going to decorate it tomorrow night. Want to come over for hot apple cider and help us?"

An ache shot through Cindy's heart. She'd like to be decorating her tree with someone. "No, thanks, it's your first Christmas together. You guys should be alone, but tell them thanks for bringing me a tree. That's sweet."

"Don't be silly. You're family."

"Actually, I have plans for tomorrow evening. I'm picking up Nana's dress for the wedding. She had to leave it here to be altered. I'm taking it out to the ranch for her." Cindy was looking forward to seeing everyone at the ceremony. And it would give her a chance to step away from what had transpired with Jack and look at it from a new perspective.

"I enjoyed meeting them. They're all such nice people."

"My dad and I moved there after mom passed and when he went to Florida, Nana kind of took me under her wing. She's very special to me, like a grandmother when I was growing up." She grinned. "Grace and I had to talk her into buying the dress. She's going to be a beautiful bride."

"I'm sure she will be. She's a sweet woman. But if you change your mind, you know you're always welcome to come over tomorrow night. Briggs likes you."

Cindy pushed a strand of hair behind her ear. "I like him, too. I'm glad you found each other. Strange, how things work out, isn't it?"

"Yeah, that's for sure. A few short months ago I was footloose and fancy free. Now, look at me. I'm a happily married two-ton Tess with a baby on the way."

"Like Grace told you, you'll lose the baby weight. But, if for some reason you didn't lose it, you'd still be the light of his life." She was happy that her friend had found her true love. "The man absolutely adores you."

"You're the best. I'm so thankful I have you as my friend." She winked at Cindy and locked the door to the school behind them.

"You've been a great friend, too, always been there for me, even with this mess with Jack." She sighed. "Thanks for listening to me whine." And she had done her share of that over the past few weeks. "But now, it's time to move ahead."

Sam gave her a side glance. "You know, I'm sorry things turned out the way they did. I believe with my whole heart Jack has a thing for you and I still do. I know he'll come back one of these days and make it up to you."

"Yeah, sure," Cindy snorted as they walked down the street, each lost in their own thoughts. "Prince and I will go to the store in a few days and buy decorations to decorate our tree. It's nice that we don't have to go to the mountains and chop one down. Must be a guy thing." They laughed together while they walked through the shops on the Sixteenth Street Mall checking out the Christmas decorations.

All of a sudden, Cindy pulled Sam to her side and stopped in her tracks, looking inside a shop window.

"What's wrong? What do you see?" Sam asked.

"There, by the ESPN zone door. I can't believe it, it's Todd and that crazy woman, Lola."

"How on earth did they get together?" Sam's brows arched in a puzzled expression.

"God only knows, but they deserve each other." In her mind's eye, Cindy could still see Lola waving that knife above Jack's head.

"Okay, you never did tell me why you broke it off with Todd." Sam stood there looking at him. "He seemed nice when he came to my paint party. What really happened with him? Fess up."

"Let's get something to eat." She took Sam's arm and led her into the Tabor Center. "It's a long story."

"Tempt me with food but it won't work. You have to tell me."

"All right, we went back to his place and he was an Austin Powers wannabe in silver sequined speedos, with the flashing strobe lights and everything just like in the movie."

"What? Todd did that? He seemed so straight laced."

Cindy laughed. "If you only knew."

"Okay, that's it. Spill it. We'll eat here." She stood in line at the Chinese food place.

They carried their trays over to a table in the center of the food court. "Okay, we have food. We're sitting down, tell me everything." Sam folded her hands on the table, waiting in anticipation.

Cindy glanced around the tables to see if there was anyone close enough to hear them. "You're not going to believe me. This guy was crazy about my feet."

"Your feet?" Sam's laughter flowed around them. "Why your feet?"

"Don't ask me. I don't know. Anyway, he gave me a foot massage and started sucking on my toes. It was sick. You would've had to have been there to believe it."

"I've heard of stuff like that, but in my dating days I can't say I ran into anyone with the desire. It must be your gorgeous toes."

"Yeah, right. You do realize the toe next to my big toe is longer than the rest." Cindy laughed. "My cross to bare."

Sam almost choked on her diet Pepsi. "Different strokes for different folks, I guess," she said, with a gleam in her eye.

"That's what I thought when I ran out of there." Cindy sobered for a moment. "I wonder what Todd and crazy woman have in common."

"That's simple." Sam winked at her. "They're both nuts."

"Crazy or not, they have each other." *And all I have is Prince. What's wrong with this picture?*

"Everything is going to be all right." Murph spoke to Jack in a soothing voice.

"What are you doing here?" Jack mumbled as he tried to

open his eyes. Ready to go in for his surgery, he was drugged to the gills. One eyelid lifted at the sound of Murph's voice.

"We wanted you to know, Murph and I are here and we'll be here until it's over," Briggs croaked. He squeezed Jack's hand before Jack lost consciousness.

"We have to take him in now." The operating room technician wheeled the bed toward the operating theater. "I'll come to the waiting room and let you know how he's doing as soon as I can."

"Thanks," Murph said when they wheeled Jack through the wide double doors.

"Can you believe he didn't want us to come? There was no way I wouldn't be here for him. What is going on in his mind? Why is he trying to cut us out of his life?" Briggs asked.

"Dr. Jones said it's common for people with these types of injuries. In their minds, they've made the decision they aren't good enough to be around other people. With counseling, he'll come out the other side. And yes, we'll stick by him, no matter how stubborn he tries to be."

"Damn straight. We're here for him, whether he wants us to be or not." Murph snorted.

"Come on, let's grab some coffee. It'll be awhile before they tell us anything."

"Okay, what do you think will happen between him and Cindy?"

Murph chewed his lip, before he answered. "I think in time they have a good chance of getting together. Something happened between them on Thanksgiving night. Jack wouldn't tell me anything, but I think it was a good thing. If you ask me, she's the reason Jack is finally getting the help he needs."

"Yeah, that's what Sam keeps telling me, too. I hope she's right. Jack needs somebody. I didn't realize how lonely I was until Sam came into my life."

"I know what you mean. I feel the same way about Rhonda." He stared down into his coffee. "As I've said many times before, Cindy would be good for him, if he would let her in."

"Well, maybe this place will help him. Everybody seems to be well informed about what these people are going through.

When Jack called me last week, he said he realized how lucky he was to be alive and have a chance to walk. He said there are people here who don't have a prayer of doing anything like that."

"Yeah, he's coming around. It's going to take time and he knows it. He's not going to get well over night. This sort of thing takes accepting and living with it, in order to finally adjust to the way his life has changed."

Settling down with coffee and magazines, they watched the time crawl on the big black clock on the waiting room wall. Finally, in the late afternoon, a man dressed in green scrubs came toward them.

"Good afternoon, gentlemen. I'm Dr. Lyle, Jack's neurosurgeon. I have some good news. I was able to repair the damage and he should be able to walk in the near future."

"That's wonderful. Thank you, doctor." Murph and Briggs shook his hand. "When can we see him?"

"He should be coming out of it in an hour or so. I'll tell the nurse to let you know when he's ready to see you."

"Okay. We'll wait here."

"Good day, gentlemen, if anything changes, I'll let you know." He turned and walked back through the double doors into the operating area.

"Great news," Murph smiled at Briggs, "this is incredible news. I wish we could tell the girls."

"Yeah, me, too, I hated telling them we were coming up here to cut Christmas trees. At least we did cut trees, so it wasn't a complete lie."

"Yeah, I didn't like it either." Murph sipped his coffee. "That's it, we have to change Jack's mind and make him let us tell the women where he is and what he's doing."

"I agree."

A little while later, the nurse brought them to Jack's room.

He lay there looking at them as if he couldn't believe they were real. "I thought I imagined you guys were here. I told you guys not to come," he mumbled.

"You did. But you of all people should know better than to give us orders." Murph grinned at him. "How are you doing?"

Jack glanced at Briggs. "And you, with the new wife and

baby due any minute. Why are you here? You need to be with your family."

Briggs towered over the bed. Leaning down into Jack's face, he gave him the once over. "Listen to me, and listen to me good. I'm only going to say this once. You are family and you can't shut us out. Now, how are you feeling? The doctor told us it was a successful surgery."

Jack frowned, then it turned into a grin. "Yeah, he told me, too. I actually have a chance to walk, again."

"Jack, that's such good news." Murph stepped forward with a glimmer of moisture in his eyes. "Thank goodness."

"Yeah, you old coot, I'll be chasing you around before you know it."

"It's amazing what medical technology can do these days." Briggs spoke from the chair next to Jack's bedside. "You're one of the lucky ones."

"After being here for the past few weeks, it's made me realize how good I have it, even if I had to spend the rest of my days in that chair." He fisted the sheets in his hand. "Cindy was right there are a lot of people worse off than me."

"Speaking of Cindy, Briggs and I have come to a decision, especially since you're doing so well. We want to tell the girls what you've been up too."

"Please don't. I promise I'll tell them soon. I want to surprise everyone for Christmas."

Briggs and Murph glanced at each other. "Will you be out of here by then?"

"That's what they tell me. With hard work, which I've already been doing, I will get out of here on Christmas Eve and head home. Maybe, be able to walk." He glanced at the fellows. "Come on. I'm only asking you to keep my secret a few more weeks."

"Why is it so important for us not to tell them? What does it matter? Is something going on we don't know about?" Murph asked.

Jack sighed and bit his lower lip. "You've probably already guessed, but I want to get to know Cindy better."

"Really?" Murph grinned.

"Yeah, we assumed that one, after the way you two got

along at Thanksgiving dinner." Briggs frowned. "But I don't get it. Then, why wouldn't you want her to know how well you're doing?"

"Yeah." Murph added his two cents. "Why don't you tell her so she can come and visit you?"

"I don't want her to see me here. The next time I see her, I want to be walking. When I ask her what I have in mind, I want to do it on my own two feet."

"Don't tell me. You're going to ask her to marry you?" Briggs appeared to be stunned. "Great. Sam will be thrilled. She keeps saying it's written in the stars. You and Cindy are meant to be together."

"It's about time." Murph added. "But the way you left things. I know she is going through a tough time of it. She's being strong, but seems confused as to why you didn't want anyone to know where you are. I told her you needed to work through some stuff, but I could tell she was feeling pretty low."

"Why did you leave things the way you did?" asked Briggs.

Jack felt like they had put him under a microscope. He'd have to tell them the truth or they'd never go along with his plan. "All right, I'll tell you. We were together and it was incredible. Everything worked, but the next morning when I woke up, she was gone. I thought she realized during the night she didn't want anything to do with me, because I was in the wheelchair."

"Cindy isn't shallow. I'm sure she had a good reason for leaving." Murph snorted. "That isn't the reason she left you."

"Let me continue. After I've had weeks to think about it, I know she isn't like that. I was a coward to face her and let my own insecurities take over, before we could talk." He hit the bed with his fist. "That's it in a nutshell. I made a stupid mistake."

"Yeah, you did. You know she might meet someone else while you're making your plans, leaving her not knowing what's on your mind. Just a few weeks ago, some friends of hers from her hometown came to the city to shop. Sam went out with them for dinner and said they were trying to get Cindy to move back home and marry some guy she used to date named Travis."

A hard cold knot formed in Jack's stomach. *Damn, had he lost her, before he had a chance to tell her how he felt?*

Travis, she never mentioned anyone named Travis to me."

"And why would she? I keep telling you, she's a beautiful, kind woman and you'd better act quick, before you lose her. Why, the way you left her, no telling how she thinks you feel about her." Murph stood there with a smug grin on his face. "You'd better call her right now and worm your way back into her good graces, before it's too late."

"Murph is right. You know how women can be. You better let her know you're interested or she might go home and marry that guy." Briggs hesitated. "I overheard Sam talking to her on the phone the other night about wedding dresses."

"Damn. I can't do anything yet." Panic ran through Jack's veins. "I can't walk."

"Do you think it matters to Cindy? She has taken care of you for months and put up with your crap because she cares for you. It doesn't make a damn bit of difference to her whether you are in a wheelchair or not." Murph glared at Jack. "That's your baggage—not hers."

"The bottom line is you have to decide what you want and take charge of the situation. Stop putting off important decisions because you are in a wheelchair. It's not your legs that aren't working—it's your head." Briggs leaned over and squeezed his shoulder. "Call her. Talk to her. Don't take the chance of losing her."

"Yes, call her. Soon as you're up to it." Murph shook his head in agreement. "Listen, you're on the mend and going to be fine. We need to be heading back to the city. We told the women we were coming to the mountains to cut Christmas trees. Because of you, they think we're nuts."

Jack laughed. "That was your excuse. How lame is that? They know you can buy one on any street corner."

"Whatever, it worked. We're here and they're none the wiser. But you owe us—big time." Briggs squeezed his shoulder again. "If you need anything, call us. You know we're here for you. Murph's right, we have to go."

Looking at the two of them, Jack realized how grateful he was for their friendship. He swallowed. *Thank you, God, for these two wonderful people.* "Get out of here. I'll figure out something about Cindy."

"Good, it's the smart thing to do. We'll call you," Briggs said. The bear of a man stood in the doorway grinning.

"We'll keep your secret until Christmas. That's it." Murph gave him a stubborn look. "We can be as ornery as you."

Jack watched them go. So Cindy had an old flame who wants to marry her. The last thing he needed. "Damn, what to do? What to do?" Jack mumbled as he dozed off into a drug-induced sleep.

CHAPTER TWENTY-THREE

A few days before Christmas, Cindy sat her suitcase in the entryway. Her mind was more at ease since she'd received a beautiful bouquet of red roses from Jack wishing her a happy holiday. It warmed her heart to know he thought about her. Maybe they still had a chance. But for the life of her, she couldn't figure out his cryptic message, saying, 'Wishing you a happy holiday season. Don't do anything until I come home. Jack.' What did that mean?

No matter, it was time to leave for the ranch. Travis was in the city and had agreed to give Cindy a lift back to Cedar Falls. It would be good to see everyone. She did miss her home town. After all, she'd lived there since she was ten. The doorbell rang, jerking her from her thoughts.

Peeking through the hole she saw Travis standing on the other side. Prince sniffed at the door. "It's okay, boy, he's my friend." She smiled, remembering some of the good times they had shared together until she'd decided they were better friends than lovers. "Come here, you big handsome cowboy." She gave him a hug and kiss. The man was like a brother to her.

"Hi, Cindy. You look great. It seems the city life is agreeing with you." He stepped through the doorway.

"Come in and let me show you my place." She closed the door. They had grown up together and it was good to see Travis. He was the brother she never had.

He leaned down and let Prince sniff his hand. "This is the

critter Grace was telling me about? He's not much to look at, is he?"

"Yeah, well, he makes up for it in other ways." Cindy attached his leash and rubbed behind his ears, hoping Prince couldn't understand what Travis had said.

"Gee. What a view." Travis walked to the glassed in balcony, staring out across the city. "I sure wouldn't want to fall from here."

"Me either, but I love the view."

"Quite different from Cedar Falls." He gazed at the skyscrapers in the distance. "Grace tells me you really like it here."

"Yeah, I do. It's different from back home, but in a good way. Sure, I miss everyone. That's the hard part." But she had fallen in love with the hustle and bustle of the city.

"Well, they have lots of things planned for this shindig, so I guess we oughta be moseying out of here."

"Yeah, you're right. I heard the higher elevations might get some snow. I hope we beat it home." It would be fun to be at the ranch in a big snow storm but she didn't like driving in them.

"We'll be okay. I've got my jeep. Not much can stop us in it."

"Thanks for picking me up." She'd sold her car and didn't really need to replace it. Living in the city in the downtown area, she could rely on the public transit system for all her needs.

"Not a problem. Where's the stuff you wanta take?"

"There, the suitcase next to the door."

"Great, let's get to gettin."

She closed and locked her door. "Oh, I forgot Nana's dress. Here, hold Prince." She handed him the leash. "I'll only be a minute."

Travis stood in the hall with her suitcase in one hand and Prince's leash in the other. She came out the door with the wedding dress over her arm.

"Okay, I think I have everything. I'm ready to go." She smiled at Travis. "I can't believe I almost forgot the dress."

"It seems like everyone is getting married. Must be

something in the water these days." He frowned. "Actually, I have some news. I want to ask Gloria to marry me." He glanced sideways at Cindy.

She turned to face him. "Travis, good for you. Gloria is perfect for you. When are you going to ask her?"

"That's just it. I came to the city to find a ring and I can't find anything I think she'd like. I want to ask her on Christmas Eve at Nana's wedding reception, but I can't if I don't have a ring."

She grinned. "Well, listen, we'll have to find a ring before we leave town. I know where there's a jewelry store that has some beautiful things at good prices."

"Oh, would you help me pick it out? You know Gloria. She doesn't like fancy stuff. Just something simple. Everything I've found seems too fancy."

"Your problem is solved. We can stop on our way out of town." She knew just the place.

A short time later, they were leaning over the counter at a jewelry store on the Sixteenth Street Mall when Murph came through the door.

"Hello, Cindy." He was in uniform and on duty. "I'm surprised to see you here."

"Hi, Murph, how are you doing? This is my friend, Travis from back home. We're looking at wedding rings." She gazed longingly through the glass case. "Aren't they beautiful?"

"Yeah," Murph said uncertainly. "Real nice. Joe has quality stuff. I need to speak to him about his security system. It keeps tripping the alarm. Nice to meet you, Travis, I'll see you later."

"Sure, Merry Christmas." She said and glanced up from the display case. Murph sure was acting strange.

Murph glanced back at her to see the woman behind the counter opening the case for her and Travis. They had their heads together, whispering.

"I think this one would be perfect for Gloria." She picked up a simple gold band with a small diamond on it. "What size does she wear?"

"Six and a half."

"The same size as me." She tried on another ring next to it, shaped in a cluster of diamonds and held her hand out in admiration. "Now, this is the kind of ring I'd like." She laughed.

"That suits you, but I think Gloria would love this one." He glanced toward the clerk. "We'll take this one." He pointed to the one with the small diamond and wide gold ban. "Can you wrap it for me?"

"Sure, what a beautiful ring. Simple and elegant. Your lady friend will love it." The clerk turned and walked away.

Leaving the store, Cindy smiled. "Travis, you're going to make Gloria a great husband. I'm so happy for both of you."

"Why, thank you." He hugged her to his side in a companionable gesture. "Gloria is going to be grateful to you for helping me find her a ring."

Across the street, Murph stood watching them with a heavy heart. This was going to kill Jack.

The next day, Sam came home to find Murph and Briggs with their heads together over the coffee pot. "What's going on with you two?"

Briggs glanced at Sam. He shuffled his feet, making Sam aware he had something on his mind he didn't want to discuss with her. "Oh, I see. This is a guy thing. Okay, I can take a hint. I have Christmas packages to wrap in the bedroom. You boys have a good time."

"Honey, we're just talking. You don't have to go in the bedroom. It's okay." She didn't like this one little bit.

"I was teasing you. I do have packages to wrap. You enjoy your coffee." She smiled at them and disappeared around the corner, stopping to listen to their conversation. "He's not going to start keeping secrets from me. That will be the day," she muttered under her breath.

Murph's voice was low, but she could understand him. "I told you, Cindy and that Travis guy were in the jewelry store buying wedding rings. I saw them and Joe said they bought a set of rings."

"Jack is going to be sorry he didn't get his butt back here and ask her to marry him. Should we tell him?"

Sam put her hand to her mouth, listening intently. Jack was

going to ask Cindy to marry him. Super! She could hardly contain her excitement. This was the big secret they didn't want her to know?

"I hate to bring him down with this. He's working hard to be able to walk out of that hospital."

The hospital? So that was where Jack had been all this time. These imbeciles hadn't bothered to tell us about it. They think Cindy is marrying Travis. She would get even and teach them a lesson about keeping secrets at the same time.

"Time is running out. He will be here on Christmas Eve or the day before. I have to think about this. What do you think?"

Sam snorted. She'd heard enough, serves them right for jumping to conclusions. If the boys wanted to play, she knew how to play rough. She didn't have to think about anything. She walked back through the living room to the open kitchen.

"I need the scissors and I'm about to die of thirst. Did you guys hear the news?" She filled her glass with ice water.

"What news?" Briggs and Murph glanced in her direction.

"Cindy and Travis are getting married. It was unexpected, but he asked her and she said yes. Kind of sudden, but I guess she was just tired of being alone."

"When? They're getting married? Isn't it too soon?" Murph muttered.

"They were childhood sweethearts and I guess they're having some kind of double wedding back on the ranch where she came from. She's tired of waiting for Mr. Right. With the way Jack treated her, I suppose she decided to settle for Mr. Almost Right. Can't blame her. Jack was a jerk."

"When's the big day?" Briggs asked, ignoring her dig about Jack.

"Christmas Eve. Tomorrow. And we're all invited. We've got reservations at the nearby hotel and hot springs so bring your bathing suits. I talked to Rhonda and she said it should be fun. Maybe, we can ride up together. It's only a few hours out of town." She grabbed the scissors from the junk drawer and picked up her glass of ice water. "Too bad Jack didn't have the guts to ask her. She really cared about him." She left them with their mouths hanging open and smiled when she went back into the bedroom.

Murph glared at Briggs. "Now, what are we going to do?"

"We have to tell Jack. Maybe he can get there in time to stop her from making the biggest mistake of her life," Briggs said. "I know they love each other."

"Okay, but not tonight, he sounded exhausted when I talked with him earlier today. At least, let him get a good night's sleep. I'll call him first thing in the morning. Lord, how did we get to be matchmakers?" Murph grumbled as he went out the door.

On the other side of the hallway, Sam was thrilled, doing the happy dance. *Yes! With a little help from his friends, Jack was going to get his rear in gear and ask Cindy the big question.*

The next morning, Murph dialed the hospital number, connecting to Jack. "Hello, Jack, this is Murph. How are you doing, old son?" He gritted his teeth, not wanting to drop this bomb on his friend, but he had no choice.

"Great. For the first time, I was able to walk by myself yesterday. It's happening, it's really happening, I'm walking. I'll be checking out of here later this morning. I can't wait to show Cindy."

Murph swallowed the hard lump in his throat. "I don't know how to sugar coat this so I'm just going to say it. I heard Cindy is getting married...tonight at that ranch she came from."

"What? This can't be true. I sent her flowers and told her not to do anything."

Murph sighed. "Sam says she's tired of waiting and this guy, Travis, used to be her childhood sweetheart."

"Sweetheart, my ass, she loves me. I know she does."

"Well, that may be true. Did you tell her how you feel about her? Women like to hear that sort of thing. And when they don't hear it, they jump to all kinds of wrong conclusions."

"No, fool that I am, I didn't have a chance to tell her, but she isn't like most women. She has a level head on her shoulders. Damn. I have to get out of here and go find her, but I don't know where she went...do you?"

"No, but I can ask Rhonda. Hold on, I'll see if she has the

address. This is happening fast. They didn't bother to send out invitations. I'll be right back."

Jack listened to the silence, trying to formulate a plan in his mind. Bottom line, he would go there.

"Hey, I'm back. She doesn't have it. She said we were riding up with Briggs and Sam. She didn't write it down. I do know it's only a few hours out of town. I'll find out and call you back soon as I know something. You figure out what you want to do."

Jack held the phone in his hand, still stunned from what he had heard. He would stop this wedding if it was the last thing he'd ever do. He had to have Cindy in his life. Why, even his late wife had told him to live a full life. He'd been a jerk not to call her and tell her he loved her.

Throwing back the covers, he slid out of bed and stormed into the bathroom fully intent on getting dressed and getting the hell out of the hospital, then it dawned on him. He was walking. He gripped the edge of the sink as his legs started to turn to jelly. Walking back to the bed, he made his decision. Soon as Murph called back, he'd go to Cindy where ever she was and stop the wedding.

The phone rang and Jack grabbed it. "Yes, where is she?"

"It's a ranch called the Cactus Rose and the ceremony is at six this evening. You're not going to believe this, but it's located somewhere around where you are, near Cedar Falls. The fates must be on your side. You should be able to make it with lots of time to spare. Do you want us to come and get you? We can be there soon."

"No, I'll get transportation. See you there." Jack smiled when he hung up the phone.

He slowly walked to the bathroom to prepare for the day. *Today is a good day. It's Christmas Eve and I'm walking. I'm going to ask the woman I love to be my wife and she's going to say yes. Nothing is going to go wrong.*

"Good morning, Jack. It's a frosty morning out there. They say we might have a white Christmas." The male nurse set the breakfast tray on the table.

"Thanks, Bud. Yes, it's a great day. Hey, do you know where the Cactus Rose Ranch is located? I think it's near here."

"Why yes, it's not far from where I live out past Interstate Seventy. Do you know the people who own the Cactus Rose? Mighty fine folks."

"No, but I have a friend who is going to be there for a wedding tonight and I was invited. Thought I might try out my new legs." He'd get there in plenty of time to stop the wedding.

"Well, if you like, you can ride out with me. I get off here around two. It only takes about an hour to get there from here. I'd be happy to give you a ride."

"Bud, that's great. I'll take you up on that ride. I'll be ready at two. Say, do you know where there's a jewelry store around here? Want to get the bride a gift." He'd buy a ring that Cindy couldn't turn down.

"There's one about four blocks from here. You can't miss it. The cab service will be working until two, then the whole town will shut down until after the holiday. That's how it is in small towns."

"Thanks, Bud. I'll catch up with you later." He grabbed the phone book, looking for a taxi service.

"No big deal. You're welcome to ride with me anytime. Glad to do it for you." He left the room, leaving Jack alone with his thoughts.

Jack leaned back against the bed and rested. He loved her and he knew in his heart that she loved him back. She was just confused. When he got to the ranch, he'd explain everything and make it right. She would say yes...wouldn't she? Doubts began to seep into his tortured soul. She had to say yes. He didn't want to spend the rest of his life without her.

Jack sat on his bed, dressed and ready to go, waiting for Bud to come pick him up. He was ready to get out of the hospital and get on with the rest of his life. During the afternoon, second thoughts twisted through his mind. What if Cindy didn't love him? What if she really did love her old sweetheart? He flipped open the jewel box for the fiftieth time staring at the ring. *Please, Lord. Let me get there in time to stop this wedding. Let her want me.*

Bud stuck his head around the door. "Ready to go?"

He stuffed the small black velvet box inside his jacket pocket. "Oh, yeah, let's go." Jack walked out of the room under his own steam and the help of a cane. Dr. Jones had told him it was best to have the extra support until his muscles were used to walking again.

"The snow is really coming down out there." Bud made casual conversation as they walked out the hospital doors. "The weather man says we're in for it."

A snowstorm. Not now! "We can make it there okay, can't we?" Jack brushed snow from his face while they trudged through the parking lot. *I've got to get there in time.*

"Oh, yeah, there's nothing to worry about. I'll get you there." He paused. "Here, this is mine." He stood before an old beat up truck that looked like it had seen better days.

Jack shivered as he climbed inside. "Man, it's cold."

"Yeah, the temperature is dropping like a rock." He pulled out of the parking lot onto the main highway. "Not much traffic."

As Jack thought of being married to Cindy, the snow continued to blow across the road, nearly making it impossible to see. "How far did you say it was?" They'd been driving for about thirty minutes and hadn't seen anybody else on the road. He grimaced when Bud's truck fishtailed toward the side of the road.

"About twenty miles. Must be ice under this white stuff." He gripped the steering wheel and slowed down. "You better buckle up."

Jack fastened his seatbelt. The truck crawled along at a snail's pace in the near white out conditions. *Damn, can't you go any faster?* Jack glanced at his watch. Three-thirty, he should have time, even if he had to crawl there.

All of a sudden a deer ran across the road. Bud swerved. "Hang on." The truck slid to the side of the road and down an embankment into a deep ditch.

"Are you okay?" Bud asked.

"Yes, and you?" Jack glanced at Bud.

"Yeah, fine." He gunned the motor. "But we're stuck." He peered out the window at the sheets of snow pelting the truck. "We can't stay here like this. We could freeze if we sit here long enough. I'll go for help."

"I'll go with you." Jack couldn't believe this was happening. "I have to get to the Cactus Rose Ranch."

"Don't be a fool. You've barely left the hospital. This storm would wear you down before you could get a hundred yards."

Grudgingly, Jack listened to the man. *Damn. He was right.*

Jack became more unhappy by the minute as he realized he might not make it to the wedding in time.

"Wait here. I'll get help." Bud opened the door and a blanket of snow blew in. "I promise. I know a shortcut. I'll get back soon as I can."

It seemed like Bud had been gone for hours. The sky had turned dark and the blizzard continued to howl outside the old truck. Jack's feet were frozen. The truck had run out of gas an hour ago. Leaning his head back, he drifted off to sleep in a dazed state. Jerking awake, he sat straight up. *I will not freeze to death, sitting here like a helpless invalid. I can walk it.* He thought the words tentatively as if testing the idea. Easing his way out of the truck he was hit by a blast of cold, wet snow. Shivering, he leaned into the storm and drove his way forward, using his cane to keep his balance. He had to get up the steep embankment to the road or die trying. Finally reaching the road side he saw snow-covered trees on each side of the road bent in the wind. A branch blew off and knocked him to the ground, stunning him.

"*Jack, get up. Get up, Jack.*" A voice came out of the blizzard.

Jack opened his eyes and felt a gash at the side of his face as warm blood gushed out of it. "What, where are you?" He stumbled to his feet.

"*That's it Jack. Get up and keep walking forward. You are almost there. You can do it.*"

"Who is it?" He was still dazed. "Who's speaking?"

In his mind's eye he saw a vision of an angel who looked like his late wife. "*It's me. Hang on, help is on the way.*"

He reached out to touch her, and the vision disappeared. "*You can make it.*" He felt the words in his head.

"Yes, I can make it." He pushed himself up and into the storm. Up ahead, lights came toward him, out of the storm.

A snow plow stopped in the middle of the road. "Damn, Jack, I told you to stay with the truck." Bud grabbed him around the waist and pulled him toward the truck.

"He looks frozen. Do you think we should get him back to the hospital," the driver spoke to Bud.

"No," Jack screamed. "I have to get to the Cactus Rose ranch to stop a wedding. The woman I love is about to marry the wrong guy. Please, get me there."

Bud and the driver exchanged a strange look. "You want to stop the wedding?"

He met their accusing eyes without flinching. "Yes. My life depends on it." He ran a hand through his hair. "I love her and she loves me. Please. Just get me there," he begged.

"Well, okay, mister, if it means that much to you. I can get you there in about ten minutes. You hold on." He pulled his handkerchief from his pocket. "Here, wipe that cut with this."

Jack forgot he was bleeding. He had to reach Cindy before it was too late. He sat in the warm snow plow between Bud and the driver, pulling his thoughts together, trying to figure out what he would say to her. He had to convince her to marry him, not this Travis guy.

"Here we are." The driver drove down a long winding road. "See the log house on the hill, over there with all the lights on?" Bud pointed toward the side of a mountain.

Jack could barely make out the image of a large log structure in the distance amid the blowing snow. He vowed to tell her how much he loves her.

"That's the Cactus Rose Ranch. Been in their family for generations. How do you know them?" Bud asked.

"It's too long a story to tell. Please, take me there as fast as you can. I've been a fool. I have to stop this wedding." Joy danced in his heart at the thought of seeing her again. He touched the wisp of black lace stuffed in his jacket pocket, feeling closer to her.

Bud and the driver gave each other that strange look again. "Okay, Mister. Since you're so determined, I'll get you there." He stepped on the gas and they sped the heavy snow plow into the circled driveway, in between a number of cars.

"Thanks." Jack pushed Bud out of the truck and made his way up the steps. Bud and the driver followed.

Jack opened the door. The bride and groom were standing in front of a huge stone fireplace in a cozy living room. Several people stood around watching the ceremony. The bride stood there with her back to Jack, next to an older man. *My God, he's old enough to be her grandfather.*

"Do you take this man to be your lawful wedded husband?"

"Stop. You can't marry him. I love you. Marry me." Jack shouted in agony and stumbled up the aisle with his cane to the bride.

The bride and groom turned toward him with total surprise showing on their faces.

The blood drained from Jack's head. "You're not Cindy. Where's Cindy?" He shook his head trying to clear his blurring vision. Was he at the wrong wedding?

Bud stepped forward. "I'm sorry, ma'am. He came straight here from the hospital. Wouldn't take no for an answer." He stepped forward to take Jack's arm. "We'll take him back with us."

"Jack, here I am. You're walking!" Tears sprang to Cindy's eyes. She stood to the side of the bride. She was a bridesmaid.

"Oh, Cindy." He grabbed her and held her close. "You're here." She welcomed him into her arms. "I thought I was losing my mind."

Murph and Briggs stepped up to help Cindy hold Jack. "Jack, come over here and sit down. You've been injured. Let us look at you."

He clung to Cindy. "Not yet, I have something to ask her." He stood there, drowned in a floodtide of emotion. "Pulling the ring box out of his pocket, he fell down on one knee. "Cindy. I love you. Will you marry me?"

She looked at the huge marquee cut diamond set on a wide gold band, then back at the hopeful look on Jack's face. She glanced at the sly smile on Sam's face and everyone watching.

"Jack, get up." She helped him to his feet. "Before I can answer you, there's something I have to tell you."

His heart nearly stopped as he stood next to her. "Whatever

it is, it's okay. Just say yes and we can work out anything that's bothering you—together."

She smiled. "It's nothing bad. It's just I think you should know. I'm Snow White from the e-mails." Passion pounded blood through his heart while he listened, too stunned to speak. "I have to know if you are really ready for a step like this."

"You're Snow White?" The pleasure was pure and explosive. "Oh, my God." He kissed her deeply with a hunger that belied his outward calm. "That's great." The real world spun on its axis as everything was righted in her arms. Gently, he held her, and captured her with his eyes. "While I was in the hospital I had lots of time to think. I want to live again." She held him close. "I want you, kids, commitment, the whole shebang. I want to spend the rest of my life with you. Yes, I'm ready for this type of commitment."

Her green eyes were lit with a warm glow. "What took you so long. I love you, too. Yes!"

Jack couldn't believe his good fortune. *Thank you God for this wonderful woman!* She had said yes. Reclaiming her lips, he crushed her to him.

"Okay, that's enough for now. Let's get you patched up so we can get on with my wedding." The older groom took Jack by the arm, pried him away from Cindy and led him to the sofa.

"I'm so sorry for barging in like this, but I thought you were marrying, Cindy." He glanced at the bride and she gave him a kind smile. "Please forgive me for this intrusion."

"Don't you worry about a thing, young man. If you are marrying our Cindy, you're family. And we take care of family."

He sat there, holding Cindy's hand while Murph patched him up. "I promise to make you happy."

Cindy gazed into his warm brown eyes. Her face was full of strength. "Yes, you will."

Murph and Briggs laughed. "Old son, she has your number," Murph said. "More power to you, Cindy. You're just what this stubborn mule needs."

Jack pushed Murph's hand from his face. "I'm okay. Long as I have this woman by my side, I'm great." He took her in his arms. First he kissed the tip of her nose, then her eyes, and finally, he satisfyingly kissed her soft mouth. It was a kiss for his tired soul to melt into. The others stood around and clapped their approval.

THE END

NOTE TO MY READERS

Just saying hello to my *Sweet Home Colorado* readers and fans. I hope you have enjoyed *Fly Away Home,* Book Two.

For an update on the next book in this series, *Home Sweet Home,* Book Three, and to be the first to hear about all of my Colorado quirky, crazy fun books, sign up for my newsletter at www.judewillhoff.com (Note: Your email will never be shared and you can unsubscribe at anytime.)

And please share your love for *Fly Away Home*, from my Sweet Home Colorado series! Word–of-mouth is vital for an author to succeed. If you enjoyed the book, please leave a review at www.Amazon.com, even if it's a sentence or two. That's how other readers find my books! Your reviews make a ton of difference and are so appreciated.

Also, feel free to email me at jude2@prodigy.net I do answer each and every email—unless you're spamming me (lol!).

You can connect and hang with me in and on the following places:

Website: www.judewillhoff.com
Facebook: www.facebook.com/judewillhoff
Twitter: judewillhoff@judewillhoff

You may purchase *No Direction Home,* Book One, *Fly Away Home*, Book Two and *Home Sweet Home*, Book Three of the *Sweet Home Colorado* series at www.amazon.com or www.judewillhoff.com Watch for Jude's nonfiction books, *Writing Secrets of 33 Bestselling Romance Authors* and *Living Well With Chronic Pain* coming fall 2013.

ABOUT THE AUTHOR

Jude Willhoff is a bestselling and award-winning author in both romance and nonfiction genres. *Fly Away Home* was written while Jude lived in a highrise in downtown Denver, Colorado. There's nothing quite like living in Denver. It has its own positive pulse, a unique heartbeat to the city, an energy that makes everything exciting and new. There's always something going on and something to do.

With her husband, while sitting at the outside tables at the Rock Bottom Brewery on the Sixteenth Street Mall on a warm spring day the idea about the characters in *Fly Away Home* came to Jude.

Jude is an avid reader and a believer in all things romance. By day, she works alongside her husband with their real estate business. "Though I could always use more time to write, the hours spent working with real estate are never dull and are a constant source of ideas for plots and characters." By night, she writes her contemporary romance and nonfiction books.

To celebrate Jude's official launch of the *Sweet Home Colorado* series she has happily included the first chapter of Book Three, *Home Sweet Home,* Jenna Myers' story for your enjoyment.

HOME SWEET HOME
~ SWEET HOME COLORADO ~
BOOK THREE

CHAPTER ONE

Panic rose like a freak desert flash flood, one minute everything was calm, the next, it was raging out of control. Jenna Myers stood on the dark crimson stain that had seeped into the hallway carpet.

"Torrie?" Jenna pounded frantically against her friend's apartment door, her pulse racing, her throat dried with panic. "Are you all right? Torrie, open the door."

No answer.

Terrified of what she'd find on the other side, she forced herself to turn the brass knob. It wouldn't budge. With trembling hands, she found the master key to her friend's apartment. Hoping against hope, the stain wasn't blood she placed the key in the lock and pushed the door open. Near the entrance, Torrie Saunders lay on her side. Sightless eyes gazed at nothing.

Oh God. Jenna choked back a frightened scream as she rushed toward her friend. Instinct took over as icy fear twisted around her heart. She scanned the studio apartment for an intruder and found none. A curtain flapped against the wall from the breeze of an open window as she examined her friend. There was no pulse. No breath. Nothing. Torrie was gone.

Only Jenna's ragged breathing broke the silence as she stood, grabbed her cell phone from her jacket pocket and dialed.

"This is 911. Is there an emergency?"

"Help me...m..my friend has been murdered," she said in a voice that seemed to come from a long way off. Closing her eyes, memories of her father's death floated past her eyelids. She squelched them.

"Where are you?"

"Aspen Valley Apartments...four twenty eight East Vine, apartment number twelve."

"Stay on the line. A police car will be right there. Did you check for the victim's pulse?"

"Yes, there isn't one. And sh—she's covered with blood. It's everywhere." Scarlet blood had splattered on the wall. Jenna took a deep breath and tried to control her nervous shaking.

"Is anyone else there?"

"No. It's a small studio apartment and I can see into all the rooms. It's just me."

Turning her back to the grisly sight, Jenna pressed the phone close against her ear and breathed in shallow, quick gasps, forcing herself to calm down.

"Don't touch anything. The police are on the way."

Sirens wailed in the distance. Would the police help this time, or would it be like the last? Jenna had sold her bookstore and moved from Cedar Falls to Denver to solve her father's murder and keep the apartment complex from being sold. It was all she had left of her family. She couldn't sell it. She hadn't been able to solve anything and was holding on to the complex by a thread. And now this.... A police car screeched into the parking lot and the shrill sound ceased as it jerked her from her thoughts.

She had to get away from the clogging metallic scent of blood—Torrie's blood. Jenna ran out of the crimson entryway, averting her gaze from the blood-soaked carpet.

Two uniformed policemen and a plain-clothes detective moved quietly down the sides of the hall with guns drawn. The well-built detective whirled and aimed his gun at Jenna as she rushed toward them.

"Police. Up against the wall," he shouted.

"I called. Thank goodness you're here."

"I said, up against the wall. Now."

She noted the hard suspicious glint in his eyes. Stunned, she quieted, stuck her hands in the air, and faced the white plaster, her world seeming to spin, yet move in slow motion at the Bobe time.

"What happened here?" the plainclothesman demanded as he patted her down, his voice threatening. He turned her around, searching for a concealed weapon.

"I don't know." Embarrassed, she felt the strength of his large warm hands through her thin jacket as he touched her body.

"Who are you?" His voice was deadly calm as he yanked her arms down and roughly handcuffed her hands behind her back. She guessed he was taking no chances since she was caught running from the crime scene covered in blood.

"I'm Jenna Myers," she croaked. With the cell phone still clutched in her cuffed hands, she nodded toward Torrie's body beyond the open door. "I found her like that and called 911. I don't know what happened." Her voice cracked. "I own the apartment complex. M...My office is down the hall."

"Johnson, stay here. Watch her." He moved away.

She leaned against the wall in disbelief as the detective and another officer entered the apartment.

The first policeman stood near her watching the open doorway. The officer inside signaled thumbs down. The one near her spoke into his radio. "Dispatch, this is Johnson. I have a cold wiggler at four twenty-eight East Vine, Aspen Valley Apartments, unit number twelve."

A calm voice crackled over the wire. "Understood. Response team in route. Coroner notified."

Jenna shook her head in dismay, nauseated by how casually they had accepted her friend's death. They were talking about Torrie as if she were an object, like a bag of trash to be discarded. A tear slipped down her cheek. This was someone with whom she had shared her triumphs and frustrations over the first cup of coffee each morning.

Two paramedics and another policeman raced by Jenna. Johnson stopped them and stood on the other side of the hallway whispering in low muted tones.

Straining to hear the conversation, she glanced at the bloodied body by the open door. A loud roar vibrated in her ears and worked its way up to the top of her head. Bright pinpoints of light flashed in her brain and everything turned dark and hazy. Her cheek touched the cool plaster. Dropping the cell phone, she slowly slid down the wall.

Strong arms caught her. She was shifted and pressed against a hard chest. She caught the woodsy scent of a familiar after-shave. The scent her father used to wear. It somehow comforted her as she tried to gather her strength. The voices around her were magnified, even as blackness threatened to envelop her. She was safe, wrapped in an invisible warmth and solid strength.

A growl vibrated beneath her ear as the shadowed man held her close. "Johnson, cordon off the area. Keep everyone away from here and bag her hands."

Groggily, she tipped her head up to meet his gaze, surprised to see it was the Bobe detective who had cuffed her. Raw hurt glittered in his warm brown eyes. They were deep, expressive and had seen too much, too often.

He stared down at her and raised his hand to smooth her hair in an infinitely tender gesture she wouldn't have expected from the man who had treated her so roughly only minutes ago. His fingers seemed to tremble as he brushed a tear from the corner of her eye. Abruptly, he averted his gaze. "I don't need this, today of all days," her rescuer mumbled. "Johnson, keep her out of the way," he said gruffly, handing her over to the policeman.

Johnson helped her to stand. "Take a deep breath, ma'am. You'll be all right."

Disoriented, she gazed at the man who had just held her. Breathing in gulps of air, she watched his well-formed backside as he leaned over and examined a pillow with a hole in it, pained tolerance in his expression.

Leaning against the wall, watching through the open doorway, her stomach churned as she attempted to focus on the changing scene around her. Someone came over and recuffed her hands in front and put a paper bag on each one. Why were they putting bags on her hands? My God, she was handcuffed, she'd been frisked. Could they think she did this horrible, unimaginable thing?

Her face flushed with humiliation as she recovered from the shock. What was going on here? She glared at the detective, with anger consuming her.

She intended to shout at him, but some confusion distracted her. A short balding man with Medical Examiner emblazoned on his jacket entered the apartment. Suddenly overcome by the reality of what had happened Jenna stared at the body and blinked back tears as her heart twisted in her chest. *Poor Torrie, I'm so sorry this happened to you.*

It would be like the last time. The real killer was getting away. She must do something. One policeman took pictures of blood spatters on the wall. Johnson turned his back to her and stood in a small group, talking. Seizing the opportunity, she inched her way inside the doorway of the apartment, hoping to find a clue.

The detective had his back to her, but she couldn't help noticing his dark wavy hair, tapered neatly to his collar. He had held her earlier, and her body still tingled from his touch. The momentary tenderness he'd shown her was gone. Now, he stood over Torrie's body, writing something in a notebook as he spoke in low tones with the medical examiner. Much to her surprise, he bent over and gently brushed a strand of Torrie's hair behind her ear. It touched Jenna's heart, but it seemed an odd thing for him to do.

He glanced up and his eyes narrowed when he spotted her. "This is a crime scene. Lady, stay in the hall." His voice of cool authority flowed over her. "Who let her in here?"

Startled, she jerked her gaze from Torrie's body to him as he strode toward her. Although his dark brown eyes showed compassion, he radiated a fiery anger.

Her own ire rose to the surface. Determined not to let this man intimidate her, she clenched her sweaty fists inside the paper bags and looked him straight in the eye. "She was my friend." Despite the quivering in her knees, she lifted her chin and met his intense gaze straight on.

"You still can't disturb the crime scene." He frowned and glanced at the body. "There's nothing you can do here. Go back to the hall. I'll talk to you soon as I can."

She noticed the strong cleft of his chin and the stubborn glint of his warm brown eyes. Then, the look he gave her suddenly made her afraid. The man wasn't to be trifled with. Maybe he would solve the crime. "You've got to find the person who did this." She straightened her spine and stood her ground.

Showing no signs of relenting, he rubbed the back of his neck. "Look, Miz. I understand how you feel about losing your friend, but you've got to go."

Not thinking clearly, Jenna was annoyed that he was talking down to her. In one glance she sized up his stony, set face, his clamped jaw and fixed eyes. "You don't understand. These people depend on me. I have elderly and disabled tenants living here who can barely care for themselves. They're not safe in their beds. I want to keep them safe." She reached her cuffed hands out toward him, beseeching him to let her help.

He glared at her. "You must leave. Now." He stepped toward her, making her heart skip a beat.

She lifted her chin. "Never mind, I'll protect them myself." She dropped her hands in resignation, knowing she was getting nowhere with the stubborn detective.

He snapped his notebook shut with a bang and moved into her personal space. "Lady, that's not your job; it's ours." He motioned to the police officer. "Now, let us get on with it. Johnson, take her down to the station. I'll get her statement there." To protect and serve, he thought. That was his job. The big, burly cop emerged from behind Jenna. "Yes sir," he said calmly. "Ma'am, Detective Locassio wants you to come with me?" He guided her by the elbow out of the apartment.

Fuming with righteous anger, she shot an indignant glare at Locassio. Even though she may have acted foolishly, she resented being hauled off as if she were a criminal. "Yes, but I'll only go because I want to help," she said firmly.

Locassio tilted his head and looked at her for a long minute. That look stripped her bare, naked to her soul. It was if he could see inside her, getting into her innermost feelings, making her feel vulnerable and exposed to him. Then he shook his head with disapproval, rolled his eyes and turned away.

"Detective Locassio will come to the station as soon as he's done here," Officer Johnson said apologetically.

She swallowed hard. "I had nothing to do with this," she whispered fiercely. Tears crept out of the corners of her eyes. "Torrie was like family to me."

The officer held her arm and walked her down the common hallway. The smell of someone's fish dinner lingered in the air from last night as he led her out the door to the patrol car. At least no tenants were around peeking out to see her in this sad situation. Luckily, most of them had already gone to work or were still sleeping. Sitting behind the reinforced glass in the patrol car, she steeled her emotions as she waited for him to finish talking with a couple of other cops. Jenna couldn't believe this was happening to her. She had her hands bagged and she was in handcuffs. What were they thinking? She didn't do it. Why were they messing with her when the real murderer was getting away?

They'd have to let her go. She clenched her jaw. They had nothing to hold her on. When they released her, she'd keep watch over the complex to make sure everyone would be safe. She couldn't afford to lose anyone else who mattered in her life.

She frowned as she crinkled the paper bags with her fingers and stared at the cuffs gleaming in the bright sunlight. In a perfect world, protecting her tenants would be Locassio's job. But the world wasn't perfect and neither were the police.

Sinking lower in the seat, she stared out the window. Biting her lip to keep from crying, she watched two men carry Torrie's body out of the apartment building and place the large black bag in the County Coroner's minivan. A single tear slid down her cheek as she watched them drive away with their quiet cargo.

Locassio turned from the window as Johnson tucked Jenna Myers into the back of the patrol car. The petite red-headed woman said she was innocent, but it wasn't something he could deal with now. He stared at the blood-soaked carpet where the body had lain. He'd handle her later. Right now he had to take care of business. He stared blankly at the spot. Torrie Saunders, alias Detective Ann Stone, was an undercover cop from his department. A good cop. His friend. Now she was dead. He took a deep breath and vowed he would find the scumbag who did this to Ann.

The medical examiner interrupted his musings. "Locassio, just the guy I want to see." The man pushed his wire rim glasses up on his nose and approached from across the room.

"Hey, Bill." Locassio accepted Bill Walker's extended hand. He had been the man on the scene for the Denver Police Department for a number of years and he knew his business.

"Sorry about Ann. She was a good cop. We're all gonna miss her."

"Yeah." He nodded. "Tough." Ann's death made Locassio physically sick. "What did you find?"

"There was no sign of a struggle. She didn't have time to react. Died instantly."

He gritted his teeth. "At least she didn't suffer."

"One bullet, fired through the pillow into the frontal lobe." His expression was grim. "Used a twenty-five caliber derringer. Unusual firearm. A woman's gun." He stroked his chin with his thumb and forefinger. "I see a lot of stiffs. Maybe every couple years one has derringer powder burns." He hesitated. "When a person gets shot this close, it's by someone who hates them."

Locassio rubbed the back of his neck. "What time would you guess it happened?"

"From the rigidity in the wrist joints, I'd say around midnight, maybe a little after." His eyes were full of compassion as he returned Locassio's gaze. He gripped his clipboard closer to his chest. "I'll get a copy of the autopsy report on your desk as soon as I can."

"I appreciate it." A vision of Ann playing in the park with a Frisbee at the last department picnic popped into Locassio's mind. "Take good care of her. I wouldn't want her brother to see her like that."

"Sure, not a problem. Under the circumstances, he can forgo the identification at the morgue if he wants."

"Thanks for your help, Bill."

"Anytime. I'll put a rush on it." He turned and walked out the door.

Detective Bob Reed, Locassio's partner for the past eight years, approached from the open doorway as Bill left the room. "We're wrapping things up. The forensics team will finish tomorrow."

"And?"

Bob shrugged. "Looks like a break-in. There are fresh pry marks on the windowsill."

"Any fingerprints?"

"No. They knew what they were doing. It wasn't robbery. Her purse is on the counter...has about a hundred in cash and all her credit cards. Nothing taken."

"Maybe she surprised them."

"I don't think so. This has the markings of a hit. The scene is too clean. No fingerprints. No weapon. Nothing except the pry marks and some dirt that came off their shoes."

"Yeah, I was thinking the Bobe thing. Could've been an old enemy. We need to go through her arrest records. Might be a lead there."

A look of tired sadness passed between them. It had been a long day. Locassio tightened his jaw as the silence drummed in his ears. "Do you think this had anything to do with her being undercover?" He had to ask. It had been his idea—she was here because of him.

"Of course not." Bob shook his head slowly. "Don't do this." He placed his hand on Locassio's shoulder. "You can't blame yourself. She volunteered. Ann was here because she was doing her job." He gave Locassio a look of reassurance. "She wanted to be a part of this investigation, to make the connection between the Ortega gang murder and the drug dealers. In any case, the dealers she was watching were small-time. If they knew she was on to them, they'd pack up and move, not commit murder."

"What could she have fallen into? This was a simple operation." Frustrated, Locassio hit the door frame. "Dammit. Why didn't she let us know?"

"That's the million dollar question. Maybe she didn't have a chance or maybe she never knew." Bob glanced away from Locassio, avoiding his direct gaze. "Anyway, once word hits the street, we'll be hearing from the snitches in a few days. If it was the drug dealers retaliating, we'll know it."

A few days. Locassio hated that part of his job. He didn't want the answers in a few days. He wanted them yesterday. He wanted to know who did this, to track him down and rip his guts out.

Calming himself, getting back to business, he gazed through the window. The patrol car was still there with the pretty woman in it. He saw the tears streaming down her face as she glared back at him. "Damn." He hadn't wanted to treat her that way, but she was caught running away from the crime scene. He knew she was Ann's friend, but Ann hadn't told him how angelic she was. Jenna had looked stricken, hurt and angry.

He didn't blame her—he was angry too. Ann was dead and he'd find the one who'd killed her. Then he remembered Bill had said the derringer was a woman's gun.

His eyes narrowed. Angelic? Maybe. Maybe not. He'd wait for the forensics test.

Made in the USA
San Bernardino, CA
16 November 2013